1

Stuart Gibbel

Research

A novel

(ΛΣΛ˙)ΕΙΥυмΛ

Casa del Yuma
Colombia - NYC

casadelyuma@gmail.com

Cover art : Juan P Wauters
Cover layout : Ricardo Alessio

Printed in the USA

sgibbel@yahoo.com

ISBN-13: 978-0-9984124-9-8

For Maurice and Corinne Gibbel who taught me how to read, gave me great books, and most importantly, lots of love and laughter.

With every mistake we must surely be

learning...

George Harrison

8

"Some men study the Civil War. They memorize the name and location of each and every skirmish. They can recite chapter and verse on the topography of every battlefield, the name and condition of each and every regiment, the impact of the weather, the style and abilities of the generals. They know how many bodies are buried, and where.

For some of these enthusiasts, reading about the war between the states is not enough. They need something more tangible than what can be found in the library, so they dress up in the Blue and the Grey and gather in fields far and wide. They sleep in canvas tents and eat hard tack. In the morning they coffee up and act out famous battles, complete with cannon fire and cavalry charges.

125 years after Robert E. Lee surrendered, a young boy--the great, great, grandson of slaves--rides the New York City subway. Some claimed that this tall teenager from The Bronx was obsessed with trains. In school he was an average student, in a below average school, but he knew the subway system. He could rattle off the separate histories of the individual subway lines: the IRC, the BMC, and the IND. If anyone asked, he would explain how the tunnels were built how many men were killed during construction.

The kid became an expert on the subject, but there were no groups who gathered to tell tales of the subway, no battlefields to play on. The kid only had the real thing.

One day he put on the stolen uniform and badge of a subway worker and headed to the end of the line. With the help of all the manuals he had meticulously memorized and his observations of real workers, he took control of a southbound local train.

Unpaid and having the time of his life, he made all the stops like the veteran motorman he dreamed he was. His passengers had no complaints.

Unfortunately, the emergency brakes failed on the 2nd to last stop in Brooklyn. Mechanical Failure. No one was hurt, but untrained, non-union children are not allowed to operate heavy machinery within city limits.

The judge had mercy and commuted the kid's sentence when he promised to go back to school and improve his grades. In history, he is studying the Civil War."

New York Train Tales

The Past

1. Hump Day

Their faces are always hidden.

I know what they are doing, but not who they are.

The shades are always halfway down. The room is always semi dark, enough light to see the lower half of bodies in motion, but not enough to illuminate the details. You can see skin, but not tattoos. If not for the sound effects, they could be wrestling. Whether the word fuck comes from the German word *ficken* 'to strike' is debatable, but the action that takes place less than a dozen feet away is not.

Words like fornicating, banging, boinking, balling, or phrases like bashing the beaver, doing the horizontal tango, mattress dancing, the beast with two backs, don't work either. Neither do any of the more than 200 euphemisms for fornication listed in Hubbell's *Dictionary of Slang and Euphemism*. Screwing seems to fit best.

11

It's late Wednesday night.

I discovered my neighbors' weekly ritual by accident last spring. Their bedroom is directly across from the kitchen and I was thirsty. The window was open and in the dark I heard the sweet sounds of moaning and bedsprings. Ten minutes earlier or later and I would have missed the entire episode.

I thought only couples in porno films were this wild. My cock wasn't stiff, but my body was. Since I caught them in the middle of the performance, I was cheated. Something was missing —I hadn't witnessed a single kiss.

Animals don't kiss.

Humans kiss because we don't sniff each other like dogs. We kiss because the ancients believed our soul was in our breath, and kissing married our breath and fused our souls. We kiss because throughout recorded history lawmakers have attempted to make it illegal and religious leaders have sermonized against it. We kiss our lovers with passion, because whores will take our organs in their

12

mouths, but refuse to have anything to do with our lips and tongues. A kiss is never just a kiss.

Later that night, I tossed and turned next to Susie who was calmly sleeping on her half of the bed. As I struggled to find a position that would induce sleep, I wondered what I would tell her about the neighbors. And When?

I had no idea if I would ever catch them in the act again, if this was a once-in-a-lifetime-event or a regular occurrence--but I knew one thing for certain: in the middle of the night I would be thirsty.

2. Upstream

It's me or him. There is no compromise— since two bodies cannot occupy the same space, at the same time, one of us is going to yield. It's me against the thousands of sleep-deprived Long Islanders marching behind him, so let's just say the odds are even.

I focus on the *Daily News* on the ground and keep walking. Dozens have stepped on the mayor's face, but he keeps smiling.

13

The man hesitates just enough for me to pass.

Tactic number one: never make eye contact.

I continue staring at the ground, but two men with umbrellas are approaching at an angle, attempting to cut me off. Left or right?

Studies on commuting have concluded that workers who travel more than one hour each way to work are sleep deprived.

My side step to the left was effective, but not the best choice; I misjudged both their speed and direction and was treated to an elbow and dirty look.

The image of the salmon swimming upstream comes to mind. Instead of water, the current I make my way through determined commuters that collectively believe they are working for a better life or at least a backyard with barbecue and lawn furniture.

Both White Shoes after Labor Day and Fancy Suspenders Man progress like they can walk right through me. I keep moving and they slow their pace just enough so I can move around them, clearing

14

them by no more distance than the width of Mr. Suspender's shiny gold watch.

Tactic number two: always keep your legs moving-even when standing in place.

My train departs in four minutes.

To commute this way is to not only travel against the crowd, but to enter a funnel. The closer you are to your train, the less space you have to work with. The thicker the crowd, the more they believe you should be the one that waits for them.

Front or back? Trains have been missed, lives permanently altered, fortunes lost, by the wrong choice of stairs. Closer to the subway or a slightly longer walk with less congestion?

There is no polite way to descend. I stay to the right, but the disembarking passengers insist on going up the stairs side by side. I stand my ground and make them clear a path just for me.

As I reach the bottom of the stairs, a black and white advertisement for Bartleby's Beer catches my eye. Bartleby is sitting at the end of the bar, holding a full tankard of frosty brew. He is looking

15

off to the side, at what, we can not be certain. All we know is that he is thinking important thoughts. The tagline is missing, left out on purpose.

Is this the work of Susie? Looks like it could be, but where is the obligatory reference to suicide? Melville didn't kill himself. I soon realize my mistake, I was considering the author Melville, and not his greatest creation, *Bartleby the Scrivener.* Having committed suicide, or to be more precise, choosing not to go on living, Bartleby fit perfectly with Susie and her fellow conspirators.

As much as I would prefer not to, I was going to have to wait for the poster to be completed, or vandalized—depending on your feelings about such things--to learn what evil forces of the corporate world Susie and her team were currently battling against. Before I get another chance to study the poster, the doors close, and the train nudges its way underground.

The nature films do a great job of depicting the salmon's journey upstream: always fighting the current, jumping up steps built to bypass giant

16

hydroelectric dams, avoiding fishermen. What the Discovery Channel has failed to mention is more fish are killed on the trip downstream than while fighting to get upriver. When the dams were designed, the environmentalists insisted on a series of steps and ladders for the fish to climb upstream. What they didn't take into account is the millions of baby fish would get sucked into the intake pipes that take in the current that turn the turbines that generate electric power. In this way the souls of baby salmon are converted into the electricity that will power the houses, offices, and even the trains that take sleepy commuters to work and back.

3.   **The Man Who Was King**

Crown Technology Publishing is the second to the last stop on the Port Jefferson Line, the third largest publisher of technology journals, the fourth largest employer on Long Island. In addition, it's one of the top places to work for--as selected by *Working Women* magazine. I can only assume the editors at WW were more impressed with the on-site daycare and flexible working hours than with the free snacks, discounted sodas, and cappuccino machines on every floor.

When the company isn't patting itself on the back for its ability to retain employees at twice the industry average, or encouraging its employees to mentor underprivileged school kids, or handing out employee of the minute awards, Crown produces technology newspapers, journals, magazines, books, and newsletters.

In short, Crown Publishing brings in enough cash to give the family-owned enterprise, and its 1200 employees, the illusion of never-ending prosperity.

In the world of publishing, staffers like me —the ones not associated with writing the book or selling the ads—are the minor leaguers, the untouchables that never have an answer to the "do you work in editorial or sales?" question.

When I started at Crown, I was a research grunt. I worked my way up, mostly because I was computer literate. You would think people that make their living selling ad space to multi-billion dollar computer vendors would want to know a little something about technology—even used car salesmen know how to drive.

Over a short period of time I developed a reputation for locating information no one else seemed to be able to easily locate. It was like everyone had telephones but didn't know the digits they needed to dial to make the thing work. No one realized the large book collecting dust on their credenza had all the phone numbers they would ever need, all they had to do was open it and begin exploring.

"I need everything you can get on IBM," John Williams would ask.

"Everything?"

"What part of everything is not crystal?"

The part of everything that would fill your double office with enough paper left over to occupy your extra parking space in the executive garage.

"Is this everything?"

"Yes." *This is everything I'm going to give you.*

"Are you sure?"

"Yes."

"Great job."

The more I insisted it was nothing, the more they thought I had unique skills that would take them years to develop. I was the one-eyed man in H.G. Wells' the *Land of the Blind.*

It was great while it lasted, but I was eventually replaced by gray haired MBA and reassigned to work in Special Projects.

The Special Projects department is conveniently located next to the research department. It was believed the two departments could work together, researching and developing products for the entire company—ideas no one else in the company seemed to have the time for.

The man at the head of Special Projects, the man I report to, is none other than the founder of Crown Publishing, Joseph Crown. After more than 20 years of running the company, from a single newsletter edited and produced on the family's dining room table to the publishing giant it is today, Joe was in charge.

The light in Joe's office is on. This could mean that he came in early, or more likely, he left it on last night. I know that if he comes in and finds that he left his light on he's going to spend the entire day sitting in the dark, trying to figure out how much wattage has been wasted. Poor memory and extremely frugality is a bad combination.

His floor is covered with more than two dozen pages—like he left for the evening just after hitting the print button. A few words, a fragment of a sentence, and I know it's about baseball.

Baseball is Joe's metaphor and security blanket. When it comes to explaining the business, he always has some clever analogy or anecdote handy; he rarely leaves a base unturned. He counts the days till spring training, and is gloomy when the World Series reaches its natural conclusion.

"How old are you?" Joe asks with a hint of a German Accent. I'm caught, but not guilty; I have no desire to read it, the odds are that he will probably give it to me at some future point.

"How old are you?"

"Old enough to drink," I say, still trying to gauge his mood.

Joe shuffles the papers. I think he says, "Old enough to know better," under his breath, but I'm not sure.

4.   I saw it on TV

I'm not old enough to remember the day that ex-U.S. marine Lee Harvey Oswald shot a bullet through JFK's skull and single-handedly launched the U.S. conspiracy industry. Nor am I old enough to claim to have attended the original Woodstock. I don't remember when The Beatles were together, but I do own a large collection of Vinyl albums. I remember selecting each and every one of them, admiring the art on their covers, reading the liner notes as if they were written by men wiser than the prophets.

I am old enough to remember getting on an airplane without going through metal detectors. I remember when no one drove with seat belts and kindergartners walked home from school alone--a time when lunch boxes were made out of metal and kids were not taught to treat all strangers as if they were members of the Manson family.

I am old enough to have experienced sexual intercourse without fear or responsibility: a brief time in human existence when no disease couldn't be cured with Penicillin, girls were on the pill, and just in case, abortion was legal.

I am young enough to remember always having a television in the house, old enough to remember watching the Vietnam War on TV. I remember the grainy black and white images of helicopters landing in rice paddies with primitive huts burning in the background. When I saw those huts, I thought of the lean-tos my brother and I used to build, and destroy, in our suburban backyard.

I remember commenting that "only 43" of our soldiers died this week, but we killed more than

300 of theirs. I was not old enough to understand the look on my mother's face, nor smart enough to know that she was silently counting the years until I was of draft age, nor sensitive enough to get the fact that she had no way to teach me that life was precious without violently removing me from the cocoon that she and my father had spent so much time constructing.

I am old enough to have grown up at a time, and foolish enough to have believed, that the future would always be better than the past, that prosperity and open roads and cheap gasoline were our birthright. To top it off, we were going to live as close to forever as possible, or at least long enough to not have to worry about much until some later time. We could change the world today, but tomorrow would be soon enough.

I am at least 30 years younger than Joe—and on a good day I have about half his energy.

5. I'm the Plant Man, Oh Yeah

"If he would just open the shades and let the sun in."

I can hear George in my office.

Of all the vendors that wander the hallways of Crown Publishing, George, The Plant Man is by far the most eccentric.

"George, I need to read my screen."

He adjusts the shutters until they are halfway open, a compromise between my plant's need for photosynthesis and, my desire to reduce eyestrain.

George turns around and sticks his finger in the potting soil of my ficus tree. "Just about right."

"I guess I can follow instructions."

"It's best to water on the same day each week." He removes the red bandana from the back pocket of his overalls and wipes his hands.

George would not even consider selling a plant to a customer unless they promised to read, and follow, the carefully worded instructions. During my career at Crown, several plants in my office have died, although I believe that at least one of them was a suicide. I get that plants need water, but at least babies scream when they are hungry. By the time a

25

plant makes a feeble attempt to indicate it needs attention, it is too late—it already has one root in the grave.

I glance down to check my e-mail and when I look up all I see of him is his graying ponytail.

Since so little is known about George, the universe requires the vacuum be filled, the blank slate covered with the gossip of inquiring minds: he lives in a greenhouse and sleeps with plants. George is the love child of hippies, raised on a commune without electricity or indoor plumbing. George was a talented law student--best in his class at Harvard--until he fried his brains on magic mushrooms. He is both happy and gay. He worked as a medic in Vietnam and became insane after seeing so many young soldiers die in a stupid and endless mistake. George's father worked for the CIA. His mother invented liquid paper, the integrated circuit, and the pet rock. George was one of the founders of Woodstock, he was on the grassy knoll, he was one of the Watergate burglars, a member of the Symbionese Liberation Army, A Maoist, a Trotskyite, a Capitalist.

He was a Rabbi with a third degree black belt, a license to carry concealed weapons, and a permit to park in handicapped spaces.

George put up with my brown thumb, and perhaps even liked me because I was one of the few at Crown Publishing that called him by his real name and held my comments when he talked with the plants.

I heard him tell healthy plants that they looked great and sick plants that not only would they grow up to be big and strong, but they would outlive him and even attend his funeral.

Imagine George's funeral. A modest affair with a few humans and dozens of plants—the ones he had struggled to bring back to life--surrounding his grave. An event that begs the question, do plants water themselves when they cry?

6.   **Effect and Cause**

He stands tall and straight, as if being judged for an Olympic medal in posture. Even the back of his white shirt is as wrinkle free and smooth as the whiteboard he draws on. John Williams is the only person in the conference room wearing a necktie. We all wait silently for him to finish.

Eight years ago, when I began my career at Crown Publishing, I would have been thrilled to sit in one of the dark leather chairs that can be adjusted into more than 126 ergonomically correct positions. Prior to the meeting I would have read, and reread, the memos and reports, hoping to contribute to the discussion, or at least nod my head in agreement with the executive chairing. Sitting in the back of the room, I would have wondered if it were appropriate to grab a brownie from the silver tray or an ice-cold soda from the always fully stocked mini-fridge.

Williams takes a handful of colorful markers and starts working on an elaborate 3-D cube.

Brownies and soda are often the main topic of discussion at Crown. Sales think they are loaded with powerful stimulants that help them make their quotas. The creative staff believes they contain just enough hallucinogens to bring out their creative impulses. The editorial staff doesn't really care and chows down as many as possible--free food is free food.

New cubes appear on the board, each one a different combination of colors.

Department heads always look for reasons to schedule meetings with the president, necessitating the need for the executive conference room and access to the executive goodies. The executive conference room is one of the only places at Crown Publishing more equal than the others, and everyone knows it.

The new cubes seem to be attempting to communicate, or perhaps mate with, the original cubes.

Williams steps away from the board so we can all see what topic has brought us together: The *Internet: Crisis or Opportunity?*

"Crisis or Opportunity?" Williams states in case some of us can't read and then gives us plenty of time to think about it, to reflect upon our suggestions, before having them summarily rejected in front of our peers.

Things really started changing shortly after Michael Crown took over the operation of the company from his father. The changes were small, and far from subtle. Executive offices were redecorated, conference rooms enlarged. Changes that were not earth shattering on their own, but together, they made one wonder about the priorities of the new president.

It started with the soda.

Michael Crown liked his soda very cold, almost to the point of freezing---cold enough that ice crystals were just starting to form, but not so cold the can exploded when opened. After much trial and error, and the best refrigeration engineers on Long Island, the perfect settings were determined, and the world was safe from room temperature Pepsi and exploding Diet Cokes.

"What does the research say?" John Williams asks, as he carefully adjusts one of his silver cufflinks with the shiny Crown Logo.

He uses the word research as if it had the same effect on users as the Zyklon B[1]. Research is unnecessary when you have gut instinct or are at least willing to keep pounding on the square peg until it finally slides through the round hole.

I don't mind presenting, but not without lots of preparation. I clear my throat, because when he looks at me, I'm going to have to say something.

"John, as you know, research for any new technology, such as the Internet is limited at best." I know I have to expand my answer, and I know there is a fifty percent chance that he will ignore whatever I have to say and a fifty percent chance that he will find some fault with my statements. I can't say which outcome I prefer.

Officially, research can be divided into two categories: Primary and Third Party. Research we conduct ourselves, or stuff we purchase from one of more than two dozen research houses that hawk studies to the technology industry. I, and everyone

---

[1] The Glossary at the end of the novel has been provided for your review.

else in the department, divide research into our own categories: research that tells the client exactly what they want to hear, and everything else.

"Is the Internet the next big thing or what?" he demands. The "or what" is almost too tempting to resist. *I would like or what' for $2,000--Alex.*

I do know this: never, ever, use the term correlation in an answer to Williams--the term produces a Pavlovian response in the man. He hears the term and immediately howls: "Correlation is not cause and effect."

"Most companies are just beginning to form an Internet strategy…"

Williams's official title is Executive Vice President of Publishing, but his real function and source of power is as the right hand of our president. He has been with the company for more than 15 years and is known for setting sales records, drinking heavily, yelling, and chasing skirts. I can't say how much of it is true, but I can say he does almost nothing to mitigate his reputation.

In about ten seconds I'm going to have to continue.

"The Internet is CB radio of the Nineties," booms a voice from outside the conference room. Once again the room is silent.

Saved by stupidity.

Tom Gordon enters the room dressed like a man late for a party at the yacht club. "The Internet is just one big fad," he glances across the assembled looking for support.

No matter how well I have thought out arguments and counter-arguments for every possible point of view, there is always someone that states something that is free of facts or logic. The fact that this person is usually in upper management, or in this case, a member of the board of directors, only makes it worse. Fighting stupidity is like peeing into the wind.

Gordon scans the whiteboard for something to comment on. Like a man in a karate match, Williams keeps his eyes locked on Gordon. Perhaps, the Internet is just a fad, like the printing press, radio, television, the steam ship, sliced bread.

In grad school, at the end of a long night of training white rats in Skinner boxes or compiling data on the mainframe, we would gather in The Pub and discuss ways we could use psychological research to seduce women.

Eventually, we designed an elaborate experiment where our subjects were asked to answer detailed personal questions. The subjects, freshman co-eds earning extra credit for their Psych 101 class, would be asked to return the next day.

When they returned, it would be made to appear that they had been randomly assigned to a specific room with another subject. Of course, like most events in life, it wasn't random, the second subject in the room was one of us, and we had selected the young lady based on the profile completed the day before.

Our plan was to scare the crap out of them. Since our hero would have memorized the subject's questionnaire he would be able to connect with her as if they were a match made by the goddess of love herself. What woman wouldn't be interested in a man who just shared a terrifying experience with them and who also shared their interests in politics, religion, music, movies...?

We rationalized that if Milgram could get subjects to electrocute a stranger and Zimbardo could get strangers to totally humiliate their fellow citizens, why couldn't we facilitate love? We even decided to fill out an application for a research grant. We called our study: The *Effect of Fear on Interpersonal Interaction*.

"Tom," John Williams comes to the rescue, "Many of our largest advertisers are getting on the Net."

"They'll be sorry in eighteen months," Gordon replies. "CB radio."

"Let us at least hear what the research has to say," and Williams stares back at me. He wants me to completely back him up--that's not my job. My job is more nuanced than Williams will ever understand.

"Online users continue to grow at more than 10% per quarter, mostly via proprietary networks."

Research is a tool, not a religion. Sometimes it works, often it doesn't--but it is usually better than just guessing or going blind. At the very least, it's a starting point.

I sense neither Williams nor Gordon are listening. They are both thinking what to say to each other when I finish. I might as well be reading from the phone book.

"So far, most people online are involved in technology or academia, but some early adopters are showing an increased interest."

Much to our relief, our research application was never accepted. We all swore we would reject the money if it came through. Our ethical concerns outweighed our need to get laid. Or maybe we were just chicken.

And while John Williams and Tom Gordon are each attempting to get the last word on the impact of technology on society, I take an extra-large brownie and sneak out of the conference room.

7.   The Song Remains The Same

"*Ice Nine.* It's their new album." Dave stands and extends his hand.

"Sounds like the sound track for a failed suicide."   We shake.

"I'll get you a copy."

"Thanks."

"The name of the group is from a novel by Kurt Vonnegut about the end of the world."   He hands me a very generic looking CD.

"*Cat's Cradle.*"

"How'd you know?"

He seems disappointed, as if most, if not all, the pleasure of listening to unknown music is derived from being able to impress your friends with your knowledge of the band's origins.   The names of the bands may be cute and colorful--*Cereal Killer, Donkey Hate,* for example, but the music all sounds the same: monotonal chanting that could easily be mistaken for the soundtrack of *The Tibetan Book of the Dead.*

37

"Lucky guess." I keep turning the CD over and over, each time expecting to see the title. "What's the name of the album?"

"It doesn't have a name."

"It doesn't have a name?"

"You just have to know."

"Doesn't that only work, when you are already famous?"

"They have a following locally," he says as he grabs a pile of boards. Dave is a graphic artist.

It is an unwritten rule in magazine production that obscure music must be played at all times. Trendy computer mags aimed at the general public even list the albums that were imbibed while the book was assembled. If you recognize any of the bands you must be related to, or sleeping with, at least one of its members.

"I have some stuff for you to look at." *Stuff* to look at is not what I want to hear. I need a simple layout for an internal presentation, and instead I'm going to get an art show.

"I took the basic idea and played with the layout."

"Much better." And if it ended here I would be satisfied, and this silly project would be off my to-do list and I would be able to devote my attention to the Comdex presentation.

He removes the top board and displays the next one.

"Which typeface do you like better?" He flashes the boards back and forth.

I know what a serif is, I just don't know what the minimum daily requirement is.

"It's all good."

"Which one is best?"

I feel like a colorblind man looking at paint swatches for an outhouse. I flip a coin in my head. "I like the first one."

I know it's not really over, protocol requires I make another suggestion. Something for Dave to work on, tinker with; something that will allow him to use his artistic skills, hone his craft, justify his college education or at least the tens of thousands of

39

dollars of computer hardware and software in his office.

"You could, maybe, make the titles a little bigger."

"I'll do that," he says as I get up to leave. "Thanks."

"My band, *Tequila Mockingbird*, is playing in the city next week—you can bring your girlfriend."

"Sure."

"We are putting the final touches on our first CD."

"Cool."

8. **Windows in the Rear**

The title of Alfred Hitchcock's 1954 film, known in the U.S. as *Rear Window*, stars Jimmy Stewart as a wheelchair bound Photographer. Stewart's infirmity, along with his profession gives him license to spy on his neighbors. He is not a voyeur. No, the only voyeurs in 1950s America were sexual deviants or spies.

Jimmy is just a working guy stuck in a wheelchair whose only fault is that he's unwilling to get hitched to his girlfriend (Grace Kelly). If the future Princess Grace can't persuade you to walk, or wheel down the aisle, you are my hero.

I don't think Hitchcock would dare film what I see out my windows. He had no problem with Ms. Lonely Hearts and her imaginary dinner parties or Miss Torso's workout sessions. Murder, even discussion of the dismemberment of a woman's body or the offing of a puppy, didn't seem to make the master of suspense blink. But raw sex, that's different. Vivisection is sometimes okay, but absolutely no fucking.

For the past several months the neighbors-- who I have named Adam and Eve--have kept up their pattern of regular intercourse. Late Wednesday Nights, or early Thursday mornings, they act out a different chapter of the Kama Sutra. They almost always do it with the lights on, but dimmed, the curtains down halfway, but never completely closed.

The strangest position I have witnessed is what I like to call the backwards spider. She was on all fours, but face up. How she kept her balance while he thrust in and out of her was beyond my comprehension. It was exhausting to watch. I was glad when they switched to something more conventional.

I've never seen either of their faces. As far as I know I pass both of them on the street every day. I've caught myself staring at kissing couples wondering if they were Adam and Eve.

Of course, Jimmy was doing what comes naturally. Maybe it makes the act more exciting for Adam and Eve when they know there is a chance someone might be observing. Perhaps it fuels their passion. Maybe the murderer in Rear Window expected, and even needed to get caught. The real voyeurs are the audience in the theatre, the people watching the person watching.

All I know is this: about a week ago, Eve was cleaning her bedroom window. Wearing nothing more than an extra-large Crown publishing T-shirt, she sat on the ledge and meticulously wiped the upper half of the outside pane. Next, she climbed back inside and did her best to reach the lower half of the outside. When she was finished her windows where spotless. .

Was it to better see out with or better to see in with? Perhaps she's just a neatness freak. Whatever the case, Eve has the cleanest windows this side of Eden.

9.   **The Twinkie Defense**

In November 1978, City Councilman Dan White murdered the mayor of San Francisco and a city councilman. At the trial, White's lawyer argued Dan was depressed and therefore not responsible for his actions. He pointed to White's excessive consumption of snack foods, including, but not limited to, Hostess Twinkies®, as proof White was despondent.

After Dan White was found not guilty by reason of mental defect and sent to a state mental hospital, the media jumped on the Twinkie defense story.

Twinkies are no match for brownies in the executive conference room.

It started like many mornings in the world of technology, a last minute e-mail marked extremely urgent—a message insisting I join a meeting, first thing Thursday morning.

If, and it's big if, some future archeologist is able to decode electronic communication from this moment in human history, they will be treated to tons of banal, and more banal e-mail. What they will learn, is hard to say, but I would argue, they would be forced to conclude the more recipients an urgent e-mail is sent to, the less likely it is too be answered.

The more people involved, the less that each is responsible.

Ask Catherine Susan Genovese. At least 27 New Yorkers heard her screams as she was being stabbed to death in the courtyard of her apartment complex. Either they didn't want to get involved or assumed someone else would. Social scientists call it diffusion of responsibility.

Before taking my seat in the back, I gathered my supply of soda and brownies and pretended to listen to the back and forth of Cassandra and Williams. A sugar rush was my replacement for sleep.

"John, I think you are misinterpreting what I stated." Cassandra lifts her eyeglasses to glance at her notes.

"Next time, say what you mean and mean what you say."

I couldn't imagine anyone having a legitimate complaint about her work. She is a great researcher.

"John, you can't merely take what people say they are going to do and expect that to correspond to what they actually do."

"Why not?"

"Sometimes people say what they think you want them to."

Cassandra's intelligence and Ivy League education could whip Williams in a fair debate. It wouldn't even be close. This is not Oxford and we are separated by more than miles from the Harvard debating society.

"But it's possible," Williams insists.

"Unlikely," Cassandra correctly protested. "Highly unlikely."

If you bring your message to the John Williams' of the world and they don't agree they will tell you why you must be wrong. If only you had more faith or were willing to work harder, you could get different results. And we all know that different results based on the same data mean that there will be more work for aspiring messengers for years to come.

"John, the correlation between computer user--"

"Correlation is not cause and effect!"

"I'm aware of the difference."

"Are you aware that in the 1930s there was an extremely high correlation between ice cream sales and polio outbreaks?

"Of course."

"Are you claiming that ice cream causes polio or is the other way around?"

"You know perfectly well the two are unrelated."

"But there is an extremely high correlation."

Is it my responsibility to step in? I need sleep, not an argument. Do I continue to listen to the bullshit or get slammed for attempting to refute it? How does one choose between gonorrhea and syphilis?

"I believe ice cream sales and polio outbreaks are what you would call a coincidence, not a correlation," Cassandra counters.

Nice. Polio is a virus that can easily be spread from kid to kid in playgrounds and parks during the hot summer months, the exact same time ice cream sales increase. In this case the correlation tells us nothing.

"You depend too much on correlations and coincidences. It undermines everything else you have presented to us."

I would love to point out to Williams that there is a very strong correlation between cigarette smoking and lung cancer. A correlation so high the tobacco industry had to hire extra lawyers and lobbyists to refute it. Sometimes, cause and effect is in the malignant tumors of the unfiltered smokers.

Cassandra starts to talk, but like a crossing guard protecting schoolchildren Williams extends his right arm.

The room is quiet. I put down my soda, without taking a sip. "And what if the Angel had been late?" Williams blurts.

Why is everyone looking at me?

"What if the Angel had been late," he repeats. I have no idea what he is talking about. *Angel, the new operating system from Microsoft? Does one of our competitors have a new Web Strategy? Can this be a new publication? Angel, the technology publication for your next life.* If I had more sleep last night, maybe I would be able to figure it out.

"Here's a clue. The Angel the Lord sends to prevent Abraham from sacrificing his favorite son." He pauses. "What would have happened to Isaac if the Angel had been just a few minutes late?" I get the feeling he has practiced this routine while performing his morning shave.

"What about the guy that misses his flight, but then the plane crashes, wasn't he better off being late than dead?" I ask.

"So now you're the expert on death?" Williams responds.

"And you are?" I too am on auto-pilot.

"I saw my share of death defending my country."

"You typed up body count reports in an air conditioned office."

Let the record reflect I was right, except for the fact the office was only air conditioned by a fan. It was easy duty; no one was awarded the Purple Heart for a paper cut. I do the only smart thing and leave. I don't blame my actions on too many brownies, or not enough sleep or the fact Susie spent the night at her office. No, the devil did not make me do it. I was awake in the middle of the night watching the neighbors.

And Dan White? Less than a year after being released from a state mental hospital he committed suicide. The coroner failed to mention if snack foods were involved.

10. This is going on your permanent record

Hello Kitty and all her stuffed friends stare down at me from the bookshelves. I can afford to smile back. I still have a job. They only axe/fire/ downsize people in one of the HR departments conference rooms—with witnesses that are not manufactured in China.

"You could take some time off," Lisa says, as she scans my personnel records.

On the middle shelf, teddy bears snuggle. The smiles on their faces are so wide, I'm surprised one of them is not smoking a cigarette.

"I have work to do."

"We all keep busy," Lisa says as she runs the pink feather of her pen across her cheek. Lisa is well dressed, articulate and without personality. I can't imagine her uttering a sentence that isn't written in the secret book of HR phrases. Yet her office is decorated as if the ten-year-old Lisa decided this is what an adult's office should look like.

"It's Comdex season." In the tech world, the calendar is not divided by something as arbitrary as the tilt of the earth or phases of the moon, but rather which trade show is coming into orbit. None has a larger gravitational pull than Fall Comdex, the black hole of technology. If your tech company isn't at the Comdex trade show, it doesn't exist.

"I've been asked to help develop the presentation on the impact of the Internet."

"I would like to suggest that you work from home."

I can't be the first male to be attracted to her. But why?

"Maybe I could do it for a few days."

Perhaps it's the conservative dress.

"We were thinking about two weeks."

"Two Weeks?"

She remains silent. The Garfield clock indicates at least 30 seconds have passed.

"John Williams is really upset. He doesn't like to be challenged so publicly." she continues. "If you didn't report to Joe, and if he didn't respect your work, well, let's leave it there."

"Comdex is less than two months from now."

"I am aware of this."

"I really need to help Joe with the presentation."

"Joe is not giving the presentation."

"Of course he is--"

"--He had a stroke."

11. **I See U**

"Room 639, down the hall, towards the right," the nurse points, and looks back at her chart.

"Thanks." I make no effort to move. "How's he doing?"

"You need to speak with his doctor," she says without looking up.

"Okay."

"I can tell you he is going to have to relearn to speak."

Before I enter the room I hesitate. I know from the nurse that he has visitors, but I hear nothing. I expect to see several people sitting glumly around a hospital bed. Perhaps one is holding Joe's hand, while another carefully wipes the drool from his chin as he gazes at the flickering images from a cheap hospital television set.

There is no television.

Everyone is reading.

His son, Michael grasps a page that looks like it was ripped from a notepad. His daughter looks back and forth from her page to her father. Only, Lillian, Joe's wife, doesn't concern herself with secret notes. She knits.

Joe sits in bed, writing. His pen moves across the page as if it is being chased by a posse that has no intention of taking prisoners. He motions me over. I thought he might want to say something. His hands shake, but his intention is clear. I hold onto the page like maybe it is the winning lottery ticket.

"I just wanted to stop by and see how you are doing."

Joe wags his finger at my paper.

The writing on the page looks alien. Did the stroke cause him to regress and write in German, the language of his youth?

Years of staring at computer screens, or only reading items that had been neatly printed, have trained my brain to not recognize handwriting. I almost wish that I couldn't make out what is in front of me. It's a to-do list written for a committee of fully caffeinated Harvard MBA graduates. Every project Joe has thought about, mentioned in passing, or threatened to work on, is on the list. The stroke didn't kill him, so he has to clear up all his unfinished business before the next one.

"Spending a lot of time on the presentation." I say.

Joe looks up, points to the note, and attempts to speak, but like a car that can't get traction on an icy street, he's unable to move his lips.

The Doctor enters, followed by his residents/groupies.

Outside the room Michael is absorbed with his note. I usually have no idea of what to say to the President of the Company, but understand it is good for my career to engage in conversation. "I think he's going to be Okay."

"He's dying."

It seems I am keeping my record of saying the wrong thing to anyone who works in upper management unchallenged. Michael once again glances at his note, says he has work to do, and leaves.

12. Sex Girl Receives Sunburn Near Pool

On the train home I read from the *Book of Joe,* my name for the memoirs of Joseph Crown. The current section stored in my backpack is from the Baseball = Apple Pie chapters.

"Is there a more pleasing sound in the universe than the cracking of the bat? When the batter swings and the ball explodes off the bat this is a sound that can't be found anywhere in nature. You can have your singing birds and bears that break wind in the forest. Keep the buzzing bees-- nature is no match for a Louisville Slugger in the mighty arms of a skilled batsman.

My brother and I waited for the cracking of ball and bat during batting practice. This was my older brother Charlie who died of cancer and not my younger brother Sam who disappeared in the war.

I remember our first trip to the stadium. It was early spring. Very cold. The sun was shining, but like a Bronx landlord refused to give us warmth. Charlie would always say, any day without rain was the perfect day for baseball in New York City, the baseball capital of the entire world..."

And on and on it went, an inning by extra inning recap of a random game written by a scorekeeper that was under the impression that this was the seventh game of the final World Series.

Joe's story was interesting, but who cares how the sunlight reflected off the infield while the players stood like Greek gods during the playing of the Star Spangled Banner or if the beer man did his James Cagney imitation while pouring cold ones?

I keep reading, because for every five pages about bat boys and peanut salesmen who could accurately toss a bag of nuts across three aisles there was a line or two about a young Mantle or a majestic shot over the wall in right field by DiMaggio.

Joe needed an editor, but hated being edited. I'd encourage him to cut it down. He would then sneak it back in. We went back and forth.

When I first started working for Joe he wanted to know how the sales and editorial staff at Crown Publishing were using the Internet. What type of information did they seek? What were they searching for?

They were searching, searching for pussy—porn consumers have always been early adaptors of new technology. Romans had nude frescos that served as menus in whorehouses. Although not pornographic by today's standards, the first Steno scope images were of Victorian woman with uncovered ankles. A majority of the first VHS tapes available for rental were X-rated. VHS became the standard because Sony would not let its superior BETA technology be used for porn.

The Internet server logs at Crown indicated that not only were porn sights popular, but many of them were hosted overseas, captioned by non-English writers. Some of my favorites:

She is virginity!!!

To her Eighteen years!!! She did not have men!

She is dissolute and the coitus wants!

She is ready to suck thy member and ovums!

Welcome in my pussy cat!

Learn her to be adult!

The headline writers for the New York Post have no fear of losing their jobs to their comrades overseas.

I wanted to do an analysis of the different sexual interests and appetites of various departments at Crown Publishing. Imagine what I could do with the findings. 28% of your department prefer women that are made to look like they are still in high school or younger. Your magazine is less gay than the rest of the industry. Do you think that last quarter's slip in advertising sales has anything to do with your departments viewing habits? Your senior sales staff seems to be obsessed with anal sex, can you explain why? What would the HR department think about interracial porn? On one hand, your department believes in equal opportunity, but on the other…

I weeded through the Web logs and gave Joe a list of non-porno sites the staffers were using on a regular basis. I also noted that one of the top applications was e-mail. He read the report and concluded that the Web was a useful tool for sharing information.

"It could catch on," he said.

"Maybe you should give it a try," I suggested.

13.   Office Home

My work at home started out extremely productive. I got up early, brewed a pot of whatever blend Zabars had on sale the previous week, cleared off Susie's old desk, set up my loaner laptop, read my e-mail, and even responded to a few of the less urgent ones. I hung my to-do list on the bulletin board above the monitor, where I could ignore it in plain sight.

Crown Publishing produces a newsletter that explores both the practical and technological aspects of telecommuting. I've never read an entire issue, but I do get the gist: workers love telecommuting; bosses hate it. Staffers love the flexibility and the ability to get the job done without the typical workplace disruptions. Supervisors complain that they have no way of knowing what their workers are up to. Yes, they get the work done, but is there more the employees could be contributing to the organization?

Susie is AWOL. It's not like this is the first time. She traveled on business and worked late. She had a couch in her office and often did the opposite of telecommuting.

I never assumed she had other lovers, but who the fuck knows for sure. On the few occasions that I stopped by her office, it looked like the habitat of a workaholic. The wastebasket was overflowing with coffee cups, empty snack-food wrappers, and the obligatory Chinese take-out containers.

Into the kitchen for my 2nd cup of coffee. "Hallelujah," I hear from the sidewalk. "Hallelujah, "Hallelujah." His screams grow louder and than fainter like a slow-moving ambulance. "Hallelujah." I have heard his screams many times; his trips are frequent, but not regular enough to tell the time by, just more noise in a city that doesn't need more noise.

I look out the window, across the corridor, and see Eve with her back to me, Eve studying herself in the mirror. Her fingers work through her short, dark hair—she is getting ready to go out.

I find my shoes and hit the stairs.

First mistake, I'm downstairs before her and have to loiter in front of my own building.

Eve steps out and I'm an agent on a secret mission.

She heads towards Broadway. I don't want to get too close to her, but I want to be close enough to hear what she sounds like when she talks, as opposed to when she moans, or screams, with pleasure.

Good surveillance requires teamwork. Different people following at different times. Each one careful not to get too close for too long. I can talk into my sleeve as much as I want, but no one is listening. The men in the surveillance van are not eating donuts and whispering witty remarks in my ear. I'm on a solo mission.

She appears to be on her way to the subway. As I descend the stairs I can hear the downtown train approaching. Eve places her subway token in the slot and moves through the turnstile. I do the same.

Decision time. If I get in a different car, will I be able to see when she exits? If I'm in the same car, will she notice?

Why worry? New Yorkers are notorious for their ability to ignore their fellow travelers. We use an endless series of tricks, adapt a million different personas, prepare sarcastic things to say--just in case. It's a skill set we covet, passing down our secrets of how best to ignore our fellow riders to only our best friends or offspring.

She isn't a beauty, but she isn't ugly either-- she has the type of body that other women would jealously say is a "nice figure." A figure capable of bending into acrobatic positions that would drive any man wild. But if I didn't know that, I wouldn't give her a second look.

She is reading a book. One of the things I was going to do today was to take inventory of our book collection. This is how I keep track of Susie. I knew that if she left for good she would take all her books with her.

Both of us were readers and over the years we culled our collection, we had to, our entire home library was a bookcase with five shelves and whatever volumes we could stack on our end tables. At New York rental prices, it would have to be our Library of Congress.

I had no idea as to the rhyme or reason of her permanent book selections. Why did Hemingway make the list and not Faulkner or Fitzgerald? I understand treasuring John Kennedy Toole's masterpiece, a *Confederacy of Dunces,* but why Jerzy Kosinski, Richard Brautigan, Michael Dorris, Yukio Mishima, and Primo Levi? I'm not afraid of Virginia Woolf, but I'm really not interested in rereading *To the Lighthouse* or *Mrs. Dalloway.* Is there an author of short stories more obscure than Breece D'J Pancake?

Susie loved her books and when she disappeared for a day or two she would just take one of her favorites and that was it. I still had the library, but the librarian was missing.

I read and reread the subway ads, and reaffirm advertisers believe underground riders must all suffer from sore feet, bad skin and hemorrhoids. In addition, are the ads for the subway system itself. I'm already on the train, why tell me how wonderful it is? If I had another way to get around, a method that was faster and cheaper and didn't smell like urine, I would take it every time. Subway ads in subway cars make as much sense as recruiting posters inside of an Army barracks. *Uncle Sam wants you! To be here.*

Eve stays engrossed in her paperback. She doesn't look up each time the car stops, she has made this trip many times.

What makes a person collect the works of authors that insisted on writing their own endings? I was ashamed it took me so long to figure out the suicide link of all of Susie's books. Perhaps, if she appreciated poetry and included Sylvia Plath it would have been easier to see, but Susie never did strive to make anything easy. This was the point: if you don't get the joke, you don't get to laugh, to be in the club. Your loss.

She even went so far as to organize the volumes in the order the Suicide Authors had each ended their writing careers. I never got an answer when I asked her about the collection, perhaps this was because I never pressed hard enough. What was I afraid of?

The train stops. Luckily for me, New Yorkers are impatient; they always telegraph their next move. The station is Christopher Street; we are in The Village. I try to not get too close, to keep the appropriate amount of distance and when she stops at the newsstand to buy some gum, I'm left standing there. If someone is watching me, they would know exactly what I was doing.

She finishes her transaction and continues. I hesitate (my second surveillance mistake) and miss the light. I have to wait until several cars pass before jaywalking. She turns the corner onto West 8th street. When I get to the corner, she has vanished. I continue up the street, look both directions at the corner. Nothing. I look back and to see if I have missed anything. Not a trace of Eve anywhere.

My career as a character in a Raymond Chandler novel is over before it starts. I head back to the subway and my home office.

In a study on management effectiveness, two groups of bosses were asked to supervise a worker. One group of bosses observed their charge for only ten minutes every hour, while the 2nd group watched their workers for more than 30 minutes each hour. In both cases, the workers did the identical amount of work. It was no surprise that the 2nd group of bosses, the ones who were in the position of watching more than the first group, claimed their workers were lazy and needed more supervision than the supervisors of the first group, who were judged to be both more independent and reliable.

14. Great Exaggerations

Everyone has a list.

Rumors of Joe's upcoming death were greatly exaggerated. Although his birth certificate was still without an expiration date, his fear of dying, as opposed to his actually passing, was much worse for everyone. People who only think that they are dying have tremendous amounts of energy to threaten, menace, guilt, or simply annoy their children, employers, bosses, underlings and coworkers. The might-be-dying may not be the most powerful people on earth, but they have no compunction against using their position to get exactly what they truly believe they deserve.

The scuttlebutt at Crown was that Michael's job was somehow on the line, that the company was in play and had even received offers—from competitors. Joe was not running the company, but he did have controlling interest and if he sold his shares, the company would soon have new managers.

Mergers, buyouts, hostile takeovers, whatever you name them, they all mean the same thing. Times, they are a changing, and someone is going to get axed. Combine two fairly stable, basically well-run companies, and you have an extra set of accounting, human resource, marketing, and research personnel. One minute your career is sailing along, you are happy and safe and then, in a brief—New York, New York minute you have a forced smile on your face and a resume in your hand.

The posters on the wall all say that change is an opportunity, that change is good. But employees who might soon get axed are the patients waiting in his oncologist's office to find out if the tumor is malignant or benign. *Oh please god, I promise, if it's benign, I'll go to church every week, I'll never steal cable again, I'll recycle.*

There is no more talk about brownies or sodas or sex and relationships. Instead the discussion is all about the future of the company, the latest, up to the minute, rumors and gossip, which are all recycled from yesterday's rumors and gossip.

I monitor the news via e-mail. The distance does not give me any perspective, but it does give me an opportunity to ignore much of it and get some work done.

15.   De Nlle

"In ancient Egypt, much like today, farmers depended on the Nile to flood and irrigate their crops."

I've been given a reprieve from my banishment from Crown Publishing so I could work on the Comdex presentation with Tom Gordon.

"Each spring, Pharaoh would send his high priests 1,000 miles down the river. They would then send a message back to Pharaoh letting him know how large the crops would be."

"I didn't know that." I also didn't know that Gordon was an Egyptologist, and hoped that I wouldn't have to use the Rosetta stone to translate the presentation into hieroglyphics.

"Do you know how they did it?"

"No idea." I didn't have a clue and if I had one I would have said no anyway. I know that he is dying to tell me and I had the feeling that the answer was somewhat interesting. I also knew that his answer would last longer than my interest, but that was punishment for committing an unknown sin in an earlier life. Perhaps I wrote graffiti on Pharaoh's tomb.

"The priests had not merely watched the river, they observed it, you understand the difference?"

"I think so."

"They knew that if the water was clear, it was because the White Nile, which flowed from Lake Victoria, dominated the flow. Flooding would be at a minimum and so would the crops.

"If the water was dark, it was because stronger waters of the Blue Nile were predominant and flooding would be just right, and the crops would be perfect. Pharaoh would be able to raise taxes and send his armies to conquer more territory."

So Pharaoh was both a Democrat and a Republican.

"Green-Brown water indicated that more water was coming from the Atbarah River—this meant too much water too early, flooding would be early and high, and crops would be ruined."

"Interesting," is all I can say.

71

Gordon plays with the trim on one of his model sailboats. "The priests were almost 100% accurate."

"Amazing."

"Do you think that any of your forecasts or predictions has even been close to being as accurate as the priests?"

I predict that by the time that he is finished, the cafeteria will be closed and I will be forced to eat my lunch from a vending machine.

"I'm not quite sure how this is going to help our presentation."

"My presentation."

"Your presentation."

"Unless you can predict something as accurately as the priests of ancient Egypt, you shouldn't make any predictions."

I keep nodding my head, but I'm no longer pretending to take notes.

"You think you can sum this up?"

"I'm guessing that you think that the jury is still out, the flag is still on the flagpole, but no one is saluting,"

"Exactly!" he says.

All I can think is that I hate people that love clichés and I have no idea what he wants to say in his presentation. Or what should be said. I get up to leave.

"Do you know what happened when the priests were wrong?"

They were promoted to upper management, elected to Congress, appointed to the Board of Directors.

His phone rings, he glances at the display.

"I have no idea."

"Think about it." He picks up the phone and says "hello."

16. All about Eve

Eve strolls through SOHO. This is only my second attempt, but I have already learned how to match her speed. I too must stroll. From Grand

Street she turns right and heads South on West Broadway. My notebook is in hand in case I come up with an idea for Tom Gordon's presentation. Like the presentation, Eve is still a mystery.

The name on her mailbox says Jane Gold. There is a listing for a J. Gold on our street in the Manhattan phone book. I dialed the number, when I knew she wasn't home, but just got the factory-installed voice asking me to please leave a message and someone will get back to me before the end of time.

She stops to gaze into a shop window, but I am far enough back to stop without fear that she will notice me. Just to be safe, I pretend to tie my shoe.

Remembering that she once wore a Crown Publishing T-shirt, I searched the employee and vendor databases and found nothing. T-shirts are the inflated currency of the tech economy. Employees hoard them and give them as cheap gifts. At trade shows, the herds wait in line, sit through mind-numbing presentations just to get a free one. Many tech workers have enough t-shirts to wear a different one every day for the rest of their lives, and still have new ones left over for their cremation or burial.

Eve finishes her window-shopping and continues down the street. I searched every database and found out that she doesn't own real estate (not unusual for New York), has never been convicted of a crime (somewhat unusual), or named as a plaintiff or defendant in a lawsuit (off the charts unusual).

I drew a blank with all organizations and associations that are available electronically. She may be a butcher, baker or candlestick maker, but she is not listed as a Doctor, Lawyer, advertising, or financial executive in the state of New York. The same goes for the fields of acting, nursing, and public relations. I had no idea what Eve does for a living. With the exception of her Wednesday night fuckathons, I had more knowledge of the Biblical Eve than the namesake that lived across from me.

It's easy to live off the grid in this city. For every actor, there are 1,000 waiters, for every writer, 10,000 bartenders: workers with day jobs that exist in a dreamworld just under the radar of success. They move around Manhattan like they own it, only a break away from fame and fortune.

Eve enters the SOHO Grand Hotel. Is she meeting someone for lunch? A secret rendezvous with her lover? Just to be safe, I count to ten.

I hear my name from across the street. I turn my head and confirm that it is Susie. What am I going to tell her if she asks why I am hanging out in such a hip neighborhood as South of Houston?

"Hey stranger."

"What are you up to?" I ask.

"I'm doing a study of NY neighborhood names for a new client."

"A new client?"

"I'm starting with the Acronyms: SoHo, NOLITA, DUMBO."

"Dumbo?"

"The Development under the Manhattan Bridge."

"Sounds like housing in hell."

"It's not really under, it's below, but DBTMB, doesn't work as an acronym."

"Have you had lunch?" I ask.

"Not yet."

"Expense account?"

"Never leave home without it."

17. Let's Misbehave

Susie? I can never separate the name from the question mark.

She has a wicked sense of humor and a fascination with suicide. Her hair is so red that it would make a Hawaiian sunset jealous. Her smile is so powerful that it never fails to stop me in my tracks. She sports a heart tattoo in a location that if it was made with edible ink, I could spend the rest of my life licking it. Her mind is nonlinear to the point that it alone proves that time and space really is curved.

The waitress at the Broome Street Bar hands us menus.

"We know exactly what we want," Susie says.

"Our specials today include--"

The waitress continues as Susie and I look at each other and smile. You come to Broome Street for many reasons: to hang out with your mates, drink imported beer, and catch a glimpse of a rock star at 2 in the morning. You don't come to Broome Street to hear about fish that has been imported from another planet, marinated in the East River, and then pan-seared by a short-order cook that graduated from Denny's university and makes great burgers and little else.

"Are you ready to order?" The waitress asks.

We can no longer hold it back and both break out in laughter. It is this laughter that bonds me to her. We laugh therefore we are. We laugh when we are sober and even more when we were drunk or high.

We only get high at inappropriate times. Before family gatherings, especially the ones that included birthday parties for toddlers. Having grown up in Jesus, New Jersey, Susie had more than her share of nieces, nephews, and cousins that needed to spend the anniversary of their arrival on earth with a dozen of their untamed peers. This was OK with us, until we learned that adults were also expected to attend, to pay tribute, to admire her friends and relatives for failing to use birth control.

It became our tradition to smoke some grass before the event, just enough so the diet coke tasted like wine, the cold pizza--cut into little squares-- tasted like manna from heaven, and the birthday songs became permanently etched in our brains.

Susie orders and dismisses the server with the efficiency of a drill instructor. "You seem stressed." She says.

Stressed? My job is crazy and my girlfriend disappears for a day or two at a time. "The Comdex presentation," is all I can mutter. "Everyone is going to hate it, they'll all complain that it says too much or too little. Some will complain that it does both, say too little or too much of nothing"

"Presentations suck."

The waitress brings our iced teas.

On our trips home from Jersey, we spent the time laughing like teenage girls under the influence of nitrous oxide. We would start singing the party songs. It's hard to say whether it was the drugs or the insipidness of the songs but within seconds we were adding our own, more adult lyrics. "If you're happy and you know it" became "if you're horny and you know it." Before our train found its way into Penn Station (we often had the car to ourselves) we had hundreds of versions, including, if your mother is a looker, I will treat her like a hooker, although Susie's personal favorite was something about fucking and death. I was stoned; I can't be expected to remember all the lyrics.

Our lunch comes and we are in Broome Street burger heaven.

We believed that we were in good company. Cole Porter had a reputation of writing humorous and often very dirty lyrics before he wrote the real ones. The fact that Mr. Porter was interested in making music with both sexes must have given him twice the opportunities for double entendres. Who knows what a collector would pay for the x-rated versions of *My*

Heart Belongs to Daddy, Adam and Eve, Ace in the Hole, and *What is This Thing Called Love?*

And when we got home, it was as if the event never happened. We put away our pot, fucked like crazy, read our books, and went on with our lives.

The waitress returns to collect our plates and attempts to entice us with desserts made in a bakery on the outskirts of heaven.

I finally have the nerve to ask Susie. "This project that you are working on?"

"Yes."

"That's an opening for you to tell me about it."

"I can't. Really."

"Because?"

"Sworn to secrecy. Besides you always find out at the end."

"When everyone else does."

"That's the best time. It's like seeing a movie in a crowded theatre as opposed to watching it alone on a small screen."

"But we're a couple."

"Yes, we are."

The most recent visit to Susie's family was for a baptism. Why should I object to getting high before entering someone else's house of god? I'm a non-observant Jew, not a Catholic. The Latin mumbo jumbo starts making sense under the influence. And when the padre said that if the baby died, it would now go to heaven, I didn't protest. I didn't stand up and scream at the father for discussing the death of a baby in front of nervous parents. I didn't mention to the parishioners that if I were the parent, I would be more worried that a priest would molest my child than my baby being sent to hell. And while we are on the subject Padre, what religion condemns babies to eternal damnation? Can't they find enough murderers, child molesters, rapists, and lawyers to fill up the place? Do they have so much room down below that they need babies—Hell, we're expanding to meet the demand. Open 24/7. Childcare available.

Susie and I notice the couple two tables away. They hold hands under the table. Neither one has touched their food. Susie glances at the woman and then back at me. "Would you do her?"

"She's not my first choice."

"That's not the question."

I take another quick glance. "Nice figure. Hair's too short; you know how I feel about blondes. The smile is nice, but I've seen better. You?"

"She's not my type at all." Susie smiles. "Oh you mean him. He's good looking enough, but has that Wall-Street feel. The sex would be okay, but he would have nothing interesting to talk about afterwards. I do like his chin."

Great. I have plenty to talk about after sex, but if I could I would rather roll over and go to sleep. I win this round by a technicality

"Think they're married?" She asks.

"Not to each other."

Laughter may be the best medicine, but is it enough to make love stay? The evidence is inconclusive. Sometimes the laughter lasts, sometimes love does. Maybe Mr. Porter had the right idea by attempting both.

"I should be back tomorrow," she says as we leave the restaurant. "I've been sleeping on the couch in my office."

"The couch must be very comfortable."

"It is."

Another day in the life of Susie Sullivan. If I have learned anything from this relationship it's that women who leave without warning return without warning. Once they have the key to your heart, the front door takes care of itself.

18. Everyone Loves Lisa

"How is working with Tom Gordon?" Lisa asks.

"It's different."

I know she's going to keep asking until I say something that can be jotted down in an employee folder.

"How is it different?"

Compare and contrast night and day, sane and insane, people who drive pick-up trucks with gun racks and carry firearms to church and....

"We are almost done with the Comdex presentation. We're going to make the deadline." At least I hope we are. Failure may be option, but never admit that in advance.

"Any problems communicating?" She asks. The question is simple, but that doesn't mean I know what she is really asking or how much I should reveal.

"You send him an e-mail and his secretary prints it and gives him the hard copy." Did that just come out of my mouth?

She says nothing and I know, and she knows, that I am going to get tired of listening to the sound of the sounds of silence and elaborate. "The man that is going to represent a large technology publisher at the largest technology trade show in history, hand writes his e-mail replies before he hands them to his secretary so she can manually input them."

Lisa glances at her notes, but writes nothing. The new teddy bear on her desk catches her eye. Both remain silent.

"You probably are aware of the fact that the E, in E-mail, stands for electronic," I say.

"I think I read that in a book somewhere."

I see it as a sign of progress that I get her to make a witty remark.

"Has he, or anyone, said anything?"

"I'm just checking in."

She writes something on her notepad. We continue to stare at each other. I have no idea on why she is staring at me, I'm just doing my best to not try and imagine her naked.

"Thank you for making my life so interesting," I say as I get up to leave.

"Good luck with the presentation."

How would Bartleby handle the situation?

On the way into Crown, I observed the next step in the evolution of Bartleby. In phase I, Bartleby was the thinking drinking man, but we had no idea what he was thinking about. Now he has a thought bubble, with the words "What If." A bubble that would surely change, if not burst into a thousand smaller bubbles.

The beauty of Susie's art was that it forced the viewer to take a second look. Her satire was often so subtle that one could never be sure at first glance, and sometimes not even then. If the counter message was not subtle, it would be immediately torn down. Even the idiots at big tobacco can figure out that a cigarette ad with *smoking kills* across the front is not going to increase sales. They are much slower to figure out that "I'm dying for a smoke" is not the marketing message they are hoping to brainwash the masses with.

Bartleby was not finished, and neither was Susie. That was the beauty of the operation. By day, she worked for Urban Advertising, and at night she worked with her women's group thinking of new methods of sabotaging the same ads that they were paid to create.

What better method of sabotaging something than creating it in the first place? Starting in the 1960s, when companies started shipping their operations to places like Hong Kong, the manufactures started noticing the counterfeiters were producing better and better replicas of their goods. Little did they know that the counterfeiters were working out of the same factories as the original manufacturers. First shift comes and churns out the real product and then the swing clocks in and produces the knock offs. The factory owners not only get counterfeit goods that are royalty free, but they maximize their real estate holdings. One man's theft is another's capitalism.

Susie's clients often wondered why their ads were being targeted and were told that only the most popular and effective ads were vandalized. Sales often went up after an attack. Susie and the girls got their message across and the client made more money. Like the pilot fish and the shark, one couldn't prosper without the other.

Susie needed a twist, a bigger challenge. The subjects of her ad campaigns were all associated, in one way or another, with suicide. The links might all be obscure, but the connection was always there. I was told that there was a bigger picture, something that I would be able to figure out all by myself.

And so Bartleby sits patiently, thinking his deep thoughts, offering little, waiting to finish the thought before being replaced by new campaign for deodorant, maxi pads, or the next blockbuster. Someday I would be able to figure it all out. Someday.

19. Sail On

A ship in the harbor is safe, but that's not what ships are built for, or so states the framed poster on the wall outside of Tom Gordon's office.

Wall art is another method of telling the difference between sales and editorial staffers at Crown Publishing. Editorial favors an eclectic mix of unknown bands, film noir movie posters, and the musings of third-world dictators. Got Che?

Sales prefer the color photography, generic philosophy, and mantras that can only be found on motivational posters that preach to the converted and inspire the faithful. *Teamwork. Climb the highest mountain. Soar like a fucking Eagle.*

It doesn't seem to matter that the themes sometimes contradict each other, that one poster extols the virtues of putting in the extra effort on the job while another insists that the only thing that matters in the long run is raising your children. *Eagles soar, but chickens don't get sucked into jet engines.*

"Come in. I want to show you something," Gordon says as proudly as a man in the maternity ward showing off his future Hall of Famer. I heard the voice, but could not see the man. Tom Gordon was hidden behind the largest computer monitor I have ever seen. A full-color monitor is attached to the latest model computer, a fully loaded system that would make the hard drives of tech crew even harder.

I walk around his desk to see that he is online.

"People from all across the globe discussing sailing," he whispers, as if there was something top secret or illicit about an online forum. "You can get information about boat maintenance, ports of call, the best fishing spots."

"Cool."

"I wish I'd known about this ten years ago—before I purchased the Crown Princess."

"It would have been useful." If Columbus had a map of the world, he might have known that he was in the Dominican Republic and not India.

"Here's this guy from Newport that wants to sell his yacht and this poor guy in San Diego has a case of merulius lacrymans."

"Interesting."

"Merulius lacrymans is the scientific name for Dry Rot, a fungal infestation, turns wood into dust. Can destroy the best of ships."

"Dust?"

"The Internet is a social organism. Humans need to interact more than they need information, that's why there's more bars than libraries in this country."

"More bars than libraries," I repeat, but I have no idea what this means. Perhaps drinkers are less efficient than readers. Perhaps they could encourage reading if they played darts in the stacks.

"Yes, I'm here to give you the final changes for the presentation," but I fear that the winds have shifted—I need a drink more than I need a bestseller.

"We need to take a new tack. The number of online users is increasing exponentially."

"In inverse relation to the time we have to finish this presentation."

"You have a couple days, just wrap some of that research that you are so proud of around an image and you have it.

"Any image?" I ask.

"How about sailing into the future."

Or sinking into the past.

"Or something like smooth sailing into the age of discovery."

Lost in the Bermuda Triangle of hype.

"You can quote me on this; the Internet will one day be seen as important as the discovery of America."

When the Americas were discovered, the land was spoiled and the natives were screwed. Next, we imported "natives" from other countries and made them slaves. And if that wasn't enough of historical irony, we then freed the slaves, hired them as cheap labor, and sent them to hunt down the few remaining natives—all in the name of progress.

"Any image?"

"Son, you just need a metaphor."

"I'm glad you have faith in my work."

"It's not that big of a deal. Finish it tomorrow and I'll meet you in Vegas."

Gordon is the poster boy for one of the iron laws of computing: the more prominent the executive, the bigger the computer and the less likely that it will be used for anything related to useful work. Computers in corner offices are used primarily to pursue personal interests, find annoying projects for others to work on, and, last but not least, play solitaire.

Once he figured out the @ symbol I was bombarded by e-mails.

11:00 AM. Subj. The Invention of the Internet.

2:00 PM Subj. Dot Com. A lengthy cut and paste job explaining the differences between The Domains .COM, .NET, .GOV, and .EDU.

2:15 PM Subj. Suggestion.   The Internet: The Next Stage in Evolution.

7:10 PM Subj. Knot tying.

8:45 PM Subj. Sailing around the world.

He was the teenage boy discovering that his penis could be used for more than urinating; he just couldn't stop playing with it.

9:30 PM Internet. Gateway to the new economy

11:23 PM Subj. Presentation. How is it going?

My reply is simple. The Internet is bigger than the printing press, the telegraph, and the telephone. I tell him that the presentation will included such tidbits as the increase of users, examples of growth information sharing, etc, etc. I

94

even included the infinite amount of commercial possibilities.

I set my computer to log in and send the e-mail at 1:23 in the morning. I do this for two reasons. Gordon will think that I'm burning the midnight oil working on the presentation, and, more importantly, maybe I'll have made some progress by then. In two days, I'm headed off to the city of sin.

20. I'm the Plant Man, Oh Yeah (Version 2.0)

Is there a more New York snack than a slice? Always fresh, available 24/7, custom made with your choice of toppings. Pizza is like everything else in this city; we stole someone else's idea, improved it slightly, and then pretended that we invented it in the first place.

I enjoy late-night pizza often enough to recognize many of the customers, a cross section of my fellow citizens: cops and cab drivers, college students and drunken executives. Folks I would never see in my living room, but that I feel

95

comfortable discussing the important NY topics of the day (the weather, the Yankees and the idiot mayor) while waiting on line. What I didn't expect to see is someone from work seasoning two giant slices of pepperoni/mushroom.

An outsider might think that New York is a city in search of surprises, but that's because they fail to understand the difference between the Big Apple and the rest of the universe. Pack enough people into a city, take away their cars (forcing them to use their feet or take the bus) and sooner rather than later they will bump into each other. It would be a bigger surprise if they never did.

I was not surprised to see George's pony tail on the Upper West Side on Wednesday night. I glance at his selection to confirm that he eats both animals and vegetables, so much for rumor. We acknowledge each other, and he waits a minute while my order is neatly placed in a bag and paid for. We exit the pizzeria and head in the same direction. Surprise meetings are one thing, forced conversations are another. The city that never sleeps offers many avenues of escape—you meet, greet, and head off in separate directions.

George and I were headed in the same direction, I knew where I was going but where was George headed? And why?

"They say rain is coming."

"Feels like it."

"Too early for snow."

"Not for another month, at least."

"Hallelujah." I hear from up the street, heading in our direction. I have heard the voice many times, but have never seen him.

"I've hear him nearly every time I come to this neighborhood," George nods towards the short, dark man in the well-worn suit. The man screams again as if talking to no one and everyone at the same time. The bible he holds looks to be as worn and used as his suit. Perhaps it was the only thing he brought with him when he escaped from hell or whatever institution he was living in.

As Hallelujah man passes us, I look at his face, if he is rude enough to wake me on Sunday mornings with his screams; I feel I have the right to figure out why. His face is wrinkled and worn and what hair sits on his head is the grey of a wreck in the junkyard. As he passes I glance at his eyes, but they are not the eyes that hope to convert me, or anyone else. His eyes focus at a horizon that he will never reach.

We arrive at the building next to mine and George says this is where his friend lives and walks past the doorman like he owns the place. I thought he lived on Long Island. What are the odds of him having a friend right next to my apartment? What's his connection? Something doesn't compute. I have all the information I need, but not the program to put it all together.

Back in the apartment I pick up a folder with the Crown Logo. And it hits me. George. Eve with a Crown T-shirt. The pony tail. The Plant man is Adam. Another myth about George killed like mosquitoes in a bug zapper. He's not celibate. That's one mystery that I really didn't want to solve.

* * *

I was too distracted to work on the presentation and didn't dare look out the window, so I read from the works of Joseph Crown.

I ask myself for the millionth time, why I allowed myself to be volunteered for this assignment. Of course it was because of Joe. I enjoyed working for him reading and reworking his material. But Joe was incapacitated and Gordon wanted me to say that the Internet was both a flop and sliced bread, CB Radio and the invention of fire.

All I know is this:

1) The presentation is not finished.

2) In 18 hours I must get on a plane to Vegas.

3) The truth about the plant man is better than anyone ever imagined.

I turn off the stereo and listen to the sounds of the city. Perhaps Hallelujah man has something to say about the presentation, but alas, no. Another messenger of god lets me down when I really need it.

21. Stuck in the Middle with You

"I cut out the dead parts."

As sure as the sun sets in the west, as sure as airline food is not much better than the slop they serve in the state penitentiary, every heterosexual man that has ever traveled by air is hoping to be assigned a seat next to an attractive member of the opposite sex. Flying to a strange city, you meet a lonely traveler, make a connection, have a few drinks and the next thing you know, you are in hotel room fucking like crazy, raiding the mini bar—all on company time and expense. Forget the miles, frequent flyers want to be frequent fornicators.

I'm not looking to hook up, just hoping that my seat mate would at least offer some eye candy--just because I'm on a diet, doesn't mean that I can't read the menu.

"Everyone wants to know how I keep the plants so green."

I know that voice. I open my eyes and watch George stuff his duffel bag into the overhead.

No hello, no what a surprise to see you, no acknowledgment of the others existence on the same planet.

"It's okay to ask, everyone does," he continues.

Funny, that isn't the question that I want to ask. I want to know how you fuck so hard and fast, and for so long. I wanted to know how he found a girlfriend that liked to be spanked in the ass. A spank that was so loud you could hear it across the courtyard.

"It's important to remember to cut, with sharp blades, and never tear or pull."

George sits, and immediately fastens his seatbelt. His seat is in the full and upright position, but he pushes the button anyway. He picks up the card and reads the emergency instructions. He turns back and forth, scanning the layout of the plane.

"It's always good to know where the emergency exits are located."

This from a man who doesn't wear condoms.

Still holding the emergency card, he closes his eyes. I've never seen anyone looking at one of these, and here George is quizzing himself. Being prepared is one thing, but this is like studying for a urine test.

"Never tear—plants can feel," he opens his eyes.

"I've heard that."

The plane bumps its way from the gate. George swallows.

"Of course the plants need the water and their vitamins and minerals, the goal is to mimic their native environment, but you can't keep them perfect. That's why you need to prune."

Three hours and 59 more minutes.

"You see a lot of dead plants in the rainforest," he continues. "Decay is part of the cycle."

Your girlfriend begs to be fucked up the ass, I want to scream, although I'm sure it would have been against some sort of airline regulation, I can imagine the flight attendant walking up to me and sternly saying, I'm sorry sir, no screaming about anal sex in economy.

"The proper amount of sunlight is always a concern."

"Yes."

"Most people either over or under water their plants."

If the root causes of root disease ever becomes a topic on Jeopardy, I'll have all the questions.

George is nervous.

Give me bad weather, turbulence, crying babies, let the plane run out of fuel, alcohol, air sickness bags--what I fear most at this moment is that I might say something to indicate that I know more about George than anyone should.

"So George, how did you get into plants?"

He was the Plant Man for the simple reason that he wanted to be the Plant Man. It wasn't just his day job, it was also his night job, his passion and avocation.

In high school he got a part-time job in a nursery. He had a green thumb, learned everything he could about plants and soon was selling plants on the side until it became his occupation/lifestyle. When he wasn't planting and maintaining corporate gardens he donated his expertise to nursing homes and other care facilities.

"Plants supply oxygen and make people very happy," he says as he hands the flight attendant his third or fourth empty.

"Seeing anyone special?" I ask. George is about to answer, but the pilot announces that we are now flying over a part of the country that I will never visit, let alone live in, and George buys himself another brew.

22.   Geeks Bearing Gifts

Welcome to the Las Vegas Convention Center, home of Comdex. The center has approximately 2 ½ million square feet of space, give or take enough footage to place several strip-malls, parking lots, or junkyards in.

The problem with Comdex, the world's largest computer trade show and lovefest, is that it has always been just a little past its prime. One gets a nagging feeling that at last year's Comdex, the exhibits were larger, the product announcements more earth shattering, the parties more spectacular.

It was not that everyone at the show doesn't worship at the altar of technology. Technology is, and always will be, the one true god, but tech is quickly becoming mainstream, and we all know that once this happens, there will be less and less need for a trade show. The more the masses are converted, the less the urgency to throw some unbelievers to the lions.

The show's organizers knew that the Woodstock for geeks was on the verge of becoming passé' so they did what any responsible entrepreneur would do: they made it bigger. And like an aging movie star that keeps applying more layers of makeup in an attempt to look young, the producers of the show keep adding more of everything.

With my exhibitor's badge I get into the exhibit hall. I walk through half-erected booths, not because I want a peek, but because I have no idea how I'm going to finish the presentation. I have eighteen hours. Maybe I'll get inspired, or find an idea to recycle. Lucky for me, Gordon doesn't want to see the presentation before he gives it. He, like every other executive, wants to read the PowerPoint slides as they magically flash across the large screen.

Rows and rows of workers assembling exhibit booths, unloading boxes of t-shirts, promotional literature, and tons of made-in-China-by-slave-labor giveaway crap. Like blindfolded tykes trying to strike the piñata, every exhibitor wants to deliver that blow that connects, that stands apart from all the clutter.

Golf: Swing into the future

Police lineup = Computer Security

The History of computing, from caveman to modern times.

Computer networks are represented by spider webs, kids with tin-can telephone lines, a gypsy fortune teller with a crystal ball makes a point about something.

When all else fails, place girls with large breasts in front of your booth—tight shorts optional, but usually recommended. This tactic used by the truly desperate works, because we all know that the larger the cup size, the more technology expertise a woman possesses. To make the presentation complete, the slogan for the campaign must be overtly suggestive, and include phrases like download and market penetration, or explosive technology. One company markets a product called Lovebox, another advertises that their network is always up.

The Crown Publishing booth is a huge two-story affair with private offices for making deals. The plants are in perfect shape. Thank you George.

I wander through rows and rows of exhibits each more soulless than steel, each one making more promises than a virgin on prom night.

I don't know the name of company or have any idea what their product is supposed to do, but their display is nothing short of awesome. In the middle of the night, hundreds of miles from any ocean, a team builds a sandcastle. This isn't a typical castle built by a toddler with a plastic shovel and pail. This is a massive structure with towers and turrets, moats and drawbridges.

The builders work like monks: each seems to know what the others are working on without speaking. A woman painstakingly adds texture to the walls, stopping every few inches or so to check her work and redo the slightest imperfection. The detail is so good, that I swear that I can see faces in the windows, and soldiers standing behind the turrets.

I watch silently. I can't help but admire their patience and dedication. I have my concept, my theme: Castles made of sand. Sandcastles in the desert. Building sandcastles because someday they might prove useful—and profitable. Because without the builder, sand is just something between the ocean and the parking lot. Worthless, just like the Internet without the dreamers, the builders, the innovators

And like monks, in just a few days, they will have to destroy what they built—no chance that a huge wave will do the job for them.

I close my eyes and am transported back to the shore. I hear the waves and smell the sunscreen, but mostly I feel the sand as I press it together to form shapes and build structures that can't last, but need to be built anyway.

I shouldn't be surprised that sand is the answer. After all, sand is mostly made out of silicon, the same substance that they make into computer chips and breast implants.

23. **89109**

"It's for a good cause."

"It's all for charity."

"A really good cause."

No one remembers what organization the event supports or opposes--the cause is only a cover. The annual chili cook off is yet another opportunity for companies to compete, to win a prize. If your new products didn't please the tech editors, you can still claim the best chili West of the Mississippi.

The charity chili cook off is held in a sporting arena, a sight usually reserved for a different type of gladiator. The uniforms are different, but the competition is just as fierce.

In theory, the chili is prepared only by employees of the firm, but that rule is often stretched to include company consultants that just happen to have experience at such technological enterprises as Barney's Beanery and Charlie's Chili.

The chili may be prepared by pros, but sales assistants serve it with a smile. And just in case you didn't get enough marketing propaganda during the day, they hand you a wad of napkins, with their slogan imprinted on each.

I was not here to taste chili and wipe my face with someone's logo. My plan was to hand off the presentation and drink.

"What's our exotic ingredient?" I ask Dave, my favorite graphic artist/guitarist. I take a sample.

"Red fire ants from a secret Indonesian Jungle."

"You can't be--"

"We don't actually put ants in the chili, we just want to suggest something unique."

"Because?"

"Maybe there's one ant for every 20 gallons of chili just so we can say that we have something that no one else has. You need to make the judges believe that you have something that no other company is capable of producing." He goes on to explain how software companies are notorious for announcing products that don't exist—and may never exist—just to keep customers from considering their competitors wares. It's standard operating procedure, scare away the competition.

"Where is Tom Gordon?"

"If you go back to last year's Comdex and read the product announcements, you'll find that most have still not come to market," Dave continues.

"Does anyone know where Tom Gordon is?" I ask again.

The room is set up with tables in a series of smaller and smaller Us. Like a maze without mice. I'm surprised someone didn't insist on rodent for their recipe. Rat the other, other, white meat. While I survey the maze metaphor for a sign of Mr. Gordon, his assistant catches my attention. I must be close, Gordon would be lost without her in both the virtual and real world.

"Where's Tom?" I think her name is Wendy.

"He's not here," the assistant who may be Wendy says.

"When does he arrive?"

"He's not coming," she says.

"What did you say?"

"He wants you to give the presentation. He said he would follow up in an e-mail."

She turns to leave. Why should she care that I had to stand up and speak in front of thousands of technology and business experts. She is happy her boss is not in town and she can party for the next three days on company expense.

"Good luck with the presentation," she says, already at a distance, she didn't fly to Vegas to earn the frequent flyer miles.

Leaving the cook-off was the closest I ever hope to come to having an out of body experience. I can see myself leaving the hall. What the fuck am I going to do? I can't give this presentation. I wrote it for someone else to give. It's not me. It's bullshit.

I watch myself make my way through the gauntlet of tables. As I pass each one I'm accosted by tech vendors that charge at me with a level of zeal that would make a Bloomingdale's cologne sprayer jealous.

"Try this."

"This is the best chili that you've ever tasted."

"It's made from a secret recipe smuggled into California by the Donner Party. Chili with lamb, pork, imported sausage, fried yak lips. Made with chilies from the Gobi desert. An Ancient Incan concoction. Special ingredients that we can't mention."

A braless creature wearing a T-shirt many sizes too small hands me a cup. She claims, without a hint of irony, that her chili is an aphrodisiac.

A woman in a trenchcoat and fedora is attempting to relate her company's secret chili recipe with their ability to network computers and the prospect of peace in the Mid-East.

A surfer dude is claiming that his Hawaiian style chili is the most radical just like the venture he fronts for. Dude, we will change the world, one computer user at a time.

As if I wasn't having enough of a Fellini moment, I slam into the king of the geeks and his disciples. Before I can figure out why this guy is standing in the middle of a crowd he asks: "What's your zip code?"

"What's your zip code," comes in unison from several members of the geek's entourage.

"Zip code please," the geek repeats, as his hand brushes his long, wavy hair.

"10025," I mumble.

"There's a Greek restaurant on 114th Street, called Symposia?" The eyes of more than a dozen onlookers stare at me from all directions.

"Yes."

The nerds are pleased.

A man in a Hawaiian shirt calls out: "64114"

"Jake Smoke house in Kansas City, Missouri."

"68132," was the next challenge.

"Trovato's Italian 4013 Underwood Avenue, Omaha Nebraska."

"How about MSR 1B9?" A man states confidently as if he was going to receive a prize for stumping the band on memorize that postal code.

"Toronto, Ontario--a Thai joint called Spice of Life. Any other foreign visitors?"

An English gentlemen gives his postal code and we are rewarded with the name of a semi-famous pub, followed by more travelers from mostly flat states in the middle of the U.S. who probably would have been impressed if someone outside of the

Central Time Zone could locate their state on a map, never mind name a restaurant within their neighborhood. Zip Code Zagat didn't miss once. He follows up with his sales pitch that his company is everywhere.

I bet that most of the assembled will not remember the name of the company, but on the way back to their hotel rooms, they will all have the exact same thought: how many hours did this guy spend memorizing maps and restaurant guides, and how much money was, name of company that no one will remember, paying for his bizarre talent?

On the street in front of the convention center, a middle-aged woman with no front teeth hands me an advertisement for, "Girls Direct," an in-room escort service. The company promises to send a large breasted college cuties to my room and make my dreams come true. Perhaps if I pay extra she'll give the presentation.

24. Escaping the Country of the Blind

The Country of the Blind is located in a remote valley, cut off from the rest of the world by the slopes of the Andes. The inhabitants believe that the world ends at the stone walls that surround their village.

Before they became completely blind the ancestors of the village built paths with markers so they could navigate with their feet. Their small world was built around their ability to use their other senses. For more than fifteen generations they maintained their simple lifestyle. They were not only blind, they had no concept of sight.

It is easy to understand how a sighted man, observing the blind, would believe that he would be a king, if not a god. His sight would be superior to anything they could imagine.

The moderator is listing my credentials.

I can't say exactly when my out-of-body experience ended. It's like waking up from a nightmare and realizing the dream was better than the reality in front of your eyes. I'm sure that they wanted to be announcing someone with the credentials of Joseph Crown or Tom Gordon, instead he is babbling on about my research expertise and years of being on the cutting edge of new media. An area of expertise that even in dog years was still a puppy.

Here I am, on the stage, instead of in the back row making snarky comments. I reflect on the fact that in myths and fairy tales, people are always punished perfectly. King Midas had his magic touch, Sisyphus his rock—and I had this presentation. Although I don't know the exact crime that I have committed, I know that someone or something believed that my reading the presentation was the perfect penance.

The presentation is scheduled to last 30 minutes, but the very technology that I was about to extol is not my friend. I know that the gods, and my coworkers, are watching me. They will all do their best to catch it on the 100 foot-high screens that it will be projected on. They will preserve it on video tape. What happens in Vegas…

I am the visionary, the guy that can predict the future without the experience of having actually been there.

This would not be a presentation to end all presentations, it would merely be an opportunity to end my career. Perhaps George was hiring. I could be an assistant plant man. I do know that plants need to be watered.

The only way out was to share the vision with the conviction of a reformed sinner. To ignore the naysayers and proceed with the confidence of a man starting a new religion that was destined to be the one and only path to salvation.

I clear my throat.

My vision begins with a picture of nothing, or what geologists classify as desert. Wasteland. Another picture of nothing. Not a building or cell tower in sight. I sense the restlessness of the audience, but if I don't start with nothing then the rest of the presentation will make no sense.

"The convention center looked like this a mere 50 years ago." More photos of desert.

A black & white photo of Las Vegas circa 1920, population 2,304. Most high schools in Manhattan have a higher population.

"From a very humble beginning."

Black & White Images of hotels and casinos being erected.

"The cynics laughed when the first hotels and casinos were erected in the middle of nowhere."

I knew that when I put this presentation together that I would get a kick when Gordon had to say the word erected. Once again, I am being punished by my sins.

Now the pictures of modern casinos are in full color.

"The concept that the masses would come from miles away to willingly give away their money. And when they returned to their homes and villages they would recommend the adventure to all their friends and then return year after year proved to be correct?

Yes, the city of Las Vegas was built by visionaries and grew larger than even the maddest of them had ever imagined. I conventionally leave out the fact that the visionaries were mobsters. I do point out that every innovation (neon lights, A-list entertainers, cheap food) was originally laughed at, but soon imitated.

The phrases information superhighway and interactive multimedia come out of my mouth and disappear into the microphone. I remind the audience that there is a reason there were more bars than libraries. In other words, the Internet is sexy. The Internet is hip. It was the new thing to end all new things. It would change the world and then change it again.

Just to be completely obvious, I make it clear that today's pioneers must build their Internet presence in the middle of nowhere. They must be willing to be laughed at, to take a lot of heat. The work was hard, but the rewards were more than gold. And as the Internet grows it would be bigger than anyone could ever imagine: The Taj Mahal/ Buckingham Palace/Great Wall of sandcastles.

Perhaps I will get an award. *Best presentation written for a person who talks about the future growth of technology but doesn't use e-mail and presented by a person afraid of speaking and cynical about most things related to the business word and human nature in general.*

I reminded the audience that this was the country that put a man on the moon, built the Panama Canal, mass produced the Model T, was on the verge of placing a computer on every desk, etc, etc, etc. I vaguely implied that not believing in the Internet was not only a really bad business decision, but un-American as well.

If I would have listened to my own research or contemplated the history of high tech, I would have had no worries. In the lingo of the tech industry, I was merely asking an audience of Kool-Aid drinkers to supersize their drink of choice.

After the presentation comes the Q&A session. I fear that I will have no answers.

"Are companies that jump on the Web going to make more profits or lose their shirts?"

"Yes."

"Will it happen in my lifetime?"

"Ask your doctor."

"Have you every considered using your skills as a research analyst?" A man asks.

"My firm is hiring. Do you have a card?" A woman asks as I gather my notebook computer.

In the Country of the Blind, the sighted man who wanted to be king, stumbled in the darkness. His eyes prevented him from relying on his other senses. When he spoke to them about sight, and the amazing world outside their walled village, they thought he was a simpleton, or worse, going crazy.

The wise men of the village gathered and studied the man. Feeling his face, they detected strange orbs below his forehead. They concluded that these strange objects were the cause of his odd behavior and must be removed. The man considered letting them operate, for he was falling in love with a young, attractive woman. She loved the man, but wished that his imagination was not so active, that he would stop his talk of seeing and outside worlds. She hoped the operation would end his madness.

And he loved her, but love was not enough for the man to let a blind surgeon remove his eyes, so he waited until the villagers were asleep to make an escape from his kingdom. As he climbed out of the valley he repeated the refrain that he now understood to be a total lie: "in the land of the blind, the one-eyed man is king."

In the field of technology, "eating your own dog food" is when a company believes so strongly in the technology that it develops, it only uses their products. In theory this contributes to better products and services, but can also lead to blindness to what works in the real world.

And what better method of washing down a metaphorical meal than drinking Kool-Aid? * Kool-Aid became the drink of choice based on the legend it was consumed by the followers of Jim Jones to commit mass suicide, thus drinking this particular brand of flavored water signifies a real commitment to the project/company/technology you are working on. Kool-Aid drinkers are not just committed, they are true believers.

It has never been documented whether or not the rocket scientists that worked on packet switching technology in the 1960s digested Alpo or drank Kool-Aid, but they did develop a simple network of computers called ARPNET. Since packets of information could be sent from any computer to any other computer on the network, the system would work if any one computer or even a few dozen computers were disabled. In other words, the network could survive a massive attack, such as, but not limited to, a nuclear war. This made the folks at the Department of Defense very happy: if 99% of the population of the planet was incinerated, at least the few remaining computers could communicate.

The system worked, but was less than user friendly. To communicate, users had to memorize various protocols and the location of computer hosts. If that wasn't cumbersome enough, users had to use the keyboard to type in their commands.

Meanwhile, halfway around the world, a man was working on a method of adding a visual interface to what we now know as the Internet. After months of labor, and without the benefit of stock options, Tim Berners-Lee merged the concept of hyper-linking text with a graphical interface to develop what is today called the World Wide Web.

Scientists and academics built sites to share their research findings and interests in such diverse topics as Greek Poetry, government conspiracies to hide UFOs, and butterfly collecting. In the first year alone there were more than 300 Web sites.

At a technology investment conference in San Francisco, a thirsty man stood up and wondered, "can make money off this Web thing?"

*Kool-Aid is a trademark of Kraft foods. To say that Kraft had nothing to do with Jim Jones and Jonestown is an understatement. The inhabitants of Jonestown drank their potassium cyanide in Flavor-Aid, an obscure competitor to the more popular drink. Since most reporters had consumed Kool-Aid as children, the more popular drink got credit for the

largest example of insanity in the modern world and was also blamed for the 700 plus deaths at Jonestown.

Dog Food and Kool-Aid: The Early Years of the Internet Explained

Part II   (The Past + 1)

1. A Nice Place to Visit

Dickens wrote "We were all going direct to heaven, we were all going direct the other way."

Is hell really the opposite of heaven?

Sigmund Freud said that the opposite of love is not hate—it's indifference. It should follow that the opposite of heaven is not hell, but what the heck is it?

In a classic episode of Rod Sterling's Twilight Zone, a two-bit crook named Rocky is gunned down by the cops as he flees a robbery. Rocky goes to the afterlife, his guide—in keeping with our allusion to Dickens, is named, Pip. Pip shows Rocky around an afterworld that looks like a simple re-creation of his old stomping grounds—smoky pool halls, wannabe gangsters hanging out on the street corner, sleazy bars with card games in the back. Rocky doesn't lose at any of the games he plays and gets any doll he sets his eyes on. He concludes that he is in heaven. Even a lowlife like Rocky has great expectations.

This is a nice place to visit, he states to his guide, but it gets rather boring when you always get what you want. He asks Pip what he did to get here and requests that he be sent to the other place. His record is reviewed and no mistake has been made, he was an evil person in life—not worthy of redemption. "This is the other place," he is told with a devilish laugh.

I got the new job.

I got the cool office.

I have an assistant (Translation: I no longer have to stand by the fax machine waiting for that stupid noise).

A cappuccino machine and refrigerator stocked with ice-cold cans of free soda is down the hall. For lunch I order sushi from a restaurant that doesn't exist.   There is interesting research to do. My inbox runneth over with requests for my insight on just about anything related to the net.

Adjusted for inflation, everything is about the same. George is still the Plant Man, making his regularly scheduled house calls to the Upper West

Side of Manhattan. Susie is Susie with a new hobby to keep her busy in her few spare minutes. She's a member of the band Tequila Mockingbird. She turned her long, anguished poems of corporate malfeasance into popish diatribes. I take some pride in introducing Susie to the band. It was after one of their local shows that she was hooked.

TM's first album, *It's A Sin* is a modest success. The title doesn't make sense unless you read the title of the album in front of the name of the group and are intensely familiar with the only published work of Harper Lee.

The band lived for cleverness and all had day jobs so it didn't matter to them if you don't get it. Their cult following knew this and flocked to their concerts to hear a group having fun, playing for beer and cab fare. Perhaps, this was the quirk that held them back from becoming rock legends or at least get some radio airplay, but rock 'n' roll artists march to their own beats for reasons that the rest of us will never understand.

It can't be labeled rock 'n' roll if at least one member of the band doesn't use heroin/smash equipment/impregnate groupies/insult the establishment. Tequila's kryptonite was that they had to play at least one novelty or political song at every one of their concerts. Call them parodies, call them fun, but once they are placed on an album, and they get airtime, you are branded as a novelty act and not a rock brand. They longed to be a rock band, but like the small child that can't resist one more sneak attack on the cookie jar, Tequila Mockingbird, could not quit the offbeat songs that made their audience laugh and their critics groan.

# # #

Meetings. Meetings. Meetings.

Venture capitalists are dumping money into Internet projects; everyone is playing their own version of "Let's make a Deal," or at the very least have a meeting.

Like mushrooms that grow out of shit after a storm, meetings pop-up everywhere. These were not ordinary meetings, concerned with such mundane topics as profit and loss, personnel changes, the color scheme of the corporate brochure--theses are planning sessions for a three hour tour of the mythical city of Eldorado, the search for the fountain of synergy—a magical location were $2 + 2 = 5$. The Internet will improve everything.

In short, it is the best of times, without the negative, and necessary, counterbalance.

My only counterbalance is the research. The collection and analysis of survey data. Data that can be compiled and analyzed, sliced and diced, compared with previous years, analyzed by gender, age, income, attitudes, geographic region, tabulated by interest and attitude--used and abused to your heart's content.

Our findings are interesting, but never earth-shattering. Unlike the PowerPoint presentation, the data is nuanced, the conclusions are in the delicate art of interpretation. The possibilities are just that: there are no guarantees, nothing has to happen. In the end, the answer is one that the audience never wants to hear: "It depends."

At first glance the clients were thrilled, for they believed that they were looking into the soul of the Internet user. Instead of inkblots they stared at data tables and pretended that they not only understood, but they could predict the future.

Sometimes when you get what you want it is the best of times.

When the customers wanted more than the data could support, there was always the temptation to fudge the data, just a little. We called this the ten-percent solution.

Sometimes it is the worst of times.

2. Every Day Something Else Leaks

The longer I study the framed poster of an Edsel in Alex's office, the more I'm convinced it's staring back at me. And moving. The front grill and the bumper are even moving in different directions. What were the engineers and designers at Ford thinking?

The poster was a gift from an online database that asked its customers not to let it happen

again—always do your homework. Research.
Research. Research.

"The data is almost ready," Alex says, like
he was referring to laundry in the spin cycle.

"I'm eager to get a look."

"You can't rush. If the data's not weighted
correctly…"

"Yes."

Every day something else leaks.

This is what Susie insisted that Edsel stood
for. The Ford Corporation was so eager to get its
latest model into showrooms and capitalize on all the
hype that many of the units arrived with defects.
Some of the cars even came with a note attached to
the steering wheel indicating which parts were
missing.

Susie knew hundreds of satirical acronyms
for dozens of different companies and organizations.
Some of them she invented herself, using the same
sardonic wit that allowed her to write twisted song
lyrics. Others were passed around via fax and e-mail.
She keeps files of them, both electronic and

hardcopy, because you never know when you're going to need an example of corporate insanity to launch an attack.

And attack she did. She dared to take on DARE, the anti-drug reeducation/indoctrination program. Its new-and improved- moniker was: Drugs Are Really Excellent. DARE deserved her scorn because they were a multi-billion dollar organization whose sole purpose, in her mind, was to paint a picture of the occasional pot smoker as a drug fiend. DARE's desire to build a "drug-free America" collided with her desire to occasionally get high.

"If they take away our pot, what will they take away next?"

How does one respond to a rhetorical question?

"Are they incapable of understanding that there is a difference between using and abusing drugs?"

Is it like the sound of one-hand clapping?

"Prohibition didn't work, never will work, can't possibly work."

Yes, ranting is good for the soul, but what about listening to someone rant? What is that good for?

"Do you know how much the CEO of DARE makes per year?"

If you mostly agree with the diatribe, but are not as strident in your position what can you say? After all, DARE is not as bad as the KKK, the Gestapo, or the Daughter's of the American Revolution.

"We need to take into account the margin of error," Alex bangs his keyboard.

The Edsel is the only model named after a Ford family member. It is also one of the biggest flops in automotive history. Can we really prevent it from happening again? Should innovators be punished for trying? Without mistakes, penicillin, post-it notes, or Velcro would never have been invented.

Several features of the Edsel were ahead of its time. Currently collectors point to its many innovations like self-adjusting brakes. It was a great research project. Instead of the butt of a mediocre business anecdote, it could almost be described as a good failure that in the long run contributed to the success of the American automotive dream.

"How was the conference?" Alex asks, eyes sill glued to the monitor.

"Everyone just wants online shopping projections."

"This data set will offer a great starting point."

"No one wants a starting point."

"What?"

"They all want to go to heaven without dying."

"Smith needs you in his office," my assistant Tiffany chimes over the phone intercom.

My new goal in life is to get her to teach me to use the phone system so I can buzz her and ask for something. Anything.

3.   The Ten Percent Solution

"Just take your current findings and add 10%," Smith says as if he was asking me to merely dilute soup to feed the homeless.

The John Williams role was now being played by Sam Smith. The new boss. Executive Vice President of Strategic Marketing.

Smith follows the pattern of men who brought their leadership skills honed in the jungles of Cambodia and Vietnam to the meeting rooms and cubicle farms of corporate America. Unfortunately no one told them that the metaphor of the corporate world as jungle was just a metaphor. Sometimes prisoners need to be taken. In war, and in life, carpet-bombing and torture will not win you the hearts and minds of coworkers or customers.

"I was under the impression that our work attempted to approximate what was happening in the world."

"It's standard industry practice," he says as he plays with one of his war medals.

"And what happens next quarter when clients want to see even higher numbers?"

"You can capture that bridge when the time comes," he shrugs.

I stare blankly, thinking that if men like Smith couldn't use sports or war metaphors they would be speechless.

Smith must think that I am about to argue with him about the findings and continues, "Your executive summary states clearly that Internet use is growing like crazy, are you saying you may be wrong?"

I find myself staring at the black and white photos tacked onto the bulletin board. Smith and his buddies on the streets of Saigon. Standing shirtless in front of a hut. Marching through a rice paddy.

"No, but."

"So in other words, we are presenting the data the way the clients need to understand it."

"We are?"

In every one of the photos, Corporal Smith and his buddies are smiling. Grins that put kids on Christmas morning to shame. I wonder why. Miles away from home, in a land with the heat and humidity of hell, a population that often cheered when soldiers were placed in body bags. A land where death came as fast and often as a click of a shutter. What reason did they have to always be smiling?

"You need a change of pace," Smith says.

"I do?"

"I want you to take the meeting at Fur Nation next week. They're considering signing up and a report from you would just about guarantee it."

"I don't do that type of research. My specialty is primary research. Analyzing data, not making shit up."

"It's all the same."

"Not really."

"I'll have Betsy make the arrangements."

"Great."

If a recipe calls for X and you make it X + 10% what do you have? Is it science? Is it research? Is it healthy? Can it be lethal? In fact, it is none of the above, but it is addictive. If the findings suggested that three months ago, five million U.S.

citizens were using the Internet, then add ten percent and presto, today 5.5 million are online. If the client wants to know how many will be online in some date in the future, add ten percent for every three months and the client will be pleased enough to keep writing checks.

I know that users will build up a tolerance for their extra ten percent and demand more and more. Unfortunately there are no rehab programs for the afflicted (both the sellers and users of watered-down research). Withdrawal symptoms include, but are not limited to, dizziness, confusion, irritation, blurred vision, loss of self, upset stomach, shrinkage of wallet, thoughts of doom... The Symptoms of the continued usage are, but not limited to, dizziness, confusion, irritation, blurred vision, loss of self, upset stomach, shrinkage of wallet, thoughts of doom.

4. People Eating Tasty Animals

Why do humans need to worship animals? If God wanted me to be a vegetarian bacon would taste like raw cabbage.

We not only worship animals, we form groups to protect them and we collect some of the non-edible ones to live in our homes, share our beds, and drink out of out toilets.

If there was ever an organization that didn't get its advertising message it's PETA. "I'd rather go naked than wear fur," makes no sense if the people uttering the statement are super models. What man wouldn't rather see Christy Turlington or Naomi Campbell naked as opposed to wearing anything? What if real ugly hags with sagging boobs threatened to take off their fur coats? I bet a lot of vegetarians would come out of the woodwork to keep them covered in pelts. Fur may be cruel, but at least it provides warmth and cover.

I check the shine on my new leather shoes and head into the lobby of Fur Nation.

The Nation is a competitor of Paws.com and others attempting to sell bags of dog food on the Internet. They were certain that I too would be a convert if I flew down to Atlanta to hear their story, meet their people, feel the energy, and see for myself that they have what it takes to be the junkyard dog of online pet supplies.

I open the door and within seconds my crotch is being sniffed by a breed of dog that I can't identify.

"She really likes strangers," the receptionist shouts as she slowly gets up to grab the studded collar of her overgrown puppy.

I am joined in the lobby by not one, but two young and eager tour guides. They introduce themselves, but almost instantly I forget their names, so I nickname them Chip 'n Dale.

Chip is female, short hair and a little too spunky to be taken seriously. Dale is the guy that looks like he got out of his high school awkward stage about 15 minutes ago. I get the feeling that he needs to frequently check his image in the mirror to prove to himself that he really has made it to adulthood.

"As you can see, at Fur Nation, everyday is take your friend to work day," Chip states proudly.

"They are all well behaved," Dale adds.

"The pets or the employees?" I ask.

"We treat animals like they are our equals, our friends."

The tour begins.

Fur nation is exactly as advertised, a cube farm of activity, a beehive of hipness, with a soundtrack of obscure bands to match.

At Fur Nation, the animal theme never rests. On the floor are water dishes for companion animals. For the humans there are dog dishes filled with adult treats such as Skittles and peanut M&Ms. Colored paw prints on the floor direct lost humans to various departments.

Animals are everywhere. Dogs mostly, with a few kitties and birdcages and aquariums to complete the picture. I'm sure that on Halloween a guy in pirate garb would greet me with a parrot on his shoulder. There is a doggie rec room with a jumbo television that plays Animal Planet. I wonder if animals get confused during the commercials.

I get to see everything from the computer server room to the obligatory Foosball table in the break room. The highlight of the tour is what the denizens of Fur Nation proudly call "The Kennel."

"The Kennel is for humans only," Chip and Dale squeak in unison.

This is the not so secret weapon. Simply put, the kennel is a doghouse for overly ambitious workers that need to take a catnap. This large room includes bunk beds, with paw print blankets and end tables made to look like scratching posts.

"Our business is 24/7."

"Some of us are night owls."

"Our employees put in a lot of time and sometimes need to take a break."

They show me the kennel the way a 12-year-old shows off his slick new ten-speed.

In the top of several bunk beds are programmers catching Zs before pounding down some Jolt Cola and getting back to their keyboards.

"Let's go to marketing," the Chip and Dale chorus announces.

The head of marketing is named Skip. Skippy thanks Chip and Dale. I thought that he was going to throw them a treat for fetching me.

After shaking my hand and offering me Cappuccino and M&Ms, Skip is ready for the sales pitch. An assistant dims the lights and Skip begins the Power Point. The presentation begins with pictures of puppies and kittens and their even less attractive owners.

"It starts with branding, it ends with branding, it's all about the branding. Soon, the Fur Nation Mascot will be the most recognized brand in the world—more popular than Nike, MTV, Coca-Cola." Skip says.

One of the headlines is Branding, branding, branding.

I don't know if they stole the idea from me or I stole it from them, but it now seems that it has more than used up its nine lives.

"We are the leading brand," Skip continues. "And as you pointed out, branding is key."

"I can't argue with that." I wrote the stupid report. Of course my report was an empirical analysis of how the top brands earn surplus profits. It doesn't follow that every company gets to be a top brand anymore than every little leaguer gets to play on the Yankees.

"I loved your report. I thought it really captured the landscape. Your clients might be interested in knowing our aggressive expansion plans."

"You want to expand, but you are still losing money on every transaction." I say.

"S.O. S."

"S.O. S?" I repeat.

"S.O. S. stands for sell other services."

"Of course."

"As we continue to build our client base, we will sell them premium goods and services."

"Which ones?"

"We are bringing in selective partners,"

Skip takes a few steps closer, so he can lower his voice and tell me a secret that I already know.

"We are going to use our stock to purchase other companies."

"And?"

"And make them more productive."

I was starting to believe that they drink their Kool-Aid out of dog dishes to show their support to the company. Perhaps it was part of the initiation ceremony. Do you Skip promise loyalty, and a hundred hours a week to Fur Nation, till death or stock options do you part? Good boy.

When the light comes back on, I notice a more than life sized replica of Betty Beagle, the mascot of Fur Nation. I wondered why I didn't notice her when I first entered the room.

Before I leave, I am handed a doggie bag of goodies that resemble something handed to A-list celebrities on Oscar night. I find the usual branded T-shirts, running shorts, hats and even a Fur Nation MP3 player. Of course there are the dog serving dishes and drinking glasses, suitable for a party at the frat house of your choice.

At the bottom of the bag is an envelope. Inside a letter and half a dozen gift cards. The latter advised me that I could use the cards at Fur Nation. I would be pleased with the wide range of products and friendly service. Not to mention that I would be entitled to free shipping with every purchase of more than $100.00. Of course, if I wanted, I could use the cards anywhere my heart desired.

Is it a treat or a bribe? I wonder if they know the difference.

5.   The Beginning of the End of the Beginning

"Just work backwards," Smith says as he waves the coffeepot in my direction. The substance at the bottom of the pot appears to be neither liquid nor solid.

"No thanks."

"Your generation only drinks that fancy coffee, and those girly drinks."

Smith pours the sludge from the bottom of the pot into his U.S. Army mug. He takes a swig and I wince at the thought of drinking coffee that has aged overnight—or even longer.

"You were saying something about working backwards."

"Simply take into account all the events that would make your future possible."

"My future?"

"Take the desired result--something that seems almost impossible to obtain, the more impossible the better."

"Yes."

"Fur Nation's stock reaching $125.00 a share in 18 months, for example. Work backwards— list the events necessary to make it an accurate prediction. Online shopping increases dramatically, everyone goes online and owns a pet. The investing audience wants the bottom line—the details are just filler."

"But the research doesn't support the conclusion."

"The research doesn't pay our salaries…"

"…the clients do."

They pay our salaries and bonuses and free coffee, snacks, soda, sushi and whatever else the office manger thinks she can get away with expensing. In corporate America, the office manager is your best friend or worst enemy.

"Exactly," Smith says as he takes another swig of caffeinated sludge. "I hired you to do more than crunch numbers. You need you to come up with some amazing predictions."

"But what happens—"

"--We protect ourselves by calling it a target price."

"Target price."

"Imagine your future, the bolder the prediction, the happier the client," he barks as he heads down the hall.

Three hours later, my whiteboard looks like this:

Fur Nation's stock reaches $148.50 a share

> Dogs order their food online
>
> Dogs evolve opposable thumbs
>
> Nuclear accident causes massive damage to canine DNA
>
> Internet usage increases 10% per second
>
> Population of the earth reaches 100 billion people.
>
> Hell Freezes over
>
> Wile E. Coyote finally catches the Road Runner
>
> Gilligan gets off the fucking Island
>
> Cubs win World Series

My bottom line is that I don't like inventing the future.

I head to the elevator.

As I enter the lobby I notice the Mystery Sushi deliveryman. Mystery Sushi is the new soda and brownies. Food items that everyone in the office discusses, has an opinion about. Instead of speculating if the food is spiked, we wonder where it's made and by whom.

Mystery Sushi is not on the map. They are not listed anywhere. There is no phone number to dial. You can only order online. And when I say order, I mean you simply tell them how many want lunch. They make the choices for you.

Forty minutes after you click the "bring me lunch" button, a deliveryman, that either doesn't understand a word of English, or has trained not to respond, delivers the most succulent raw fish available. Cash on delivery. If you don't have the exact change, it's added to the tip. If you don't tip, your account will be blocked.

I was not the first to suggest that we get the tech department to trace the web server, check the owner of the domain name. All dead ends.

Every time someone attempted to follow one of the deliverymen they were given a free tour of the offices and alleyways of downtown Manhattan. No one was able to locate the source of the appropriately named, Mystery Sushi.

Once again I follow a stranger. Perhaps I will be the hero that breaks the code, solves the mystery.

My favorite teacher in college was called the code breaker. He taught advanced statistics and used examples from his military service. During the Second World War he was assigned to a team in England that was responsible for breaking the coded messages sent from headquarters in Berlin to Field Marshal Erwin Rommel in North Africa.

After months of work, they were able, with a high degree of accuracy, to decipher the messages. They broke the code.

Was my professor awarded a medal for helping the Allies win the war? It would have if Rommel had regularly followed his orders. Unfortunately for the Allies, the Desert Fox had a mind of his own and often-changed course as conditions on the ground warranted. The Allies knew what he was supposed to do, where he was supposed to be, what was supposed to happen, but Rommel had other ideas, and the war in North Africa continued.

The code breakers, as smart as they were, did not significantly speed up the process of Rommel's defeat. Rommel was defeated because the Allies had more tanks, planes, fuel, and bullets than the Nazis.

I wait in a strange lobby ready to follow the Mystery Sushi deliveryman to his next delivery or the secret sushi factory, but he never reappears. I make a note of the address to enter into the Mystery Sushi database that we are compiling.

Here's the outline I hand Smith:

Fur Nation Target Share Price $158.00

The stock of the leader always demands a premium.

Fur Nation is the number one pet brand
Branding, Branding, Branding.
Online shopping becomes widely accepted
Internet Usage Increases 10% per quarter
Everyone owns a fucking dog or cat
People are more willing to spend money on their fucking pets than on their children

Online shopping saves time-people are working more than ever before

Online saves money

The report includes sections on how the Fur Nation management team will use the high value of their stock to make strategic acquisitions. The companies they want to get their paws on would be undervalued enterprises that needed a little help. I state, without a hint of sarcasm, that the gurus at FN would turn these acquisitions into the cash cows that they were breed to be.

I conclude that we live in a "Winner take all" economy that the number one brand was worth geometrically more than the number two brand.

"It's a winner, put it in PowerPoint." is all Smith says. He doesn't even ask me to take out the word fucking. No one cares about the details, the bottom line is enough.

6. I before E

"Just wanted to let you know," the PR flak from Paws.COM is on my speakerphone. "We are offering Paw points for every dollar spent. This is the type of program that is guaranteed to build customer loyalty. Guaranteed."

"Do I get paw points when I buy fish food?"

"Of course."

"But fish don't have paws."

Nothing like getting them off script.

I break the silence. "Your competitors are offering free shipping."

"Our prices are lower," she responds. "Much lower."

Bribery is quickly becoming the accepted method of encouraging consumers to shop online. How long can they continue to sell one-dollar bills for 95 cents?

"I'll keep it in mind when I write my report."

I hang up without saying goodbye. She'll call back and bother me tomorrow and the day after that.

Smith is in my office; I have no idea how long he has been standing there. "Are you ready to pick some winners?"

Mind is blank. Must say something.

"It's not one of your multiple choice questions." He says.

"I can handle the assignment."

What's wrong with multiple choice? Yes or No, True/False, does not allow the questionnaire to delve into the mind of the subject and produce the most meaningful results.

"You are representing us, and we intend to be in the vanguard. Only the lead dog gets a change in scenery."

Dividing the world into true/false, black/white works on the battlefield, not in research.

"Pick the companies that are on the verge of changing the world." He continues.

"You do realize that this is not the first time that people were convinced that the world was changing."

"This time it's different. See me as soon as you get back into town." Smith turns to leave without wasting any effort or motion.

* * *

"I thought that when you invited me to dinner, you were going to cook something, boil some water. Our microwave is fully functional."

"You don't like the selection, the atmosphere." Susie looks up from her Palm Pilot.

"I'm eating donuts in a bus station."

"Actually you're chomping on a cruller."

"If you only put your knowledge of fried dough into cooking lessons." I'm grateful that she ignores this.

"It comes from early 19th century Dutch kruller, 'to curl.'"

Only Susie can make the etymology of cruller sexy.

"Thanks."

"We have perfect seats for the concert."

The sign above the band reads *Music under the Stairs*. This is the New York version of everyone else's Music under the Stars. Local bands are given the opportunity to play underground in front of commuters. The fact that the average member of their audience listens for less time then it would take to perform the one-minute waltz does not seem to deter them. New York—if you can make it here.

"How do you pick a company based on a PowerPoint deck? I wonder if anyone has ever used a Magic 8-Ball to select the most promising start-ups?" I ask, but Susie is preoccupied.

"I have news. One of our clients is thinking of using one of my songs."

The band continues to set up.

"Hopefully not the one about the 16 year old that is determined to lose her virginity?"

"That's the one."

"But the lyrics."

"Clients don't care what the song says, as longs as they think it's cool."

"Seriously?"

"It's very upbeat."

"Not if you're the parent of the 16 year old."

"The client wants cutting edge."

"But the lyrics…"

"We know, but the client doesn't care. They never do."

"So you're saying that they never check the lyrics before they approve a song for a commercial?"

"I can give you hundreds of examples of songs that are 100% wrong for the subject matter, they just sounded cool at the time."

"For example?"

The bass player is ready to go, while the drummer is still setting up his kit.

"A Japanese car manufacturer uses the title music from the *movie Bridge on the River Kwai,* a movie about the Japanese mistreatment of prisoners during WWII to promote a vehicle in the United States?"

"That's just one example."

"Volvo used Donovan's "Catch the Wind" to emphasize that its autos are fun, and very safe. Donovan was singing about things that one can never have. Volkswagen used "Won't get fooled again," by The Who.

"Those are all foreign companies, maybe they didn't understand the lyrics."

"Detroit-based Cadillac used Led Zeppelin in an attempt to revive its stale image. Two problems. One, Zeppelin was cool and cutting edge about two decades ago. Two, the song they chose, *Rock And Roll,* is about a guy that can't get any lovin'. You think the lyrics, lonely, lonely, lonely…. might have been a clue, but they weren't."

"I'm going to go with automobile manufactures are idiots, but you'll just tell me that I'm missing the big picture."

"Carnival Cruise wants you to sail with them and in the background is an Iggy Pop song about abusing drugs. Speaking of the joys of heroin, Lou Reed's song, "Just another Day" plays while overgrown men smash into each other in a spot for the National Football League. Unless scoring dope becomes a spectator sport, I miss the obvious connection."

The lead singer mumbles something into his microphone.

"Maybe it should…"

"And what chief marketing officer would not be proud to shell out top bucks to have Mick Jagger sing about raping slaves."

"Brown sugar?"

"Who doesn't want to drink a Pepsi after hearing that?" Susie takes a gulp of her latte.

"You are saying that there is a vast conspiracy to undermine advertising led by the very people who are paid to develop it?"

"It's a consensus not a conspiracy."

If I could produce a thought bubble, it would have a large cartoon question mark above my head. "Not sure if I get the difference."

"When any campaign is unveiled, the audience sees the pretty images splashing across the screen, they hear the pop playing on the speakers, it is new and exciting, it does what advertising is supposed to do-it catches the eye, makes an impression, creates some buzz. In short, the soundtrack is the creative and everyone pats themselves on the back for being a genius."

"I still not sure if I get why they make such bad choices."

"For approximately 90% of the population the ad is experienced as planned. But, for some college student up too late, or a baby boomer that enjoyed the sixties, but not necessarily the sexual revolution, or some dissatisfied ex-employee, the lyrics of the song elicits a response that the advertiser never expected. With a little research, online or off, they review the actual lyrics, and send off an angry e-mail that no one in corporate with any authority will ever read."

"In short, people like you take advantage of the fact that the people who pay you are mostly clueless."

"I saved my favorite example for last."

"Don't be a tease."

The band is finally ready and the band begins.

"Microsoft used The Rolling Stones tune, "Start Me Up." Obviously no one read, or cared about the lyrics, about dead men ejaculating and grown men shedding tears when their OS crashed."

"You make a grown man cry."

"There is plenty of sabotage in the industry, but most of the damage is self inflicted."

The lead guitarist is so into his solo that he fails to notice the commuters forced to take an extra step around him to get to their gates. I expect he will be asking how to get to Carnegie Hall as soon as he is finished.

***

My colleagues call it "deck and a dream day." I think the official title is "Companies of the Future." The premise is simple: rent a hotel ballroom and invite prospective Internet entrepreneurs to pitch their brilliant ideas to vulture capitalists and noted industry analysts like myself.

There is something for everyone. The start-ups need funds to get off the ground and the VCs have billions and believe that they deserve to make billions more. The firm I labor for can charge our clients busloads of money to provide insight, analysis, expertise, unadulterated bull shit, etc.

If your idea is good enough, or at least not as crazy as all the others, if you can answer stupid questions, if you look like you are willing to work 120 hours a week, but also project the aura of a future multimillionaire, then maybe you will get what you came for.

I listen to pitch after pitch, from companies that didn't exist six months ago and came into being when they simply put an I or an E in front of their product or service.

"Our plan is to be the number one Web site in the universe for medical and health information."

"Antique furniture online."

"Why go to the supermarket, when we pick your food and deliver it to you."

The I is for Internet, or Interactive—E as in electronic (or energy, ennui, or egotistical).

"Religion online, because who has time to go to church anymore?"

"Pizza, who doesn't love pizza? You can pick any combination of toppings."

Wave after wave of presenters hit the podium for their three minutes. Most are shot down, but to borrow a metaphor from Smith--like good solders hitting the beach on D-day, they don't give up, each hoping that they are the one to make it to shore, to be the hero and seize the day.

"Travel information for overweight tourists."

"Online driving lessons."

"Unbiased stock market advice from autistic children."

Forget soldiers, this was more like the one out of 80 million spermatozoa that swims through the vagina into the cervix and up a fallopian tube to impregnate an egg, except in this case the man is alone, masturbating to online porn.

"Everything a pig farmer needs to be profitable."

"A dating service for victims of alien abduction."

"Fixing up your brick and mortar retail location is like saddling up a dinosaur."

"Our Web site seeks to provide everything that an exotic dancer needs."

"You mean strippers?"

"Exotic dancers have special needs, like health insurance that covers breast enlargement."

"And reductions when they retire."

"We have everything covered."

"So to speak."

This is a sporting event without rules, a trial without laws, an orgy without lubrication.

The afternoon session is when I get to ask questions to the presenters that have been invited to round two.

"Our plan is to capture the listening habits of young people and offer them CDs at a discount."

"Isn't your target audience the ones who are illegally downloading music?"

"We believe that if they were offered the CDs at a discount, they wouldn't have to."

"What's Your SOS?" I ask.

The analysts from rival firms look at me like I'm speaking in a foreign language.

"S.O. S." I repeat slowly. "S. O. S. Sell other stuff, what is your strategy for selling other shit."

"We expect to be profitable with our main products," the future Internet stock billionaire claims.

"Even at a competitive discount, we will have more than an 18% profit margin," his associate chimes in." Like Moses and the Ten Commandments, he holds a large chart over his head.

"What happens when your competitors start offering even bigger discounts?" I ask.

"If they discount too much, they will lose money on every sale."

His associate comes forward with more charts and graphs. "Customers love us. We are building brand loyalty."

"I think you are building a ladder to bankruptcy," I say, but his firm could just as easily be a winner as many of the companies that made presentations.

By the end of the day I have a headache, a pocketful of business cards, and a desire to find a remote island where I can spend the rest of my life fighting sobriety.

* * *

"You really get it"

It's one of my fellow analysts, and if he's still wearing his name badge I won't have one of those awkward moments or trying to remember his name.

"Brad," The smile on my face is not because I want to converse. I have an island to search for.

"David."

I violated my first rule of attending conferences, remove your badge before leaving the hall to avoid having to discuss with every attendee, bellhop and cabbie that needs to discuss Interactive

Multimedia or whatever is the buzzword of the day. When will I learn?

"You see right through the BS. It is all about the user."

"My background is in research." *Shit, I'm encouraging him.*

"You want to grab a beer, I'd love to hear your plans?"

"Plans?"

"You can't listen to jokers all day and not want to cash in, you must have a business plan or two in your case."

"I have some ideas I've been working on."

"Great, there's a bar around the corner."

I remove my name-tag and follow Brad.

Everyone has plans. If you deny having plans, they assume you are holding out and believe your ideas are out of this world. Every idea I've ever had sounds cliché' or insane.

We discuss what the sidewalks of New York were paved to discuss--money. Of course, like all schemers we were pretending that we wanted to do is change the world, but that was only the pretext. The Internet was simply the get-away vehicle for our next heist.

"You'll love this pub," Brad says. "A lot of techies drink there, it's called 'Unwired,' get it? Unwired."

Cliché' or insane.

7. L'Chaim

"We anticipate an initial public offering in 18 months."

"18 months and we'll be out."

"Our exit strategy is to IPO or get bought out in 18 months."

Another day, another conference.

Smith thinks I'm a genius. He also thinks that the U.S. could have won in Vietnam.

My reward for pleasing him is the opportunity to attend more meetings with more companies about to make it big.

"In 18 months we will be acquired—at a huge multiple of our current value."

"In just 18 months…"

Hebrew is only one of five ancient languages still spoken. The observant consider it holy, and only use it for religious purposes, for it is the language of the Prophets.

In Hebrew, words often have more than one meaning and are often connected in ways both simple and profound. Each letter in the alphabet, even the silent ones, corresponds to a number. Add up the letters in the word "wine" and you have the same number as the word "secrets." When you drink wine, you give away secrets or so the medieval mystics insisted.

To the believer and the non-believer alike, 18 is the magic, mystical number. The beggar in Jerusalem and the Yeshiva boy in 16th century Poland and every Jew in-between knows that 18 is *L'Chaim* -- to life. When you slam a glass of homemade vodka or delicately clink crystal stemware with Château Margaux, you exclaim L'Chaim. It even works with the overly sweet, poor excuse for wine that we would break into the synagogue's kitchen for and drink after Hebrew school. You can even exclaim L'chaim with Kool-Aid, for it is not the drink that we are toasting.

It has become customary to give to charity in multiples of 18. Bar and Bat mitzvah boys and girls are always hoping for 180 or 72 dollars, 18 is just plain cheap. When the number 18 pops up in the lottery you can bet your bottom shekel that some Jew somewhere is holding a ticket with his lucky number selected.

"Our target is 18 months."

This is always stated with certainty.

Why must every CEO speech to potential investors include the magic number?

Numbers like 27 or 22 are equally valid. Why do they hate on 17 or 19? Is the universe trying to tell us something? My vote is with coincidence.

Perhaps 18 was stated by some random individual and then repeated by others. At this point it is no longer a coincidence, it's an incantation. A mantra in search of a religion. If enough people say it long enough, eventually someone will hit the 18 month mark and cash out. When this happens, everyone has to try for the big 18. No one wants to be the one that only claims that they can do it in 20 months or 27.

Bottom line. If the dot.com world was Sesame Street if would be brought to you by the number 18.

* * *

On my desk are two documents. A heavily marked up research report and an e-mail from Joe. I guess old dogs can learn new tricks. He even sent an attached word document from his memoir. Wish I had time to read, but I've been summoned to Smith's office to talk about the report and another new client with PowerPoint dreams. The client is looking to purchase our research and services and to write some big checks. I guess I can drink to that.

The Importance of S.O.S. is the hot new report. Sell other shit has become sell other stuff, but the philosophy is still the same: attract customers, analyze the crap out of them and find additional, high-profit-products and services to offer them.

Brad stole my stolen meme and wrote a report and got interviewed on several business talk shows and quoted in the trades.

Smith used his red sharpie to circle Brad's "target" stock prices that are all higher than the ones I pulled out of the stratosphere. Why? Why? Why? Smith writes. I guess he wants to know why I'm not psychic. I wasn't able to figure out what Brad was going to say so I couldn't aim even higher in this nuclear arms race of unrealistic stock prices.

"Your work is good, very good." Smith says.

The television in Smith's office is tuned to a business talk show.

"Thank you." Give me a but.

"You know why your competition is getting all the press?" He motions towards the technology report on the screen. The sound is off, but they are discussing stock prices. All the arrows are pointing up. The stock market continues to boom as fast as the nation's vocabulary for web related terminology:

search engines, portals, eyeballs, Netscape, dial-up, DOT.COM, monetize, interactive multimedia, information superhighway...

"Because they are making the most outrageous predictions." He continues. "More quotes, more TV equals more business, more business equals more bonuses, and..."

You're only as good as your last bold/bad prediction.

"...More stock options. I assume you have nothing against capitalism?"

"Not personally." In college I screwed a communist. It was fun.

Stock prices for companies that I thought would be high, go even higher. Everyone looks like a genius. The problem of course, is not that we all look like geniuses, but that we think we are geniuses.

"The PR department wants to give you some media training so you'll be ready."

And yet something is off. Winds are shifting.

"Ready for what exactly?"

Why shifting winds are a metaphor for change, is a mystery to me. Winds are made to shift. Shifting forces create wind.

"You're just as smart as any of those talking heads. Maybe a little smarter." He pauses. "They're just more aggressive."

The real threat would be if the winds were constant, if they never changed.

***

In a psychology experiment by Solomon Asch, a test subject is asked to participate in a vision test. The subject is seated to the right of four confederates and always answers last. The questions are extremely easy: which line is longer, which circle is bigger. The correct answer is obvious. For the first few questions the confederates answer correctly and so do the test subjects.

After a few questions the confederates start making deliberate mistakes. For the first few "mistakes," the subject held his ground and state the correct answer. A few questions later and the subject

179

gives in to peer pressure and starts making the same dumb mistakes the confederates were instructed to, and had practiced, making. When additional confederates were added to the lineup, the subjects were even more likely to conform to the larger group.

Many subjects tried to have it both ways, and attempted to please their peers and their own eyes: they give a few correct and a few wrong answers. Very few of them were willing to stand up to the confederates and their bogus answers.

When confronted with the fact that they confirmed with the majority, test subjects blamed their mistakes on poor eyesight. No one wants to be labeled a conformist.

8. Selling Soles*

"If you can sell books online, why not athletic shoes? Most people know their size, know what they want. A few clicks of the mouse and you're off and running."

The only thing worse than appearing on television, is watching yourself on television while you sit next to a media trainer. If the main objective of a dog trainer is to get puppies to not pee on the rug then the goal of a media trainer is?

Julie stops the tape. "See what you did wrong?"

"No idea."

"Never nod your head while the interviewer is asking a question. It makes it look like you agree with them."

"But–"

"Your mission is to look completely objective."

"I am objective."

Unless Smith is yelling in my ear to be more aggressive.

"I said you are supposed to *look* objective. I don't care if you get up every fucking morning and read tea leaves. I'm paid to make you look, and sound like, an impartial expert."

I notice the vine tattoo around her wrist when she reaches for the play button.

"Talk to the camera, the interviewer is just a prop."

A fake-tanned, well-dressed, overly paid, prop.

"Never hesitate once you start talking."

Julie lights up a cigarette.

I could swear this is a smoke-free building. I hope the mayor doesn't hear about this.

She exhales. "Be more aggressive with your opinions. Give them something to remember and a more importantly, a reason to invite you back."

Mission. Aggressive. She's in bed with Smith, literally, figuratively or both.

"How aggressive can I be on a fake interview on a non-existent television station?"

"Consider this your boot camp."

The image of doing push-ups while a drill sergeant plants his boot on my back and screams at me to defend my Internet company stock valuations invades my cortex. Or is it the cerebellum? My brain can't keep track of its own parts.

"I thought I did OK for a daytime business show."

"Not good enough—it's also my reputation on the line." She takes another drag.

I envy smokers, they always have something to do with their hands.

"Are we done here? I need to brew a pot of tea. A nice Darjeeling would hit the spot. Earl Grey is always nice this time of day." I stand.

"Your homework for next week is to prepare answers for questions about these topics and companies." She hands me a binder. "Prepare to sound spontaneous."

"Is there going to be a quiz at the end?"

"I promised Smith that you would be ready in three weeks."

"Three weeks?"

"He's not paying me enough to go longer."

"You know you could save a lot of money by quitting." I nod towards her pack of Marlboro Reds.

"That's what my parole officer tells me."

***

"There's only one number one."

The voice is mine, but the words belong to someone else.

Number one what? Am I talking about the company or am I thinking about the guy talking about the company? For the company to be number one they need a good idea, hard work, some luck. But for the research expert to be number one all he or she needs is an opinion that is just slightly more outrageous than everyone else's.

"We think we can double our sales in the next 18 months." Kevin is executive vice president of the company that used to be called Shoe Time.

"Our research indicates that online shopping will grow faster than what you are forecasting." The only item missing from the research is a simple asterisk. The asterisk that suggests you might want to take a glance at the small print at the bottom of the page. The notes in six-point font that merely suggest that past results are not always indicative of future performance. Your mileage may vary.

"We are gaining customers every day." He turns his laptop so I get a better view. Another PowerPoint. I would ask if the devil uses PowerPoint in hell, but I know the answer. The devil uses PowerPoint wherever she goes.

They re-branded their company last month. Shoe town? Shoe hub? Heel nation? I can't remember their new name. It's written on a stick-it note on my desk. This is the tenth company I've met within the past two days.

"Why not triple your sales in 12 months?" I ask.

I-shoe? E-footware?

"I'm not sure if that's even possible." Kevin slides a stack of sales projections towards me.

Shoe World? Word Wide Foot? Soles R US? I was up half the night doing my homework.

"I can help you."

Athlete's Foot (not just a fungus). Shoepedia? Foot Fetish?

"It would help if you wrote about us, let investors know what's happening here." He gestures with his hands.

How about writing us a check.

Shoeville? If the shoe fits?

*"*Your company does not have all the information it needs to be successful. We can help." I attempt to copy his hand gesture. It doesn't come natural to me, but I know that copying a persons body language builds rapport.

A purchase order would work.

"I'll have some of my staff look into establishing a relationship with your firm, becoming a client."

Something about jogging. Runnin' with the devil? I love that song. Wish I played guitar.

"We like to think of the firms that we work with as our partners."

"I think we will have a great year." He puts out his hand to shake.

"Don't think, *do.*"

My words have become a sick combination of Yoda, Mr. Miyagi and Smith. I'm one step away from moving to California to write self-help books.

* * *

Media trainers are like most consultants, half of what they say is extremely helpful, the other half may cause either temporary or permanent insanity. The problem is figuring out which is the correct choice. You never know if you're drinking poison or taking the cure, but in either case you usually have to pay in advance.

Today is my media training final exam. And yes, I did homework for a media test. It's like studying for a urine test (distance or accuracy).

Back in the fake television studio I'm ready to go. I'm wearing a new suit and a tie that won't clash with my eyes or the capricious taste of my wardrobe consultant. The makeup guy likes my skin tone, suggests I exfoliate at least three times a week and wants to get into the Internet business. The sound guy asks for investing advice as he mics me.

I even have fake answers for the stress questions that Julie hinted they would ask. Questions that are supposed to trip you up, catch you off guard, make you make a mistake. Yes I did my homework. I talked to my own expert who gave me a list of questions that consultants love to throw at their clients. Absurd questions that make the clients think the consultant prepared them for everything, even if there is a less than 1/10 of one- percent chance of getting asked.

"Were back in five:" Someone from the control room shouts. I wonder who is hiding in there. "Four, Three." The camera operator waves her hand as if conducting an orchestra of dust mites. The light on top of camera one burns red.

"Were back for Internet Stock watch." The fake interviewer, who once worked at the fourth largest TV station in Bakersfield, California announces: "Today our guest will discuss where he thinks Internet stocks are going. My guess is up." He then spends what seems like an hour talking about my credentials. I'd rather listen to the Mormon

Tabernacle Choir sing the best of Ozzy Osbourne than hear anyone talk about me or my alleged accomplishments.

"David, the market for Internet companies continues to soar." Mr. Interviewer is reading from the teleprompter. "Will it continue?"

"I think it's safe to say that the market values growth."

Not sure what that means, but I fear that someone will eat it up.

"Many of the Internet companies that you report on have yet to show a profit."

"All of them are gaining customers daily."

Insert another asterisk here.

"Many traditional investors are sitting on the sideline because they believe that the Internet is just a fad."

My forehead is still.

"People said that about the automobile, the steam engine and about every new technology over the past 100 years. The fact is Internet usage is growing faster than technologies like the telephone, radio, or even television."

"Really?"

"It took more than 100 years for the telephone to be in only 80% of U.S. Households."

"That's a good point."

Not really, but what else can he say? We all must play our parts.

"Users are online for many reasons," I continue. "The number one is information." Really it's porn. "They love the fact that they can go online 24/7 and find what they are looking for. Companies that provide in-depth information about their products and services will convert users into long-term customers."

"Many users seem hesitant to shop online."

I studied for this?

"A few years ago some were afraid of using an automated teller machine. Others argued that the machines would never be popular. Go to Penn Station and place an *Out of Order* sign over an ATM machine on a Friday afternoon and see what happens.

New technology is often scary at first but after a few months many can't believe they ever lived without it."

"Interesting analysis."

For a Luddite with an Associate Degree in communications.

"I'd like to turn now to some specific companies that you have been reporting on."

I am pretending to have no idea who he is going to ask about.

"Of course."

"Fur Nation has yet to show a profit, yet their stock is one of the largest gainers in recent weeks. Can you explain why?"

He really wants to know if *he* should buy the stock, in case his acting/anchorman career doesn't pan out.

"The company has a solid management team, a very ambitious plan and a fantastic marketing program."

And they're a client of my firm.

"So you think it was a good idea to spend millions on a commercial during the Super Bowl?"

"I know that everyone who doesn't live in a cave is familiar with the brand and that humans are willing to spend on their pets. Man's best friend is a great market niche to be in."

Is that folksy enough for you?

"But can the stock continue to soar?"

I hear Smith talking in my ear, yet the Interviewer is the one with the ear piece.

"It's a 20 billion a year market segment."

"So you would consider this stock a buy?"

I wouldn't buy it with my money, but if you wanted to give me a few shares, that's a different story.

"Long term it's a buy."

Please, please don't ask me to define long term. I have no idea, and in fact, no one does. At some point long term equals infinity and my head explodes.

"Another hot company that your firm is following is.." The interviewer pauses. Something is wrong with the teleprompter. He's listening to the voice in his earpiece.

When the interviewer stops talking I hear Smith: Go *For It! Be more aggressive*, in my non-existent earpiece. If my enthusiasm for any of our clients drops more than a hair, Smith is in my office challenging me. He demands to know if I am a leader or a follower. Was I willing to take the risks necessary to be the alpha male of Internet research? Was I the guy boldly predicting the future or the one that gets paid peanuts to close the barn door after the four-legged clichés have left the barn?

"--experiencing double-digit growth is Health Web. Why do you love this company?"

"I like this company, because they love their customers. They understand their customers. They are building long-term relationships. They are number one in their market segment. And we know that being number one demands a premium."

Another answer, another asterisk.

And the asterisk this time is the cost of acquiring customers. Online shoppers expect deep discounts. The asterisk is the hard cold fact that only a fraction of the population is shopping online, and that online shoppers would have to order merchandise 24 hours a day, 7 days a week for a thousand years to justify some of the stock evaluations. The asterisk is the fact that rampant optimism can't predict real success in the marketplace any more than raging hormones can predict the success rate of teenagers attempting to hook up with the prom queen: just because you have a boner, doesn't mean that she's going to take her clothes off.

"One more question."

Here comes the "stress" question. He's about to pause, then read the question as quickly as possible in an attempt to get me to answer quickly and screw up.

"When did you stop beating your girlfriend?"

They're going with the classic.

One Mississippi. Two Mississippi.

"When she started behaving."

Nailed it.

"Cut." Julie screams from the control room. I hear laughter.

The laughter is from Smith who emerges from the control room with a rare grin on his face. Julie follows with a look that if put into action would put her in prison for the first, or possibly, second time.

"Someone finally came up with an answer to that stupid question." Smith shakes my hand for the first time since my job interview.

"You can't be serious." Julie takes the cigarette that has been waiting behind her ear to release its carcinogens.

"No one is ever going to ask that. All they care about is where the fuck they should invest." Smith looks in my direction and back to Julie. "You did a good job training him, but the only way we'll know if he's ready is to put him on TV. You can't judge a soldier until he's under enemy fire."

I swear, war metaphors are going to be the death of Western Civilization. Can't say we don't have it coming.

*The asterisk is a typographical symbol or glyph. It originates from the Latin word for star). It is often used to call out a single footnote and has also been used to block out letters in words that are considered naughty like b**bs, f**k, and c**********s. It has also been used, again without irony, to block out letters in the name of G*D, L**D, and J******h. Programmers use it as a wildcard, a substitute for any character. In medieval times, the humble asterisk was used to denote the date of birth in family trees. Having an asterisk next to you name in the record books usually means that something about your feats of strength and agility is in question (you cheated, perhaps). America's greatest author, Kurt Vonnegut, used his sketch of an asterisk to represent the human rectum (i.e. the asshole) in his novel, *Breakfast of Champions*. Now you know.

9. Soul Mate

These are the laws of nature: Insects lose their exoskeletons. Snakes shed. Ursine creatures void their bowels in forested environments. Executives gather with their high priced consultants and brainstorm.

On a yearly basis, the modern exec needs a new strategy. Last year's model no longer has that new strategy smell. It seems passé' to even mention the old strategy while pissing in the executive washroom.

Arrangements are made. Calendars are cleared of all non-strategy appointments and meetings.   Invitations are issued. T-shirts with clever slogans are produced in foreign sweatshops. And then the mavens gather to drink $180 a gallon coffee, eat catered lunches and strategize with the intensity of teenagers attempting to score beer before prom night.

After three days they emerge from the corporate sweat lodge with not only a strategy, but an action plan.

A plan that is guaranteed to please Wall Street and send their stock soaring.

A plan that bears a strong resemblance to what many of their own loyal, but underpaid, employees have been saying all along.

I used to be one of the underpaid employees that no one wanted to listen to, now I am one of the "experts." I can see the resentment in the eyes of the staff as I sit in the waiting room or walk down the hall. These are not just icy stares demanding to know why my firm can charge thousands of dollars a day for a bagel's worth of advice, these are people that want to see me fail, in the quixotic attempt to banish all consultants and let the company proceed in the same manner that it always did, but with a little more cash to spend on coffee, pastries, and bonuses.

Companies need to evolve, but no one needs a brand-new engine when their car is low on gas. The problem is that consultants, strategists, experts, are not willing to merely top off your tank, when they have the opportunity to sell you a brand-new car, fully loaded with the undercoating and the extended warranty.

"Why aren't you running an add during the Super Bowl?" is my opening question to the senior management team. They saw me on TV and asked for a meeting to discuss a possible strategy session.

It's a silly question, but one that is guaranteed to get the conversation flowing in some direction, because before they gather in the corporate sweat lodge, client and consultant must perform the mating dance. In other words, this is a little meeting to sell them on the big meeting.

While I wait for them to decide who is going to answer, I study the posters that line their conference room. Posters that promise relationships that include long walks on sun kissed beaches and champagne toasts in hot tubs. Perfect Match is the company that is determined to grow fast and dominate the online dating world.

"We don't believe that's it's in the best interest of the company to invest 80% of our total marketing budget for thirty seconds of glory."

"We're in this for the long term," number two pipes in.

Wall Street and everyday investors are falling in love with Internet companies. A less than perfect match, but they say opposites attract. My fear is that when Wall Street mates with Internet companies the offspring will be mutants, born without souls, destined for a life in the suburbs defined by teenage vandalism that eventually graduates to white-collar crime.

"We intend to grow organically," continues number three.

All three are dressed in the uniform of the future Internet billionaires they aspire to be: cutoffs and T-shirts. Number three is not even wearing shoes. After they go public in a few months, every employee, included the ones with no shoes, will be rich (at least on paper). My guess is that once they become multi-millionaires they will dress even shabbier.

I loosen my tie and keep silent, enjoying the fact that they are eager for my feedback and approval.

The only thing that happens organically in this business is death and decomposition. That's not their biggest problem. That would be repeat business. If they are successful in creating great matches, why would anyone return to them? Is this a long-term business? How do you plan on standing out in the crowd if you don't think big from the very beginning? So big that they shut out the competition, and have the vision and flexibility to move on to other ventures.

"We'd like to show you our very aggressive online advertising campaign." The lights go off and the PowerPoint begins.

Do people in Kansas imagine walking in wheat fields? I've never been on a long walk on the beach with anyone. Does anyone on their deathbed regret not having walked with their SO on a sandy beach? Was I willing to take this chance?

Susie, my perfect match, has been working with Tequila Mockingbird on their second album. *God Made us Horny*, is even more outspoken and rebellious than their first offering. With songs attacking the hypocrisy of a world that both sells and shies away from sex they are attempting to tap into the culture and make a statement.

The first single, *I'm a slut, but what are you?*, could have been titled what's good for the goose is great for the gander. It's angry, thought provoking, fun, and most importantly, hip.

Although some of the songs are too risqué to get play on non-college stations, the album is a minor hit, and the groups' day jobs have disappeared at the speed of e-mail. The band is ramping up for a national tour where they could play small clubs to promote the album, and more importantly sell concert T-shirts. Susie will probably hit the road with them. Once again she will be gone and I will have no idea what she was up to.

"We respect your position."

The presentation is over and the lights come back on.

"We are considering retaining your firm's services."

"We understand that we are in a highly competitive market space, but in the long run…"

"My firm." I clear my throat. "is not interested in merely cashing your checks."

Pause.

Advanced media training. Pausing makes you sound confident and subtly encourages people to listen. "We want to help you become number one, to take you public, to build something that people will look up to, and to make all of us wealthy."

I pause again, just like I did when I practiced in front of the partners. "We're still not sure that you are truly committed to being a complete success."

Smith would be proud. They'll sign with us, not today but in week or so. Smith, or one of his lieutenants will negotiate a huge fee, and perhaps some stock options.

Tomorrow I'm doing another television interview. It turns out that the bold do get quoted, asked to give their opinion, to share their wisdom. They are even sending a car to pick me up. Of course, I am responsible for getting myself home.

It's like screwing, someone is always willing to help you take off your clothes, but when the deed is done, you're on your own.

10. Souls on Fire

"You Jew."

Question or statement?

The man in black places a pamphlet in my hand. He's dressed in the distinct garb of a Hasid, a follower of an 18th century Polish Rabbi. Not exactly the person I want to have a discussion on my unwillingness to be observant. I don't say religious, for I refuse to conflate observant and religious, but that's a long discussion that I never want to have with anyone who is willing to wear a heavy-wool suit and a fur hat in the middle of a New York summer.

The Messiah is about to return.   I slip the pamphlet onto the printout of Joe's e-mail that I was looking forward to reading on the trip downtown.

"You have a Jewish soul." The Hasid persists, in a manner that suggests joy not sorrow, reward not effort--but how can I trust a man that wears wool in summer--not to mention the long beard--and doesn't sweat? I'm on fire in chinos and a short-sleeve shirt. His soul is on fire, but not his body.

Souls on Fire is a book by Holocaust survivor, Ellie Wiesel. The "Souls" are 18th Century Hasidic masters who are, to say the least, passionate about their faith. They eagerly spend long days studying how to obey G*d's commandants (all 613 of them). They insist that the messiah is about to make his appearance and bring peace to all mankind. And perhaps, if the Jews keep praying, and observing the commandments, we can encourage the messiah to ride the express train instead waiting for him to arrive on the local.

The original Hasidim lived in a world of anguish and despair, but always burned with faith. Their modern counterparts exist in a world without the turmoil of centuries past, but they haven't lost much of the fire, not to mention the inaccurate travel schedules of their savior. And yet, the reference that I can't get out of my mind is not the fire in the belly, but the fire in the gas ovens that incinerated both the observant Jew and non-believer alike; the chambers that provided equal opportunity for both the pious and the profane.

We got lucky. Joe writes. *They wanted to kill more, they thought they could knock down one of the towers into the other and kill thousands, they originally intended to use poisonous gas.*

The 1993 bombing of the World Trade Center was his Kennedy assignation: a straightforward murder turned into a conspiracy that could only be understood if layer after layer were peeled back and viewed through the proper historical prospective.

Their plan was to murder Jews.

Seven years latter and he was obsessed as ever.

If anti-Semitism was his drug, then the Internet was his pusher. Around the world and 24/7, Web page after Web page reported on Neo Nazis, white supremacist and every other hate group with enough tech savvy to post a page. The groups may have been small in number, and unable to understand the basic rules of English grammar, but the fear they inspired was real. And that, no doubt, was their intention. For if you can't scare an old man whose family had suffered greatly, then what other purpose do you have?

Why? Because we are Jews they attack us.

Joe's logic was both perfect and circular.

His paranoia was a simple overreaction to enemies who wanted him dead but didn't even know he was alive. Joe's soul was on fire, but it was the real flame of death and not the metaphorical fire of joy and redemption.

"Remember, the towers stood. The towers stood."

***

"Do you think you're making enough for the amount of effort you put in?"

What's enough?

"A lot of firms," the headhunter continues, "would love to meet with you."

Meetings to set up meetings. Interviews to set up more interviews. Does it ever end? I see the appeal of working the day shift.

I smile. I have never seen more manila file folders stacked on a single desk. There are even more on the credenza. Enough folders I suppose to build cubicles for a dozen worker bees that do nothing all day but read the contents of manila folders.

"Everybody is looking to add staff."

If I get a new job, I'll have a new commute. New trains, new schedule. Perhaps have to get up earlier.

"And signing bonuses. Out of this world." He looks up.

And I love my coffee guy. I don't even have to order. That's worth something.

"There's never been a better time to be looking for a new position."

"I'm not really looking." I can tell from the look on his face that he thinks I'm just playing hard to get, but it's the truth.

I like my job. I have an assistant. She does nothing, but never complains.

"I can see that you're thinking about it."

Susie is right, I should at least listen. I don't have to take a new job, I could just use it as leverage. Get more from the firm. More money, more stock in IPO companies. Lots more stock.

The recruiter opens the manila folder and scans something. "You deserve more than the token shares you are currently receiving."

"Yes I do."

He's glances at his Rolex. What happened to my soul? I'm starting to think like a yuppie. I used to want to work for Greenpeace and save whales. Workers at GP can't afford Caribbean vacations and farmhouses in Vermont, but maybe they sleep better at night.

The phone buzzes and the recruiter gives me the one minute sign and picks it up.

Whales sleep with one-eye open. They go back and forth between eyes so both parts of their brain can get rest. Mr. Headhunter knows a lot about my salary and perks, but I bet he knows nothing about sea mammals.

He says, "bye," and hangs up.

"Do you love going into work every day?" He asks.

"Most days."

My soul is not on fire, it is warm and more importantly, I am a stakeholder. I have a few stock options, that on paper are worth nothing, but in a few months time, if the stocks continued to surge, will have value. And I'm only getting a fraction of what the firm pulls in, but at least, I'm a participant in the great American dream/nightmare/scam that is often labeled the stock market.

I'm not a true believer. If I was, life would be much easier.

If you are a true believer, you know that things are going to work out. Failure is not an option. You will be successful. You will be rich.

If you're a believer you understand that it's the body which burns in the flames, not the soul. The soul is elsewhere. The soul survives, becomes one with the universe, is on a first name basis with the almighty, lasts forever and a day.

If you are a non-believer you are screwed, because in the end you have nothing but the flames and the ashes.

"What would someone have to offer," the recruiter asks, "to get you to leave your current position."

Money. Stock at the pre IPO price. Something that will make me a million without any significant risk. I don't want to worry so much about whether or not I'm doing the right thing. I want to care more about whales than money. But I don't. If I earn more I can send a check. But that's not the same, is it?

* * *

"You are Jewish?" This time it's definitely a question.

Another station, another salesperson. This time in a red T-shirt, with both a cross and a Star of David.

"Eskimo." Love quoting Bogart--especially when no one gets the reference.

"You know you can believe in Jesus and still be Jewish." I reject the Jews for Jesus pamphlet that he thrusts towards me.

"And vegetarians can eat steak." The look on his face is blank as I turn towards the stairs.

"If you don't accept Jesus as your personal lord and savior you face eternal damnation."

"Can you put that in PowerPoint?" I mumble, but he has moved on to the next potential customer.

What is it with fanatics that insist my soul is not getting its minimum daily requirement of irritation? Does this happen everywhere? If I travel the subway in Tokyo, will I be accosted by *Baptists for Buddha?*

Perhaps this is proof that god really exists—or just maybe, subway stations around the planet are another world's hell.

11. O Lord Won't You Buy Me a Mercedes-Benz?

Both earthquakes and business phenomena have epicenters.

The epicenter of the Internet on the West Coast is Silicon Valley and on the East Coast its Silicon Alley (New York, NY). One has better weather, one has culture. One has earthquakes, the other has culture. Choose carefully.

The day after many Internet companies in Silicon Valley were taken public and the employees cashed their stock options the parking lots went from rows of old Toyotas and used Volvos to brand new Porsches, Mercedes, Ferrari's and Lamborghini's. Luxury car salesmen in Silicon Valley were making a killing. What did they do with their commission checks? They fed the beast. They invested in the stock of the dotcoms that their customers toiled at. Why not? The market was booming. Some car salesmen made enough money on just a few stock transactions to buy their own Porsches, Mercedes, Ferrari's and Lamborghini's.

How can such a uniquely American success story end badly?

Who is more pathetic, the man lost at sea surrounded by water he can't drink or the man in the desert without any liquid for miles?   What if either the sailor or the explorer had the choice of drinking Kool-Aid laced with cyanide to immediately end his suffering?   Would they choose to drink or would they choose to continue on and endure a painful death?

If they chose the poison would they be able to get the image of rescue just a few waves or sand dunes away out of their minds? How ironic, the press would report, that they took their own life just a few feet away from salvation. Or, if they refused the refreshment and instead suffered, with no hope of escaping their fates what would the outside world think? Along with death and taxes, you can't escape irony.

You either drink the Kool-Aid or you die of thirst.

Some of us do both. Again and Again.
Diary of a dot com billionaire

Part III The Present

Jailhouse Rock

Dearest Susie,

Got your letter. Thanks. It's always good to hear from people on the outside. Feel free to write anytime. I'm here 24/7.

Sorry. Sorry. Sorry.

Once again, sorry.

I should have told you everything. I have been advised by counsel to not to say anything about the activities that have landed me here. I'm not even supposed to commit to writing the information that is part of the public record. Fucking lawyers.

I have no one but myself to blame. Perhaps I would have made better decisions if I had thought about it, or talked it out with you. Each night, while I'm drifting into sleep, I get to perform my life's autopsy. The analysis isn't pretty, but what else could it be?

It was interesting while it lasted. Although we never lived like royalty, we did have some fun and they can't take that away. The week we spent on St. ????--that island in the Caribbean was great. Someday, maybe, we'll do it again (although probably not at a five star resort—of course if the band hits it really big, and you get some royalties, and you can put up with me, feel free to buy me a ticket—it doesn't have to be first class, as long as it is next to you).

They can take away the money, but not the vacations. They can force you to surrender assets, but not memories. If you have a soul, it's yours to keep. In short, the Feds got their pound of flesh and have moved on, so when I'm out it's over. And that in itself is a relief. It's over.

Still sorry.

As for the other thing... I kept it all to myself and you want to know why. I don't really have a reason. It's not that I love secrets. The fact is that I have never been good at keeping them, especially from you. Maybe I would like secrets if I were good at them. Can't say for sure. I must admit, that I liked having at least one small (smallish?) secret from you.

You read me too well. It's a gift, that I'm not even sure that you are totally aware of. You don't just finish my sentences; you improve them. I used to resent this, just a little, but now I miss the hell out of it.

I should have known that one-day you would know. Only the very young can take all their secrets to the grave.

Remember, before we were together, we would hang out at Brooke and Dave's beach house? You and I would end up sitting together, even when we were both seeing other people and we would comment on how couples were always afraid to share information about some of the most mundane items. Neither one willing to admit that someone else was interesting nor god forbid, attractive. We both believed that it would enhance the relationship if couples shared. How much energy was wasted, we wondered, keeping stupid secrets? The smaller the secret, the harder they worked to guard it.

You said that it was phony to always have to pretend that your mate was the one, the only, the belle of the ball. I thought that it was just too much work to believe otherwise, or at least act as if it was so. Most couples need to live in a world of imaginary perfection. My spouse is perfect ... He/she is soooooooooooo wonderful. Blah, Blah, etc. Blah.

I think that more than anything, I didn't want to be identified as "that person," a voyeur, a peeping tom, a pervert. I had no idea what you would think. Would you have wanted to watch with me? Or would you think that I had crossed a line? This was all going through my mind when I thought about telling you.

I understand your point. I didn't give you the opportunity to share, to be nonjudgmental. You say that maybe you would have enjoyed it, considered it foreplay for the most intense lovemaking of our lives. You wrote that maybe you would have shared the experience, even got down on your knees and blown me while I watched. (BTW I'm happy to report that I'm currently celibate and not hoping to meet anyone special for the next 2 and a half years--maybe less with good behavior. Thanks for asking. You?).

Ouch. You really know how to push a guy's buttons, saying that I might have gotten oral sex while watching live porn. Would you have really? I know, I know, we'll never know, but it's really not like you to be a tease. Guess I deserve that.

I guess that I wasn't willing to take the chance, to let the cat out of the bag. Once you tell a secret, there is no untelling.

So this is my opportunity to come clean, to write it all down, to confess and be free (so to speak). You wanted to know everything, so here it is:

They're not total strangers. They were at first; I called them Adam and Eve. (Yes, I do remember that our favorite restaurant is the Garden of Eden and I would like nothing better to be sitting there with you eating humus and drinking really mediocre Lebanese Wine.

Adam and Eve were the first names that came to mind. The entire forbidden fruit story is just too tempting to ignore sometimes. The Bible as metaphor for life in modern New York City, who could have guessed?

The first time I discovered them was a complete accident, and yes it did turn me on, but not necessarily that way. It's not like watching two people fucking is an instant hard on. For me it's more of a heart racing, I can't believe this is happening type of event. More of getting high or riding a roller coaster than actual sex. It's like being a schoolboy and seeing your first Playboy. I imagine that it's like being a hunter and seeing the prey in your sights after days of stalking. A combination of all the above events is the best description that I can manage. It's not that it's better than the real thing, it's a completely different activity.

Sex never gets to be new again. Only one first kiss. Only once do we get to delicately touch a breast for the first time. It really doesn't seem right that we only get to lose our virginity once. Think about it, after the first twenty years of your life, the only original thing you have to look forward to is death.

So I enjoyed watching them fucking, but, believe it or not, the event was still a mystery that was begging to be solved. It's one thing to sit in a café' and wonder if the man sitting in the table near you is having an affair with the young lady next to him, and another to see two people going at it and trying to figure out the what the rest of their life is like. Before this I would have assumed that if I observed the erotic, I wouldn't care about the rest, but that wasn't the case.

I knew the erotic, but still wanted the everyday details. There were important questions to be answered. Why only once a week? Why Wednesdays? Maybe they did it somewhere else on Friday nights. Or maybe they used another room or Riverside Park? I had no idea.

I often thought that they were the ones getting the most enjoyment out of the act. Exhibitionism was their fetish. Makes sense, but again, I have no data. My research is incomplete and always will be.

I do know that it's Eve's Apartment and the name downstairs says, Jane Gold, but I can't find out any information about her anywhere, and I searched and searched. Nothing. Zilch. Nada. Zero.

Here's the freakish part. Remember that guy I told you about at Crown, the one with all the plants, the one I sat next to on the flight to Vegas, the strange guy that no one really talked with? It turns out that Adam is the plant man (his real name is George). The plant man and his paramour are our own weekly private show.

It's a little different when you know at least one of the participants. I imagine that more people would attend orgies if they didn't have to face the participants the next day, or ever again. At least more guys would.

I was afraid that I might give my secret away that I might say something that would suggest that I know about them.

222

I'm not surprised that you also noticed that he is well endowed. Hard to miss. Maybe you can invite yourself over for a cup of coffee and a threesome. I know, I know, that's not your scene. But if you could have sex with him, and not have to see him again would you want to? And if you do, will you make sure that the blinds are closed?

Remember that day I bumped into you in the village? I was really following Eve. I had no idea where she was going, but a few weeks later I found out that she had a regular appointment with her therapist. Can't tell you what issues she was working on, I'm not that good. I just know that the office that she visited was used by a Sheila Goldstein, MSW, couples and individual therapy.

Wish I knew more, but that's all. I got too busy at work to be anything more than an amateur sleuth. Maybe if I spent more time stalking and less time hyping over-valued Internet stocks I would be in a better place. At least my record would be cleaner.

That's all I know about Adam and Eve or George and Jane. It is up to you to keep up the research or not. (I am not, repeat not, asking you to take one for the team).

To answer your question about voyeurism in the slammer, there are very few opportunities. If you listen at night you can hear when your cellmate or the guy in the next cage is jerking off, but most guys wear their headphones at night and listen to music. Most of what you see in prison is mundane at best. It's the same shit every day—repeat as necessary. Can I sue the ghost of Elvis for false advertising?

Speaking of music, you asked me what my choice would be for the best song ever written and recorded or at least the one that comes closest to approaching a state of perfection. I was hoping that this meant that you were going to be sending me lots of music, but this made no sense, since we both know that you should have some understanding of the music that I enjoy listening to (both alone and with you).

I thought maybe you were doing some type of experiment and you would write a new song based on what my answer was. I finally concluded that it was one of the millions of random questions that you enjoy asking. As I've said before, being with you is like a perpetual first date/murder interrogation with dozens of unrelated questions and random statements (I mean this as a compliment). God, I miss you.

I can only assume that for most people, picking out the perfect song would be a chore. There must be, in English alone, a million or so choices. Even if we limit it down to only songs that have charted in the past 40 years, we still have a lifetime of listening to choose from.

That being said, my choice is easy.

While My Guitar Gently Weeps, by George Harrison gets my vote for the best song ever recorded. In second place is everything else.

I know, The Beatles recorded it, but the song belongs to Harrison, and Harrison alone. Who else in the Fab Four could have written something so lyrical and enchanting? So balanced and beautiful? Not Paul with his "Uncle Albert," mentality or Ringo and his fucking, "Octopus Garden." Sure John was close, and Lennon/McCartney were two of the best songwriters in history, but the question was not who was the best team based on a body of work, you wanted to know who wrote/performed the perfect song.

Harrison understood his voice, and crafted music and lyrics that fit perfectly with that voice. Can you imagine anyone singing a version better than the original? I don't think it's possible to cover the song and not murder it. You can cover most songs, and make them you own, but not this one. This one is complete exactly as published.

Saint-Exupéry, the author of "The Little Prince," but you probably know that (it's hard to have a one-way conversation, but that's all we have). Anyway, Saint-Exupéry said that something is perfect not when nothing can be added, but when nothing can be taken away.

Every note, every word of the song is perfect. (Although, I did hear there is a demo of the song that contains new verses that were cut prior to the official release. This does not change my argument one bit, because we are talking about songs as released, not as taped in some barnyard studio and then lost until the artist overdoses and some sound engineer or ex-wife cashes in).

Harrison succinctly captures one man's complete understanding of the universe, and his role in it. All human experience is in every note, in every lyric and all the spaces in-between.

He misses no detail and captures the moment perfectly. He sees the "Love there that's sleeping" and the dust on the floor. Notice how the love is sleeping, it's not dead or dormant or nonexistent. He doesn't bring the love or invent it. He merely notices it and continues on, believing that he can inspire us to come to an understanding on our own terms, when we are ready to do so, and not a millisecond before.

And throughout the song his guitar is, not just weeping, but gently weeping. His instrument does not sing, or chant, hum, nor intone, it gently weeps. For it is a sad and wise guitar, lovingly played by a caring master; one that has seen much and humbly offers to share its vision of life on earth.

George understand that his guitar is both mightier than the sword and less effective at communicating than a madman shouting in the wind.

He reminds me of that saying in the Talmud that all men should carry a piece of paper in each of his front pockets. The first should declare that "The World Was Created Just For Me." And the second should state: "I Am Merely Dust and Ashes." At our best, and at our worst, we are both.

George is our Hamlet, our Socrates, asking the big questions and suggesting that if the answers do exist, they may be slightly out of reach. Even so, asking the questions is the right thing to do. Perhaps it is the only alternative: I wonder, therefore I exist. He is both restless and at peace.

Not many artists could pull it off, to be both humble and powerful at the same time. The passion to teach, without preaching, is an obvious reflection of his studies in eastern religion and philosophy. A less talented artist would have gone too far either way, but George was balanced enough to pull it off.

In my opinion, WMGGW proves, beyond a reasonable doubt, that reincarnation exists, and for that matter, has always existed. While My Guitar Gently Weeps is not a work of art composed by a 28-year-old soul. This is a song written by someone that has been there, done that, kicked the tires and chariot wheels, had tea with God, wrestled with angels, walked across the desert for sport, mediated on top of clouds, been to the mountaintop, drank from the fountain and then reborn, at the perfect time, in the humble town of Liverpool.

If you ever need a song to get lost in, a song to live inside, this is it. You can focus on the lyrics, get lost in the lead guitar work of Clapton or the rhythm guitar of Harrison. Listen to it a thousand times and be comforted or surprised.

It is the perfect song.

I don't care what Rolling Stone says. The last time that Rolling Stone was a relevant publication was when The Beatles were together.

The fact that Rolling Stone is still published and that Keith Richards may die of old age are two of the unexplained miracles of rock n roll. (Perhaps one of them, if not both, signed a deal with the devil. And believe me, the devil will collect, if not in this lifetime, then in the next).

You may chart higher, but you won't come closer to perfection. (The above should not be taken to suggest that you should not try and write a better song. You must try. I can only assume that you wanted to know what to aspire to, as far as I concerned, while song writing. Or, it could, as I said before, be a random question. In either case, keep writing. I think that George (the ex-beatle, not the plant man/porn star would want you to. No, I believe that the quiet Beatle would scream out loud that you do your best to write the perfect song).

Speaking of song writing, how's Tequila? Heard you guys have a new album. Congrats. How many songs did you write? Are you going to tour? Stupid question. Stay away from groupies and send postcards from the road. Lots of postcards.

I have to go now; they are serving tea on the veranda.

With every mistake,

David

Upstate Correctional Facility

Minimum Security with Maximum Inconvenience

* * *

Susie,

What can we write about death that hasn't already been written and rewritten, copied and pasted?

Dead. Deceased. Expired. Gone. Not coming back. Passed away. The end.

The punishment of prison is not the isolation, the boredom, the confinement, the food. The punishment is the removal from the ones you love, and your complete inability to communicate with them in any meaningful fashion. You never get to say goodbye. To say thanks. To say anything.

You just get to wait. This is the final nail in the coffin that is the lesson I should have learned a long time ago.

I'm thrilled that he left me more of his writings, but I think that I should wait until I'm out of here to read. Keep them in a safe place. I'll be out soon enough. And then?

Love always,
David

The Near Future

1)   Y N T B E

Bryant Park.

Except for a whiff of maple in the air, it is
the perfect New York morning. I'm happy it's spring.
I'm happier I'm out. I'm happiest after the welcome
home that I got from Susie last night. This morning,
she said, "a stint in the slammer is more effective
than Viagra." Not sure if it would make a good
television commercial, but I'll take sex and a
compliment anytime.

"David."

Alex closes in quickly, like a lion chasing
the prey.

"Edsel. Great to see you."

"No one calls me that anymore. In fact, no
one that I work with even knows that the name ever
existed. I've moved on."

"Moving on is not such a bad idea." I can
sense that not only has he moved on, but he is now
moving much faster, with more determination than

ever. "From this point forward, I will only refer to you as Alex."

"Let's walk." He gestures, and I struggle to keep up.

The only clutter on the sidewalk is the small, gray patches of stubborn ice; the last scraps of a blizzard that should have melted weeks ago, but for whatever reason, holds on to its solid state, avoiding, for just a few more days, its trip through the gutters and into the East River.

"You probably want to know why I was so eager to see you."

"It's always good to see an old friend."

I thought I would have a few days to decompress, but Alex sent e-mails and text messages to all of my known aliases and I just couldn't resist his zeal. He asked to see me and I had nothing on the to-do list. In fact, I haven't even had time to write a to-do list.

He turns right and we head east on 42nd street.

"A lot has changed in the last couple of years. Industry wise. We're no longer living in a RDZ."

What the hell is an RDZ? "I've been out of the loop."

"The Internet has changed the world, and the speed of change is accelerating. Forward thinking organizations are tired of same ol' RTW."

RTW? Forget Bryant park, we should have met in Alphabet City. A minimum-security correctional facility is not the place to keep up with industry trends or the latest lingo. All I learned in my months in the slammer is more than 100 euphemisms for creamed beef on toast, the most famous being SOS.

"I think it's going to take a little while to get caught up."

"What's the problem with most Internet companies?" Alex asks and waits for a response that is not going to be delivered at the caffeinated speed that he is moving at. He doesn't wait for me to answer and I am relieved. "Why just sell socks, when you can market the entire line of footwear needs? Why stop there? Why not include everything a man would ever need, from diapers to condoms to caskets?"

"You only need the diapers, because you didn't use the condom." I may not be fully back, but I am alive.

"I'm speaking metaphorically, although it might be a great business, but that's not the point of the question."

"A lot has changed, since I took my sabbatical." I spent a lot of time trying to figure out how best to refer to my time in the big house, but so far haven't settled on anything. It's not a big deal with Alex; he knows where I've been sleeping. He was there when the Feds slapped the bracelets on my wrists and marched me out of the office, before I even had the opportunity to take a sip of my morning latte.

"I think that the problem with most Internet companies is that they promise too much," I say, thinking that I've nailed the answer.

We turn right and head south on Fifth Avenue.

"Correction! They promise too little. Way too little."

"Really?"

"They don't even come close to offering enough."

"OK." I'm trying to follow, but how can anyone that has seen so many miners not find the gold they were promised not be skeptical? I would like to believe that had I lived in middle ages, I would have been just as skeptical watching alchemists attempt to turn lead into gold. Someone had to believe, but my only goal is to keep on the straight and narrow. Get a job, pay my taxes, recycle, and live as a free man. Let someone else play with lead.

"What can you find on the typical career Web site?"

"A new job?"

"Exactly." He pauses for effect. "Suppose you're a man in your late 20s, single, mid-income, with the potential for earning more. Do you really just need a slightly higher paying position?"

Yes." I said, positive that this was not the answer he was looking for to make his point, but it was the only answer that came to mind.

"It's a start, but we're going to offer more, much more."

"Like?"

"Isn't it time to get serious about your relationships?"

"It really depends on how you define serious. But no."

"You're not the typical demo, besides, someday you'll change your mind."

Someday I'll be dead and my loved ones will be buying me a casket online, maybe I can get married in it.

"So, if I was the correct demographic, you would?"

"Think big, think very big"

"You would find me the best career opportunity in the world."

Alex stops. We are now in front of the New
York Public Library.

"Y. N. T. B. E."

"Y. N. T. B. E.?"

"You're Not Thinking Big Enough."

"How big is enough?"

"Everything is not enough."

"Everything?"

"Y. N. T. B. E. That's all I can say."
Suddenly, Alex whose mouth has been going 55
MPH in a school zone is now silent.

"I'm not sure what you mean."

"What makes a great employee?" Not sure
why he's changed the topic.

I search my mind, look around, but I've got
nothing. "Patience and fortitude."

"You have been away for awhile."

Patience and Fortitude are the names of the
stone lions that guard the library. They're very
effective; the library has never been attacked by
wildebeests. We continue walking on Fifth.

"We want you."

"You want to hire me, but you can't tell me more. I can sign an NDA."

"We want you to come onboard?"

"As a consultant?"

"As a provisional employee, see if it works out--for both of us."

"But what if I'm not thinking big enough?"

"You will, it just takes a little time to catch on to what we are trying to accomplish. It's going to be huge, bigger than Microsoft and Google combined."

"There is this problem, and I almost hesitate to bring it up, but I do have a small, but not inconsequential felony conviction on my record. And if you need a reference, I only got the warden."

"The only thing that means is that you can't be an officer of the corporation or give fucking stock recommendations, no one gives a shit about that anymore. We don't care what anyone thinks about you either. There is only one thing that we really care about."

We reach 40th street and turn right.

"And that would be?"

"You know how to make the data work."

"The data doesn't always work the way people want it to."

"It will be your job to help find the hidden relationships, that's what you have always done best. We have made great strides, but there is so much more we need to do. We would like you to be one of our code breakers."

"Sounds fun."

"Don't kid yourself, it's a startup, you'll work your ass off—for little money, until the venture pays off. It is going to be the next big thing," Alex says with the conviction of a man who just bet that the sun would rise the next morning. I'm relieved to know that I don't have to donate a kidney or promise what's left of my soul to the devil. Although in this town it's a buyer's market.

"Bigger than IBM or Intel in their Primes. Bigger, much bigger." Alex continues.

"Sounds amazing."

This offer couldn't be any worse than my former cellmate who said his brother could get my a job on the loading dock of his brother's furniture import business.

"I really want you to think about it."

"I will."

"Keep in mind that we are on a very tight deadline. Very tight."

We round the corner and pass the same spot that we started. My mouth is open wide and I'm sure that Alex thinks that I'm overwhelmed with his ideas and his energy. Stretched across a park bench, just over his shoulder is a homeless man fast asleep, holding an empty bottle of wine. The T-shirt he is wearing is old and dirty, but I can't miss the Fur Nation logo.

I comment on how perhaps Fitzgerald was wrong about no second acts in America. The reference is lost on Alex who is walking faster as he babbles on about founder's shares and sweat equity and soon the stock market will return to its former glory days, he just knows that it will. This is going to be big, really big, and with just a little luck, change the world.

I am hungry, I need work, but am I thirsty enough?

2. Wings of Wax

New day. New job. The rest of my life…

I open the door to McBucks and see Alex at the counter. My watch confirms that I'm 15 minutes early. Alex has already picked up our morning fuel.

"You need this." He hands me a grande.

"Thanks." I slept better in prison than I did last night.

"There's something you need to know, before you start."

"What?" I really want to ask why, as in why am I here?

"You have to believe that this is going to be big, the biggest."

"What if I'm still, for arguments sake, a little skeptical."

I actually wanted to talk to Susie in the middle of the night. It was a first. Seems almost unnatural to wake someone up just to start a conversation.

"That's because you don't know about Icarus."

"Icarus?"

What if I left all my knowledge and skills behind bars? It happens.

"Icarus stands for Intelligent Computing Arranged Regarding User Statistics, it's simply the most powerful system every developed."

"But Icarus."

"Yes I know, Icarus was the myth guy that died, but it was his own fault--he didn't listen to his father."

"You are going to succeed because you plan on listening to your father?"

"We are going to succeed. YNTBE is going to succeed, because it is powered by Icarus."

"How many more acronyms do I need to memorize?"

"Just Icarus."

"Here's to Icarus" I lift my cup to salute. Alex's cup remains still. "Why didn't you tell me this before?"

Why am I starting a new job? What if they are all crazy?

"I didn't want to tell you more than you could handle."

"What exactly can't I handle about a job finding Web site?"

Susie thinks I should give it a shot. I can always quit. Help whales another day.

Alex takes a sip of his grande whatever and remains silent, with a look of a police officer about to tell anxious parents that there child is still missing, or worse.

"I know, I'm not thinking big enough, it's a site that sets your career soaring," I say.

I've never been a quitter. For better or worse, I stick with it. Starting a job feels like entering a Catholic marriage or joining the Mafia. Death gets to decide when the relationship is over.

Alex looks in both directions.

"Think big," he starts off slowly. "Imagine a Web site that not only provides you with a job, but also finds you the perfect place to live and a life partner—based on your sexual preference, of course."

"Goes without saying."

"How much would people owe us to perfect their lives?"

Before I could ask if users that kept the job, but got divorced, were due a partial refund, Alex stops, turns, and whispers: "No matter what you think, you have to make everyone you meet today believe that you believe."

Sincerity is great if you can fake it.

As we continued to walk towards Hudson Street, Alex extols the virtues of the Icarus team and the terabytes of data they are collecting and analyzing. Data that will be used to make matches that will drastically improve the lives of thousands, if not everyone in the known universe.

"Bigger than Google," I lift my latte to toast Alex. He seems relieved enough to lift his cup and smile.

"By the way how do I pronounce YNTBE?"

"It's a secret," Alex says flatly.

"In ancient religions, how to pronounce the name of God was a secret. Actually, in some religions it still is…" Once again he is not listening.

"Exactly," is all he says as we enter the former factory/warehouse that now houses YNTBE worldwide, and possibly larger, headquarters.

3. Something Old, Something New

Forget Phoenix and all that garbage about rebirth in the fucking desert. If you want to see a city that is constantly reborn and don't have 500 years, come to NYC. This is a city that lives in a state of renewal.

A little more than 100 years ago there was prime farmland in Manhattan. Farms became houses, and than apartments. Apartments were sub divided and just when you thought that they were as small as someone could live in, and was willing to pay for, they were subdivided once again. A few years later, young entrepreneurs cashed in their Internet-stock options and bought dozens of apartments just to gut them and live in 3,500 square feet of empty space.

New York is a city where the Landmarks Preservation Commission and the developers are constantly at war. Old office buildings that seemed modern only a few years ago are torn down and replaced with something taller, but uglier. Less friendly, but more expensive. Meat packing plants become nightclubs. Nightclubs become million dollar lofts. Old shoe factories become modern Web shops.

The techies love their brick warehouses wired for the digital age. For years you couldn't find an article on new media without the cliché 'brick and mortar' used for everything that is both uncyber and uncool. It's as if the world turned upside down and everything that was solid was worthless while only the "objects" that were virtual had real value. The virtual world was going to soar, and the real world was going to sink into its foundations. The only exception to the brick and mortar rule is your corporate headquarters. The more bricks in your building, the more likely you were to kick the crap out of competitors, both virtual and non.

YNTBE is the only signage in the place; a single banner that you can't miss as you enter the main room.

Alex leads me to a nearly empty desk. The computer looks like it had just been taken out of the box.

"Here you are." he says. "Most communication here is electronic or F2F."

"Cool."

I've never loved the word, unfortunately it works. Use it and you don't have to say anything else. It is often used, but rarely understood, to be a touch sarcastic.

"I have to go to a meeting, but why don't you introduce yourself to your neighbors," he says.

"Thanks."

"You might notice they we are not seated by job function. Our company philosophy is that all employees are seated randomly so that everyone is part of the overall business."

"Interesting."

"Think of it as a giant jig saw puzzle that everyone gets to put together." He turns and is quickly gone.

"Thanks," I say, thinking of blind men working on a jig saw puzzle, or better yet blind men with no arms pushing random pieces with their noses and trying to make a pretty picture for the king's birthday.

I put down my coffee and turn on the computer.

"Did you have an opportunity to sign your forms yet?"

The first piece of the puzzle has arrived.

"No," I say.

"I'm Robin."

"I haven't had the opportunity to go over it yet."

I pick up the packet on my desk and notice that all the forms are filled out, all the choices made for me.

"Sometimes I get a little ahead of myself. I'm a Myers-Brigs ENFJ. You need to take your test within two days. You had a question?"

Myers-Brigs ENFJ would not be how I described her. In polite company, I'd go with: brunette, mid-twenties, nice figure, medium height-- overly perky this early in the morning.

"It seems that the human resources department has completed all of my forms."

"Departments have walls, functions have purpose."

"And the purpose of this document?"

"You certify, under penalty of death, that you will only drink your share of soda and won't steal office supplies."

Wow, a HR rep with I sense of humor, maybe there is something about this new economy. I wanted to make a crack about stealing from my last job, but thought better of it.

251

"Ok, but why are all the forms filled out?"

"Icarus took care of it."

"Oh yes, Icarus."

"Icarus, stands for Intelligent Computing-"

"Arranged Regarding User Statistics," I finish her decoding of the holy acronym.

"We simply input your data," she continues, "and Icarus selected the best healthcare, life insurance, investment, and retirement plans for you."

"Do I need to send Icarus a thank you note?"

"We like to use what we build."

"We eat our own dog food."

"Exactly." She says and smiles, but I sense she wants to finish with me and get to the next item on her preprogrammed, electronic, to-do list.

I sign the forms, and watch as she takes the entire stack of paper.

"Welcome. You will receive an e-mail confirming everything that we discussed within an hour. Icarus will remind you take your personality tests within the next two days."

"Thanks."

"Don't worry, you can come in anytime to do the tests, or do extra work. We're open 24/7—365 days of the year.

"Cool."

As I discretely watched her ass disappear into a maze of cubicles all I can think about was that Icarus was working overtime, but never drank soda, ate brownies, and never, ever, stole pens and stick-it note from the office supply closet.

I'm proud of myself for landing a real job, one based on not just connections, but at least in part, on my skills. For the first time in months I am relatively happy, that is until I think of the implications of eating your own dog food at a company like YNTBE.

4. New York's Strongest

In New York, New York, the cops are "The Finest," the fireman "The Bravest," and not to be left behind in the moniker department, the sanitation engineers--the gentlemen that collect your garbage—bill themselves as "The Strongest." They even paint it on their trucks, next to their tattered and faded, American flags.

Customers of YNTBE sign a release form that allows the company *"to gather any and all data, information, facts, or figures that will allow us to gain insight into the above individuals in order to insure quality life choices. Such information is not limited to traditional methods and may include…"*

One man's data is another man's trash. You collect the nuggets of gold and the pieces of lead and hope that you have enough sense to tell the difference between the two.

Years ago, when I first started online, I developed a reputation for being able to find info in a hurry. This was great, until every executive in the company wanted info, always in hurry. It was as if overnight shipping was the only option; ASAP the only time frame.

To make matters worse, no one just asked for one item, (IBM's sales last quarter, the number of hard drives built last year). They wanted everything.

In hard copy. If I gave them everything, they would drown in a sea of paper, a dumpster of data.

Every attempt to narrow down their request, via the assistant, resulted in a he needs *everything*, he can't say *exactly* what he needs, but he'll know it when he sees it.

So, I delivered what I though they needed, the basic info plus 10 percent, just to show extra effort. I never delivered everything (asking for everything is like asking for infinity). No one ever complained. I can only assume that that they either got what they needed, or most likely, never even looked at what I had sent. The executives that demand everything are the ones that are easily distracted by new, and more exciting, projects.

At YNTBE, we get the release signed and we start collecting everything but their garbage.

Besides the typical demographic info, we capture information from employment records to birth order. The more you know, the more you can use: older siblings get along better with spouses that were also the oldest, middle children tend to be

255

peacekeepers and the youngest more rebellious and on it goes.

You never know what useful information that you can glean from reading a list of movie rentals or the TV shows they watch (as opposed to the educational shows that they claim to watch).

Is it important for the individual to be seen as smart? Educated? Successful? Add it to the profile. Do they pay their bills on time? Spend too much or save every penny? Do they buy drinks for the girls at the bar? Do they purchase their underwear on sale? How often do they do their laundry? What are there online shopping habits? Do they steal cable or pay for it? Recycle? Drive over the speed limit? Use birth control? What Web sites do they visit? How kinky is the porn that they download?

How much time do they spend on e-mail? Texting? Do they forward stupid chain letters that some find amusing? What does their credit report say about them? Do the personality tests indicate that they got along with their parents, siblings, college professors?

Do they believe in ghosts? Life on other planets? Life after death? Sex before marriage? The Monroe Doctrine? Can they explain the no-huddle offense or the infield fly rule?

Each and every data point is a possible predicator of future behavior.

Unlike New York's strongest, our collection is not limited to the amount of stinky bags we can throw into the back of the truck and load on garbage barges to ship out of state. We are only limited by the size of our Sun servers, which is close to infinity.

Our data collecting may not be making us stronger, but we do have a brand-new, manufactured-in-China, American Flag on the wall of one of the break rooms.

* * *

And than there are the facts that we collect and have no idea how to process or what to do with. Knowledge that can't be unlearned; pieces of information that spin around the inside of our thick skulls like a hamster on a wheel or bounce around our craniums until we die.

Example: The books of David Foster Wallace now rest in peace on our shelves, next to all the other suicide authors.

Another writer killed himself.

I know this for a fact, but can't attribute it to anything meaningful.

I made a list of all the authors, sorted it by date and added a column for method of death.

Author	Method of Death
Virginia Woolf	Drowning
Ernest Hemingway	Shotgun
John Kennedy Toole	Carbon Monoxide
Yukio Mishima	Ritual Suicide
Breece D'J Pancake	Gun
Richard Brautigan	Gun
Primo Levi	Stairs/Gravity
Jerzy Kosiński	Pills
John O'Brien	Gun
Michael Dorris	Pills/Suffocation
David Foster Wallace	Hanging

Where are the secret relationships in the above facts? What can be done to prevent another writer, or your average citizen, from taking his or her own life?

I have no idea if writers are more prone to suicide than members of the general population. Not impossible to figure out, just not sure if the conclusion would matter to anyone.

Individuals are not going to forgo a career based on the suicide rate of its workers. The rates are still low, and even of they were much higher, a majority of individuals would proclaim that they were the exception to the rule, that they could have it all without any of the nasty side effects. Or perhaps, it is the nasty side effects that convinced them to be writers in the first place. Either way, no one is going to stop writing because they have a statistically higher suicide rate than lawyers, CPAs, or flight attendants.

Many of us would argue that it is far better to write one obscure novel than to spend the rest of our life's muttering to bored judges that our sleazebag client was not being treated fairly by the court after their fourth arrest for driving under the influence, or that it's time to put your seat-backs into their full, and upright position-and please turn off all our electronic devices.

I postponed the conversation as long as I could. Finally, in bed, with the lights off, I just blurted it out: "Why suicide? I mean writers that committed suicide."

Suicide runs in Hemingway's family.

"You're asking me this now?"

Levi and Kosiński were survivors of the holocaust.

"Harder to run away when you're naked."

"I'll keep that in mind next time you want to fuck."

Kosinski was often accused of plagiarism. And I almost always want to fuck. I'm a guy.

"No secrets."

"I didn't mean that."

With the exception of Mishima, all had the decency to commit their final act in privacy.

Brautigan's body was not found for at least a month after his death.

"Yes you did. If I catch the neighbors fucking. I let you know. If they ask me to do something shady at work we talk about it. When I wonder why my lover only keeps the books of writers that offed themselves, I ask."

Mishima anticipated by 30 years the advent of reality television and made his death into a public spectacle. Ritual suicide.

"Lover, I like that word, but is that all I am to you?"

"If that was all you were to me, I wouldn't be asking."

You can't blame it on their lack of success, all but one (Toole) were published to at least some critical and financial success while they were alive.

"Camus" Susie turns towards me and whispers. "believed that suicide was the only serious philosophical problem."

"Camus died in a car accident"

A few Pulitzers, National Book Awards, best seller lists, critical acclaim and still they are all dead of the most unnatural of causes. You would think that evolution would have done a better job of weeding out suicide.

"That's why he's not on the shelf."

The fact that the sales of all their books increased dramatically after their deaths became public can't be entered in the equation.

The common thread among them all is that they were depressed. Duh. Their illnesses were mental and physical, not existential. Duh, again.

Susie reaches for my hand.

And yet, they all had tremendous talent. All had stories worth telling and knew how to tell them. We all have stories worth writing, but only a few of us have stories worth reading.

Susie sighs, but keeps quiet. I'm going to have wait for an answer.

If suicide would end the human species, what purpose does depression serve? Consider this psychology experiment. A group of depressed and non-depressed individuals are asked to press a button and make a green light flash as often as possible. Part of the time the subjects were rewarded monetarily when the green light flashed and other times they would lose money if the light didn't flash.

Afterwards, both groups were asked how much control they had over the green light. The non-depressed believed that they had complete control of the light when they were making money, but when they were losing they suggested that they had no control, that there losses were due to outside factors that were beyond their control.

And the depressed? The humans with a shortage of the neurotransmitter serotonin, the individuals making many pharmaceutical companies rich beyond belief, the very people that were complete social outcasts just a generation ago--how did they do when asked to evaluate their button pushing abilities? Whether they won or lost money at the game, they believed that they had no control. Of course, their perceptions were the only correct ones; the lights were programmed to flash randomly.

The game was a complete fiction and they alone knew it. Whether being more objective makes an individual depressed, or depression makes a person more observant has yet to be established. Perhaps there are other factors involved.

I squeeze Susie's hand. She squeezes back.

5. Models

"A blind man has a better chance of finding pussy in a men's prison than our computer models have of predicting which couples are going to clique," Scotty, the Chief Information Architect exclaims to the assembled staffers in the conference room. The steel table that we are seated around looks like it was recently stolen from the county morgue. We are only slightly more alive than the customers the table was designed for, but still not awake, or caffeinated enough, to keep up with a YNTBE manger on a mission.

I've been assigned to the team that is matching-up men with women, one of the pillars of our plan to change the world, one happy couple at a time.

"We need to make our models more predictive." Scotty runs his hand through his nonexistent hair and glances in my direction. "We need this to happen now."

I am supposed to help fill in the gaps, to help connect the dots. It is true that the more data you have the better the picture, but sometimes, you can only collect so much, this is where the modeling comes in.

Suppose you don't have a subject's income, but need it to figure out his social status. If you know his level of educational, and his age, you can come close. Add his neighborhood and employment status and you are within a couple of lattes of his total net worth. Information geeks are always building models to figure out the stuff that they don't know directly. Of course, relationships are 10,000 times more complicated than wealth and social status.

The essence of a workable mathematical model is 70% data, 15% intelligent guesses, and 5%

luck. As soon as you realize that the numbers don't add to 100 you are that much closer to understanding the problem.

I clear my throat. "We believe that the personality profiles are solid, but we are going to have to make some more assumptions about our couples. There are factors that personality matches can't overcome."

I realize that Scotty's job title becomes an acronym for the CIA. Is this a coincidence? Am I being too paranoid this early in the morning? Maybe I should just cut back on caffeine. That would mean that I would need more sleep and sleep and YNTBE are opposing forces. A blind man would have a better chance—

"For example?" Scotty is either really impatient or overly caffeinated, or both.

"Two suggestions to improve the models. The men should be taller." I can already tell that most of the women in the room are waiting for the other pump to drop. "And have a higher net worth." At this point I realize that I am speaking as softy as possible. "Or at least, the men should be more ambitions than their potential partners, or at least seem more ambitious, that someday they will have more income."

"You can't be serious," Sally screams. Her short blonde hair stays in place as she moves her head back and forth. You would think that I was suggesting that young women be resettled in Utah as third wives to a cult leader.

"Many women make more money and date taller men," Sally says. I don't know what her title is, but I do know that Sally is at every meeting that I'm at.

"We're not talking about dating, we're talking about finding a life partner," someone adds.

No one wants to think, for even a second, that his or her life fits a pattern, that he/she is much like everyone else.

"A real soul mate."

We are all teenagers pretending that our conformity is truly a rebellion.

"Do you believe that all women are just waiting to spread their legs for anyone with a fat wallet?"

"We've done the research." How many times have I wanted to shout that in a meeting? It felt good, but almost no one noticed.

"This organization is not about changing society."

"Who says it is not?"

"We are what we are."

"Are you quoting Popeye?"

"The question is, does Icarus have a soul?"

Please, please, I'm begging--not the *do computers have soul's* discussion. That could literally go all day and all night and the result would be no sleep and less agreement.

"Can we at least go over what the data says, and then decide?" I turn around and see Alex. He must have entered the room after me. Once again, the man formerly known as Edsel is my savior.

I have an attentive audience, but I also knew that I have to sum up as quickly as possible.

"Based on millions of successful relationships, we know that men like to be taller, women like taller men, with at least as much money, if not more than they have. Men like their mates to be younger, you can spend your lifetime arguing, but the exceptions don't prove the rule."

"Sooner or later we have to make assumptions, we can adjust the models later as the project develops," Alex states and I once again indebted to him. "Keep in mind that this model will need to be merged with the housing and career modules."

Forget jigsaw puzzles, I'm an assembly worker putting unknown parts on some type of vehicle.

"If we take your suggestions how much will that improve the compatibility index." Scotty moves over to the white board, red marker in hand.

"Somewhere in the range of 13 to 17 percent." Scotty writes my best guess on the board.

Perhaps if I become a full-time worker I'll get to see the blueprints.

"A decent start, but not good enough. Not nearly good enough. We meet again on Tuesday--so be prepared, and David."

"Yes." I respond.

"Put it in PowerPoint next time."

"I will."

Hello PowerPoint, my old friend.

6. Stones

"Where's my stone?" I yell to Susie from two rooms away. I hate it when people do the same to me.

"You mean that rock that was on the dresser? I threw it away."

Susie looks up from her tablet as I enter the living room.

"It was a stone and I need it."

"Rock. Stone. What's the difference?"

"One's for placing on a grave of a loved one and the other is for analyzing in geology lab."

"Was it special?"

"It was the one I was going to use." I check to see if my keys are still in my pocket.

"You can't use any rock, eh stone?"

"You can't leave a rock, on a headstone."

"What's the difference?"

"Neither will bring life to the dead." I grab my coat and head for the door. "I've got a train to catch."

"You want me to come with?"

I'm gone before she finishes.

Before the elevator reaches the lobby I realize that I've forgotten half of my day of depression. I was not only going to the cemetery, but I was going to read his memoirs on the trip.

I open the apartment door and see that Susie is standing there, wearing a raincoat, manuscript in hand. "You planning on following me?"

"This is our day to spend together." Susie places her index finger over her lips. "You can thank me later."

***

"We leave stones on graves to say to the universe that the body may be food for worms, but at least one person remembers. I left some mark, I touched someone. Gone, but not completely forgotten."

The train begins its journey with a sudden jerk.

"You just want to read." Susie holds up a copy of Joe's memoirs.

"I want to know that when I die someone will think enough to visit. I want to know if I will leave anything behind that matters. Anything."

"Quit your job," She says. "You can take a class, write a novel, whatever you want to do."

"And live on what?"

"I'll support you."

"You have no idea how that makes me feel."

"I think I do."

"Really you don't. Doesn't matter, because we both know that tomorrow morning, I'm getting up early and going to work." My dad died at work. He was ill and he died at his desk. Modern man, like ancient warriors died working. One stood in the field holding a spear, the other sat at a desk shuffling papers. Both truly believed that they were doing their best to make the world a better place.

"So what do you want?"

"I don't want to fail."

"You won't."

"When I was in prison, I had trouble failing asleep. For hours I would stare at the shadows that the bars made. I got through my time by always reminding myself that someday I would be out. I promised myself that not only would I do my best to make amends, but that I would stop and smell the roses. I wold enjoy every minute of my precious freedom. I would no longer take things for granted. Since my release, when I have trouble sleeping another thought comes to mind. The only people in this world that have time to smell the roses, are usually the ones in mental institutions or the ones living on the street. I'm no different than the masses. I need to work."

I realize that for the past five minutes I've been tracing the raindrops on the window of the train.

"They bought and sold you."

"You quoting George?"

"I read that letter a dozen times and listened to the song hundreds, thousands maybe."

"Nice."

"When I listened I thought of you. A few times I become so horny that I had to masturbate."

"A girl's gotta do what a girl's gotta do."

"My offer still stands." She says. "You can quit your job and smell the roses all day long. Write *your* story." She hands me Joe's memoirs.

The train enters a tunnel and for a second we are in darkness. I live with and love a woman that is willing to pay my bills. At least I'm taller than her.

7. The Unofficial History of PowerPoint

"If the Nazis had PCs, the first program they created would have been PowerPoint."

"It's three in the morning." Susie staggers in from the kitchen, glass of water in hand.

"Imagine the presentations. Slide number 1. Total number of arrests. Slide number two. Breakdown by Race/Gender."

"—Please come to bed."

"Slide number three. Number killed. Slide number four. Fuel used in furnaces. Slide—"

"—I'm hoping all you need is sleep."

"Bullet points on the number of bullets used. I'll bet they wouldn't even notice the irony."

"I think you should cut down on caffeine."

"You ever notice how the number of bullet points is always an odd number, usually three or five?"

"Never thought about it."

"That's not the main problem with the PowerPoint presentation. What happens when a concept can't be boiled down to a bullet point? How many more people have to die before the world learns that not everything can be summed up in a simple sentence fragment?"

"I'm sure death by PowerPoint is not very common or even real."

"Really? During the wars in Afghanistan and Iraq, intelligence officers used PowerPoint to brief their superiors, who in turn used PowerPoint to brief their superiors and so on up the chain of command. Bullet points are great for body counts, but they suck when it comes to the nuances of nation building and describing your subtle attempts to capture the hearts and minds of the populace. Information was lost, bad decisions made, soldiers sent home in flag-draped coffins."

"I'm sure Microsoft wasn't planning on destroying Western Civilization when they invented the program."

"Microsoft didn't invent the program, they purchased it from another company in 1987."

"Sure."

"It was originally called Presenter, and available only on the Macintosh."

"I love you, but you need help."

"You bet I do. I can turn my work into numbers that fit into a model or I can write pages on why they should work. A single sentence doesn't work. Imagine trying to explain the General Theory of Relativity or War and Peace in three short sentence fragments. It can't be done. It shouldn't even be attempted. If I say what I have to say in bullet points, I will get slammed within seconds of the text flashing on the screen. It's, to say the least, controversial. PowerPoint makes us dumber."

"So does lack of sleep."

"When we put information in a presentation, we are pretending that we understand, that we have everything under control. Someday you'll hear about some disaster that was preventable or completely manmade. Bet the farm that prior to the incident, someone, somewhere said it couldn't happen. They had the PowerPoint presentation and their odd number of bullet points to prove that it couldn't happen. When you collect on that wager I suggest that you go double-or-nothing on whether or not the executive/officer who gave the presentation got promoted soon after the incident. The smart money says yes."

"You're the carpenter with only a hammer."

277

"OK?" I have no idea what she is talking about. I notice that she is wearing a new Tequila Mockingbird T-shirt.

"What did you do in the past when bullet points didn't fit into the presentation?"

The picture on the shirt is a Hitler-type mustache and a pyramid of vegetables. Do they have a new album?

"It's been awhile."

"Hint. Instead of bullet points, use illustrations and just say what you need to say."

"That might work."

"Hallelujah," I once again hear from the street. Hallelujah Man returns, once again screaming for everyone in the neighborhood with insomnia.

"What type of insanity causes a man to march up and down the Upper West Side screaming about god?"

"Torture." Susie says with a yawn.

"He was tortured, so now he tortures us."

"He was a torturer."

"Still is."

"In Haiti," Susie continues. "He was a member of the paramilitary group developed by Papa Doc Duvalier to enforce order. Entire families disappeared. Rape, murder, whatever it took to enforce order. They killed people, hung their bodies from trees and when the relatives came for the body, they also were killed. Now he's a messenger of god."

"I think god needs better messengers."

"Hallelujah," she says, but when I look up she is gone.

8.   Super Models

The YNTBE logo fades and pictures of smiling couples flash on the wall. Each pair has been perfectly matched in attractiveness by Icarus. My first goal today is to remind the team that attractiveness is real—and universal.

"I think that we can all agree that couples need to be initially attracted to each other."

"Please tell us something we don't know," Scotty barks. I'm not sure if he is generally upset or if he is merely testing me. My second goal today is to keep my job, and perhaps get hired on a more permanent basis.

New slide. Unhappy couples. One member of each couple is more attractive than the other. You can argue with god all day long, but every culture on the planet finds some people more attractive than others. Within each culture there is wide agreement on who is hot and who is not.

"What about improving the personality profiles?" Ann asks. Of course, the one person in the room that would have been rated a ten when Peter Paul Rubens was painting has a problem with attractiveness. If she gave up a reuben sandwich or two she might be rated higher. She would be rated higher.

"Good point," I say. "The fact is that our target demo is not giving the profiles, or everything else Icarus has to offer a chance to work."

"Again," Scotty says. "How is this going to improve the index?"

"We have re-tested all matches made by Icarus in the past six months and preformed follow up tests on all subjects that initially rejected their proposed mates. We came to some conclusions." I hit the button. The slide shows the part of the equation that Icarus uses to match our clients. The equation moves. It flashes. It pulses. It looks like something that would give Albert Einstein an erection.

"So far, you identified a problem, but haven't offered a solution," Scotty says. I need to give him something to write on his board, because once he starts writing he'll ignore the rest of the presentation and we can discuss the issues and perhaps, make a decision or two.

"Three items." Scotty draws a number one on the board. "Number one. We place more emphasis on the attractiveness when matching couples." It occurs to me that Scotty is using an old technology to copy what I have created via new technology. What to do with your hands: some people smoke, some people write on white boards.

"Two. We ask all clients to rate themselves."

"But won't clients overrate their looks?" Ann asks while Scotty writes. The fact that she is still participating in the discussion indicates that I haven't completely pissed her off. I have no idea how or who recommends me for promotion in this company or who can blackball me.

"Of course they will, that's why we program Icarus to also rate clients."

I also assume, based on limited observation, that if I'm too non-controversial, I will also not be asked to be a part of the team.

"How?" Scotty asks.

"We have hi-rez pictures as part of each profile. Icarus can provide the ratings using modified facial recognition software. Of course, we will program the system to take into account photos that have been shopped and are more than three years old."

"What else?" Scotty needs to write.

"We also need to factor in the personality profile, gender, and age of the client. Especially for males in the 25 to 30 year age range."

"Why?" Scotty asks. I may have actually piqued his curiosity.

"Their mirrors don't work," Alex takes a gulp from the largest cup of coffee I have ever seen.

"What does this have to do with fucking mirrors?" Scotty asks.

"I think what Alex is pointing out is that at first, very few people accept their level of attractiveness. We know they will exaggerate. The level of exaggeration is another data point."

"Every guy believes they deserve the fucking homecoming queen and every chick wants Charles fucking Atlas." Alex yawns. I swear he was wearing the same clothes yesterday.

"If our goal is for long-term relationships, we have to sell them on the concept of ICARUS. The key is to convince them that they are only being matched with equally attractive members of the opposite sex."

"Are you suggesting that we lie?"

"I'm saying that we need to control expectations, to guide people into making the correct decisions."

"Then go with it—for now at least."

I expected a thousand arguments and get this.

"I'm going to need to run all this past The Doctor," Sally says and everyone nods.

"Yes, the Doctor," I say, but I am alone, because I am one of the few people in the room who has not had a house call with the rich and mysterious —our CEO and president, Dr. Joseph Conrad.

I look at Sally and wonder if "run this past the doctor" is a euphemism.

9.   The Doctor is in…Sane

Take the 8:52 from Penn Station; sit in one of the first three cars…

I was not given directions to the Doctor's house, but rather step by step instructions that take into account everything but recent volcanic activity in

Iceland. What else can I expect for an interview after I had already started working?

Remember your umbrella. Weather patterns predict a 28% chance of rain by early afternoon.

Moving up the corporate ladder is old school.   In the new world, some mid-level geek hires you, your work is evaluated, people take notes when you speak at meetings and after a random amount of time you meet the boss. If he or she approves you are awarded with a smart phone and stock options —and the opportunity to go from working 50+ weeks to being available to help the cause 24/7/365.

After you exit the train, look both ways before crossing the street.

The Doctor is a beneficiary of the technology/Internet economy. He has developed and sold a series of companies that have netted him more wealth than the net worth of Costa Rica. His name appears on hospital wings; several major universities have awarded him honorary doctorates. For years his face graced the covers of business magazines.

Financial talk shows booked him as an expert on all things tech. Sometime during the past two years the covers and appearances slowed down, but The Doctor was still seen as a mover, an entrepreneur that is too busy to spend time promoting his various enterprises on TV.

Turn right, take 25 steps and the car will be waiting.

I wonder if Icarus took into account that I am above average height and will need to take fewer steps than the average person. Silly question, of course it did.

A black sedan awaits me. Nothing with a rumble seat. No solar powered motorcycle with sidecar.

I'm relieved that my driver doesn't speak much English--I want to prepare for the interview. It feels like studying for a dental appointment: you know what's coming, but the gagging, and the pain, is the same.

Techies are overly fond of their intelligence and they love putting job seekers to the test. Take

Lord of the Flies and subtract *Revenge of the Nerds* and you get the general idea. These are the kids that were picked-on in the hallways of every Normal Rockwell High School and now are in the position of extracting a little revenge. Instead of stuffing jocks into lockers they ask job applicants to perform cerebral gymnastics.

Some firms in Silicon Valley laugh at job applicants with less than perfect SAT scores. If that wasn't enough, they often give you the full MacGyver and ask questions such as: "You are locked in an eight foot by eight foot room with just a book of matches, a nail clipper, and a blender. You will run out of oxygen in approximately 13 minutes. What do you do?" The Microsoft human resources department has a reputation of asking such random and thought-provoking questions as: "Why are manhole covers round?"

The drive takes about 25 minutes, but I don't pay attention to the route or the scenery. I couldn't make it back to station myself, and don't think that I will have to. This is a job interview, not a kidnapping.

The house, one of five or six that The Doctor owns, is down the street from where Jay Gatsby used to live. The place is huge. The Doctor owns land, and trees, and more land and some horses and more land. In America, this is what happens when your stock hits it big, you get a zip code to call your own.

After we pull up to the door, the driver informs me that I should wait inside, he doesn't tell me how many steps it should take. In the gigantic foyer I notice that there are rooms off to both the right and the left. After checking both, I select the right, because it is the one with the tray of drinks. Looks like I'll pass the first test.

The room that I choose is furnished with stuff from a country that I assume is somewhere in Southeast Asia. The room that I did not choose has an African theme. That is my total knowledge of third-world furnishings. If I were smarter, or had lived in some of these places, I could use it in conversation. *I couldn't help but notice that end table from Thailand and those masks from Zimbabwe are fabulous, they really go with the hand-carved Ugandan cabinets.* Except for work, I have nothing to discuss with the Doctor.

I smell incense, but can't locate the source. Perhaps rich people have a central-incense-system installed in their homes when they return from their travels.

"Why are you here?"

There is a voice, but I have no idea where it is coming from. Heaven is a palace in the suburbs of New York. This can't be hell, because there is no PowerPoint welcoming me to the first circle.

"Why are you here?" and I am standing face to face with the Doctor.

"For a meeting slash interview."

"I mean, on the planet?" He shakes my hand. I remember to use a firm grasp, but not too firm—someone has to be the alpha male.

We are both dressed in business casual, the difference is that his clothes look like they have never

289

been worn before today, part of a disposable wardrobe—wear once and donate.

"I was not aware that there were alternatives."

He nods, neither approving or disapproving of my answer. I realize that I am at least two inches taller, just enough that I get a view of the bald spot. He motions for me to sit.

"You've never thought about your purpose?"

It occurs to me as I place my ass on his fine Cambodian couch that it is usually the rich that have time to think about their purpose on the planet, that the rest of us have to make a living. "I've never been good with the big questions."

"You're more of a down-to-earth, data guy."

"That's what I've been told."

"And yet," he pauses, and then takes a sip of his iced tea. "All your research has been about people, how they respond to technology, and most recently how they pair bond." I take a sip of my tea and wonder what to say next. The Doctor has a slight, but very satisfied smile on his face, the look of a man that is purposefully saying less than he knows and wants me to understand that he knows more than he is saying.

"Yes, but I'm not sure that any of my work has addressed any of the larger, more philosophical questions."

"What does your research say about me?"

I know that I can't lie about not doing any research. What moron goes on any interview without digging up everything about their interrogator? Of course, I know that one of his minions has done the same on me. A job interview is a delicate game of pretending not to know too much or too little.

"Is it true that you dream in code?" is the safest question that comes to mind.

He laughs. "That's one of my favorite myths, —the short answer is no, code only makes sense to me if it's directly in front of me on a screen, but sometimes in business it helps when your competition, and even some of your employees, think that you can perform miracles. Keeps them on their toes." The Doctor smiles, and so do I, but we both know that this is not the first time he's told this anecdote.

Just as I am about to say something, The Doctor suggests that we stroll through the garden.

10. (E=MC^2) Times Two

"See the guest cottage hidden behind the oaks?"

I see it, the question is, when am I going to be invited for the weekend? Probably the day after never. "It's in its own private world."

"Exactly."

"I really like the fountains."

"All hand-carved marble smuggled out of Italy via Naples."

He stresses the phrases *hand-carved* and *smuggled* as if he did the work himself.

"Nice."

"What is it like," he asks, "to always be counting. To think that life can all be reduced to simple mathematical formulas?"

"Not sure I understand."

"Everything that can be counted does not necessarily count--"

"Everything that counts cannot necessarily be counted." I finish the quote.

"Albert Einstein. The greatest business mind of the 20th Century." The Doctor says as he glances at his diamond Rolex that probably costs enough to feed a sold-out crowd at Yankee Stadium.

"I would argue that our understanding of human behavior is, and always will be, limited."

"This is true--but what, or who, is doing the limiting?" We stop to admire the Japanese flower garden and pond. Gold, orange, and even blue Koi swim up, looking for a snack, or possibly just to receive wisdom from The Doctor. Perhaps they understand the meaning of life.

"Have you considered," he pauses for effect, "that your entire life has been leading up to this moment?"

"I guess that I would have to assume that it's a possibility."

"I would like to suggest that it's more than a possibility. Think about it. Consider your education. Your research in college. The grant proposal that you submitted."

I never submitted any proposals, and if I did, how would he know? Why would he bring this up?

"Think back," The Doctor continues, "to all the times that you superiors didn't take your work seriously, when you were right—and you knew it. Not to mention your obvious ability to wait things out, to never betray your friends. You are loyal."

I'm a regular Boy Scout.

"Your soul is troubled," he continues, "and believe it or not, we believe that this is an asset. Most of all, and of course you will at first deny this, your skepticism is at the heart of what we need, it fuels our growth, makes us stronger. After healing, the bone is stronger than before it was broken."

"OK," I said, but I don't remember any of my doctors or coaches recommending I go out of my way to bust any part of my skeleton in the name of strength conditioning.

"Yet, you still have many doubts."

"It would seem to be logical that I be somewhat skeptical."

"Of course, but at the same time, you appear to be very flexible."

"I try to be."

"Good. We are a very dynamic organization. Today you are working on one project, but tomorrow you may be asked to work on something else, not 100% related to your current endeavors."

"I can do that." Eye contact to validate my sincerity.

"Good. One more thing," he adds. "I ask you to be open to the possibility that you are here for a reason." He doesn't wait for me to respond, but rather motions for us to head back towards Xanadu.

A few moments later and I'm on the train headed back to New York City and what I used to believe to be reality. The text on my phone reminds me to enter my receipts into ICARUS for any and all business expenses within the next 48 hours.

The earlier Einstein quote reminded me of another: "If we knew what we were doing, it wouldn't be called research, would it?"

11. Why manhole covers are round: A brief list of possible answers.

A. Because the holes are round.

B. A rectangle can be turned around and accidentally dropped into the hole.

C. Round = no sharp edges to pop tires if it becomes dislodged.

D. The earth is round, you know.

E. Round ones are easier to make.

F. Why do you ask?

G. Do you get out much? Alternative = have you ever been laid?

H. What the fuck does the shape of manhole covers have to do with writing code for an evil monopoly?

Note: There are no correct answers, the point of the exercise is to assess your problem solving abilities. One would assume that answers F,

G, and H would probably not be appreciated by a majority of the human resource managers at Microsoft, or any large technology company for that matter. But who knows? Sometimes fortune, job offers, and stock options favor the bold and the reckless.

12.   Notes From the Love Lab

Can love be measured?

Analyzed?

Understood?

Hook humans up to computers and you can easily record how fast the heart beats, which sections of the brain respond, how much the palms sweat. Icarus collects terabytes of data, but are we really measuring anything more than the side effects of love? Are we 16th century explorers looking for the New World—not knowing where we are going and having no idea where we are when we plant our flag in the sand?

The Lab, in the basement of YNTBE HQ, is shielded from the outside world by brick walls and a security system originally developed to protect military installations. Susan, my tour guide, flashes her card in front of the sensor and enters a security code longer than an international telephone number. The door opens; a swish of air hits my face and makes me think, if only for a second or two, that I'm entering a spaceship headed to a distant quadrant of the galaxy.

"So this is the love lab."

Susan gives me the look of a school librarian about to chastise teenage boys for looking up dirty words in the dictionary. "It's called The Underground Biometrics Laboratory for Relationship and Life Improvement."

Here's one potential acronym that is never going to roll off anyone's tongue.

Without missing a beat, Susan motions me into a room that overlooks the lab. "One-way glass, no one can see us."

The mystery of one-way glass solved.

Below us are a dozen extra-large cubicles. Some with desks, others with reclining chairs.

Human guinea-pigs are surrounded by video monitors; sensors run from fingers, foreheads and arms directly into the heart of Icarus. Staffers move back and forth, tapping on their tablets.

Susan touches a screen and a row of monitors come to life. "See the client below us? He's on a video chat with his girlfriend, who is across the room, although she could be anywhere in the world." The monitors capture both sides of the conversation and enough biometric data to fill a garbage dump.

"Intense." I say.

"Watch the monitor on the left, just before he speaks."

Electronic meters spike, but as far as I know they are measuring volcanic activity on the moons of Jupiter.

"Looks like their relationship is doomed." Susan says with the emotion of a Governor signing a highway bill.

"Are you saying he's lying?"

"More like contempt."

"Sounds a tad intrusive."

"The Doctor believes that with a little help from modern technology, divorce will become as rare as polio or smallpox." Her voice resonates like a television preacher who has repeated a biblical verse one too many times.

"I never looked at it that way." I say. "So, what's going to happen to them?"

"We sit them down, with a professional counselor of course, and just give them the facts so they can make an informed decision."

"Do they usually agree?"

"Not at first, but we are as delicate as possible"

"You want them to remain as clients."

"Exactly." Susan takes a sip from her YNTBE water bottle.

"Take a look at the man in the far corner." Susan points and then taps a screen. The displays change.

"He seems like he's really involved in his work."

"He's testing our new career advancement module. We are looking for ways to increase performance, testing what motivates people, how they learn from their mistakes."

"Cool."

"We believe with the proper testing and motivation, workers can achieve optimal performance."

Optimal performance: where the assembly line crashes head-first into a cube farm and no one gets out alive.

"I'm impressed with all the data you're collecting."

"The information that we collect and process is not more important than what your team is doing."

"Good to know."

"There is no I in team."

But there are two in insanity.

"I'm curious on how the collection process affects the measurements."

Susan takes another sip. This spaceship seems to be causing dehydration. "Perhaps a demonstration will answer your questions."

I fear that it might.

Susan taps the screen and motions for me to exit the observation chamber. We pass several offices and stop at the last one. "This is my office, if you have any questions after the calibration."

The office contains a desk, a chair, a laptop, and a wastebasket. I don't know which I find more archaic, the empty wastebasket in a nearly paperless office or the framed portrait of the 40th President.

"Big fan of Reagan?" I ask.

"TBV."

"TB what?"

"Trust but verify. It's the new motto of the lab."

"Not sure if I get the connection." Wonder what the old motto was.

"President Reagan wanted us to trust the Soviet Union; at the same time he built into the peace treaties mechanisms for us to check up on them. It's not any different for us in the lab. People will self-report that they like working with others, but when we test them the results indicate not so much. People lie to themselves about work, love, and just about everything else. Icarus is objective. Always."

"I see."

"Are you ready for the test?"

Test. Calibration. Please pick a euphemism and stick with it.

We head down the stairs to the floor of the lab.

"Looks different from down here." I want to fit in, but I'm a stranger in a strange land.

"Tracy will guide you through the entire process."

Susan turns and sprints up the stairs to her office/shrine. Tracy approaches in the uniform of the lab: khakis and a blue YNTBE polo.

"Hello David."

"Hello Tracy."

"Please follow me." Tracy is a multitasker; she is simultaneously walking, checking her tablet, and telling me about the test. "People have three questions about the process, so I'll just answer them for you. Everyone does it, it's fun, and your information is completely confidential."

Sounds like a marketing slogan for a cheap hooker.

We arrive at one of the super-sized cubicles and Tracy motions for me to sit. The chair looks like a dental chair as designed by La-Z-Boy. Instead of an examination light designed to inflict temporary blindness, Tracey slides an array of monitors in front of my eyes and hands me a pair of headphones. "Don't put these on until instructed to do so."

"OK."

Tracy begins to wire me to the machine. She places a clip on my index finger and a cuff around my upper arm.

"Doesn't all this equipment interfere with the results?"

"Good question." She selects a sensor to attach to my forehead. "That's why we ignore the first 10 minutes of the process."

"You thought of everything."

"There's been some trial and error."

"That's usually how it works."

"In a minute, I'm going to start the program. I just want you to relax, try not to move too much and let your mind go where it needs to go. You can put the headphones on now."

I'm surrounded by video screens. The YNTBE logo appears on the all three. Tracy's instructions splash across the screen for the hearing impaired.

Pictures of puppies. Videos of kittens. Smiling kids at play. At the beach. In the pool. Sledding in winter. Jumping into piles of autumnal leaves. If the classical music that's playing was ice cream, it would be vanilla. I'm glad I can close my eyes and that Beethoven's Ninth isn't playing in my ears.

Are the first 10 minutes up? I'm not supposed to look at my watch, there are no clocks mounted anywhere.

Happy couples on beaches. Smiling. Laughing. I'm going to call this section of video: one-way ticket to Cliché Island. Throw in a sunset and I can die a happy man.

What would happen if Susie and I were hooked up to Icarus?

$123 + 458 =$? 3^3. $12 \times 11=$? Math problems. Testing how I react when encourage to think. But are they taking into account that I'm thinking about thinking? Am I actually one step ahead? More generic music, but now it's rock guitar. The sounds become more intense.

Soldiers marching. Nazis Goose stepping. Images of war. I hope my blood pressure is up to the appropriate levels. I think of Joe and realize that I haven't even attempted to read his memoirs/notes in a long time. Yah, they're hard to read, but shouldn't someone make the effort? It would be nice if they were edited and polished, but life is never like that. Most of us die before our life is complete.

A blank screen. Silence. Perhaps they are cleansing my mental palette.

More love scenes. Close to an R raring here. I thought this type of material was not appropriate in the workplace? Can I sue for harassment? Icarus would probably testify against me. Claim that I enjoyed it.

Rush hour traffic. People pushing to get on subways. Crowds. Waiting in line. Music that sounds like a group of drunken hobos banging trash cans in an alley. Horns honk. More traffic.

Another blank screen, more sorbet for the soul.

Comedy time. Chaplin as the little tramp. You just know that either Laurel or Hardy is going to let go and that piano is rolling down the hill. The house falls and Buster is still standing. I once dragged Susie to a Buster Keaton festival at Film Forum. She laughed more than I did.

Shit. Three screens, three different images. Math. Love. War. What are they measuring now? I do want to close my eyes, I want to be an ostrich and stick my head in the sand. Perhaps that is what they are testing. Can I multitask? Can I handle pressure?

How do I handle ambiguous situations? Can they tell if I'm concentrating on the math or watching lovers kiss? How much longer...

Fade to black. It's over. I can breathe normally. I'm sure that some of these images will invite themselves into my dreams.

As Tracy unhooks my soul from the machine I wonder what suggestions would the mighty Icarus confidently serve Susie and me. Would the computer/program even select us as partners to begin with? Icarus leans towards the conventional: two humans, places to live, work and shop, crap to buy—white picket fence, optional. Not wishing to form a more perfect union or believing that producing offspring may not be for everyone are not within the parameters of the system. Icarus knows that the traditional relationship is the best, but doesn't know why. It just knows what has been programmed into it. Other possibilities do not exist. Some, for whatever reason, just don't want to get married – or divorced.

"Did I pass?" I ask Tracy.

"There is no pass or fail, there only is."

"Of course."

How would Icarus factor into the equation that as soon as things become as close to wonderful as one could hope for, Susie going to hit the road again? You get into a groove and life makes other plans, inputs additional data into your electronic day-planner.

"I told you it wouldn't hurt," Tracy says as I struggle to get up from the chair that is threatening to hold me hostage for the rest of the day.

My relations with Susie would soon consist of e-mails and texts from G*d knows where. The band was booking gigs in small and medium size concert halls to support their latest album, "Hitler was a Vegetarian." Suffice it to say that they continued on their path of being rockers and political junkies, more than willing to point out hypocrisy, either real or imagined. Of course this begged the question of are we also hypocrites for expecting our politicians to be free of hypocrisy. As hard as they tried to be noncommercial, they continued to sell enough albums, concert tickets and t-shirts to keep the show on the road and make a taste of profit.

I once again hear that swish of air as the doors open for me to exit the lab. I'm back on Earth. How long have I been gone and more importantly, what have I learned? I realize that there is no limit to how much data you can collect and the answers only beg for more questions.

I know that Icarus can verify, but can't trust. Can I?

13. Will it play in Peoria?

That mathematically perfect little town in central Illinois. The center of average; the epicenter of ordinary. If you're an advertising guru in New York, and you need to know if the peasants in the heartland understand your brilliant campaign you test it in a place like this. Your colleagues all love your idea, think it's brilliant, but they spend their time at the club chugging martinis, not spreading manure or square dancing or whatever they do in the middle of America.

For whatever reason our marketing function didn't start testing Icarus in Peoria. Maybe they believed that for too long Peorians have been the canary in the cultural coal mine. For whatever reason the citizens of Peoria were spared (for now) and testing began in such All-American towns as Kansas City, Buffalo, Tacoma, Austin. The same small towns that Susie and the band are currently touring in.

The plan, as far as I understand, is to test smaller pieces of Icarus in various locations throughout the U.S. All the tests will be conducted under generic brand names, the end users—and our competitors—would have no idea that YNTBE was building the last Web site you ever needed, wanted, or used.

Test results are reported in the form of a case study: Picture a semi-dark room, with multiple presentations flashed across the front walls. Bullet points far and wide. White boards with formulas that may or may not make sense to the person who wrote them. Figure there are a dozen staffers and two dozen coffee cups and/or caffeinated drinks at various

311

levels of consumption. Alex reads from an electronic file and the audience participates, serving a function that is equal parts head cheerleader, court jester, and weary business executive.

Alex: "Case study 212. Jennie."

"Not her real name."

Alex: "Jennie is a 28 year old Assistant District Attorney in Austin, Texas. She claims not to be overly interested in what her potential partner does for a living."

"In other words she wants a fucking doctor or another lawyer."

"God forbid someone that works with their hands."

"And when I say lawyer, I don't mean some slob that works in the public defender's office."

Alex: "Icarus matched her with Sam."

"Not his real name."

Alex: "Sam is a 33 year old owner of a contracting business. The housing boom has been good to Sam, putting money in the bank and several roofs over his lonely head. Sam's self profile reads: I enjoy moonlight walks on the beach, candlelight dinners, and foreign films.

"Bullshit."

"He thinks this is going to get him laid."

"He'll do this stuff to impress her and then go home to drink beer and watch sports on TV.—

"One hand on the remote, the other one scratching his balls."

Alex: "Icarus collected more than 3,500 points of data on each of them. This couple was given a 95 on the Icarus scale of compatibility. One of our highest scores. Icarus predicted that after a 17 month courtship they would marry and honeymoon in Hawaii. Three years later they would move to the suburbs, wait six months and then start their family. In addition, Icarus has suggestions for both their careers, including Sam's business. Data indicates several niches in the coming years that will prove to be more profitable than his current projects. So far, it hasn't worked out as planned. In follow up interviews they claim not to like each other."

"They were a nearly perfect match, what happened?"

"They met."

"No chemistry?"

Alex: "I think, and Icarus supports this, that if they just got past the initial rejection of each other, they would be a great match."

"We could kidnap them and force them to spend time together,"

"You got to be kidding."

"If you believe in Icarus, then you must believe that if we gave a well matched couple some time together, they would eventually bond."

"Where's the romance in kidnapping?"

"Where's the romance in singles bars and clubs?

"Is their more coffee? I need caffeine."

"Is love dead?"

"Did it ever really exist?"

Yes. Love exists. I have evidence. Evidence unseen, but evidence nonetheless. Love may be invisible, but so is the wind.

Susie.

Something in the way she moves.

When Susie is gone it becomes something in the way she texts. Or Skype's. Or whatever form of electronic communication we are using. Even at the speed of light, the distances are still greater than the heart can comprehend. This is why people dive into their work. Or drink too much. Anything that distracts.

I work as much as I can and I get electronic updates from the road.

Something in the way she knows.

Once again I'm trapped in a song; a prisoner of love and lyrics. My lone guard is a playlist with a single MP3.

Something.

The quiet Beatle returns. The one who can sum it up with a few simple chords and lyrics that say more in the spaces than most song writers accomplish in a lifetime of verbiage. The song describes not a prefect relationship, but rather how a perfect relationship would feel like. Not knowing if love will grow, but believing that it can and it will.

You know I believe and how.

Here's a man that doesn't want to leave his lover; wants to spend more time with her. Surely it is better to live in a world with a finite amount of time and an infinite amount of love than the opposite?

14. Case Study 315

"You mixed an M with a J."

"Correction. Icarus mixed an M with a J."

"Icarus should know better than to mix oil and water. How can a control freak mate with a slob?"

"Icarus has his reasons."

"Perhaps Icarus is a woman."

"That would explain a lot."

"What do you mean?"

"I don't mean anything…I'm just tired."

"Just because you're tired, doesn't mean that you didn't really mean it."

"OK. I meant it, but I'm still really tired."

"The Doctor believes—" The room becomes silent. We all look towards Sally. "—that we need to focus on what is working and ignore what is not." I am positive that she was not here when the meeting started.

"Perhaps we need to consider why they received a high rating to begin with."

"Good idea. At the same time we can see what we missed in the profiles and biometric data."

"Exactly."

"We can make this work."

"AMO."

"Agreed."

15. The Widget King

This is my favorite story about The Doctor.
A story so illuminating that it doesn't have to be true.
It merely has to be believed.

Years before YNTBE, The Doctor created a
software start-up. Let's call it Widget Corp. This
was the third, or fourth high tech company that he
had founded, and he wanted to have control over how
the company was perceived in the media, especially
among the digerati. He knew that with any high-tech
company, especially a successful one, there would be
critics and detractors; he merely wanted to do his best
to orchestrate the Internet noise.

His plan was simple: buy up every domain
name related to Widget Corp, especially the ones that
would be obvious choice of critics such as
Widgetcorpsucks and Widgetsux. Of course the

318

Doctor, or his lackeys purchased every name in all the domains (.com, .net. and org.) and from every country on the map. In total, the Doctor owned tens of thousands of domain names.

When Widget Corp started showing its first signs of success and some frustrated tech writer or college student attempted to buy up one of the suck domains they simply found that all their brilliant choices were mysteriously unavailable.

The disgruntled still had plenty of opportunities to rant, but some of the magic was missing, there would be no "reports" from widgetsucks.com. Criticism always sounded more intense, and detractors would spend more energy on a site whose name alone infuriated every member of the company that it attacked.

But The Doctor was not finished. Instead of merely parking all 10,000 of his useless domain names, he used a couple of them to set up Web sites that seemed to attack his beloved Widget Corp. To any outsider it would look like corporate democracy at its best: a give and take of corporate PR and freewheeling journalism, to create what Adam Smith considered to be the perfect marketplace of ideas.

Where the doctor is concerned, thinking that opinions and ideas were being freely exchanged would be like believing that the marionette was controlling the man holding the strings. Someone, out of sight, was doing his best to frame the discussion. What seemed like criticism of Widget Corp's software tools and applications were also indirectly promoting them.

Stories that would point out bugs in the software would also highlight features that the competitors lacked. Headlines that screamed that Widget Corp was about to miss another deadline reminded readers that the new offering was worth waiting for. Other posts suggested that some products would not be compatible with the competition's offerings. The Doctor knew that information that is leaked is often viewed as being more reliable than information that is officially released.

Other tech writers and bloggers, the real ones that were not affiliated with the fake ones, had to at least acknowledge the controlled rantings of the fake ones.

External communication was not enough for The Doctor; he used his power to go inside his own company. One of the sites reported on programming bugs found in some of the Widget Corps applications. It's impossible to prove, but some have speculated that the Doctor was simply talking to his programmers, tweaking them just enough to get them to perform better and faster. The ones that he couldn't sell the dream to, he shamed into doing their best. He got what he needed simply by anonymously challenging them, by stating publicly that it couldn't be done, that they were sure to fail.

The Doctor had developed a cottage industry of Web sites that were popular and served his purpose. They attracted enough traffic to sell ads; the sites looked even more home-grown than before. Some of the sites even ran ads for Widget corp., while a few refused to do so. It was rumored that the entire enterprise paid for itself, or perhaps even made a buck or two.

Eventually The Doctor sold Widget Corp. to a larger software vendor that didn't give a fuck about what their competitors or customers thought about anything. Soon after the sale, the attack Web sites disappeared.

16. Case Study 347

Grainy video.

Poor lighting.

Anonymous upload to YouTube.

Terrorists planning an attack or Susie promoting one?

I'm going with Susie, terrorists don't do metaphor. Or understand irony. They confuse television with reality. During the early days of the War in Afghanistan, the Taliban broadcasted propaganda to U.S. soldiers that were kicking their butts. One of their claims was that while the American soldiers were fighting in foreign countries their wives were back home fucking Homer Simpson.

Perhaps we will win the war on terror not because we are getting smarter, but because our enemies are getting dumber. Much dumber.

In the video faces are obscured by caps and scarfs. Clothing is generic track pants and sweat shirts many sizes too large.

Looks like a bus station, but the video is shaky, and considering the project, I have no idea if the videographer is nervous or just attempting to be avant-garde. The camera finds a poster. Five smiling lads. All hunky. One can imagine that the art director spent hours picking out the lineup. Too thin. Too blonde. Too hairy. Too gay. Not gay enough. Please tilt your head. Lift your arm. Act like you give a damn. Don't smile too much.

The original advertisement that Susie and her team are about to deface is for cologne that promises to make you the coolest dude on the planet.

And the spray painting begins. I don't know who you are, but I know that you have practiced. In less than 30 seconds the poster has a new slogan and URL. The crew disperses, but not after capturing the image of the six smiling lads and the new slogan: *Which one of us gave you herpes?* Before I have time to check the URL, I hear Alex clearing is throat.

"Case Study 347." Alex reads. "We have a unique situation here."

At this point his hair would have to be on fire for the assembled to think that anything was different about this case, to make anyone start tapping on their pads, checking their notes, searching their mental and virtual databases.

Alex takes a sip of his Mcbucks super latte and continues, "Thanks to Icarus, Ann and Dave met 12 months ago. As predicted they dated, bonded, became engaged and are planning an October wedding.

Still not sure what we are meeting about here. This is how the system is supposed to function. I want to use my computer to check my e-mail, but I know that's frowned upon.

Alex: "They don't like their apartment."

Now he has our attention.

"But the square footage was perfect."

"As for location, the commuting distance was completely optimal."

"They don't need a larger kitchen, neither one of them cooks much."

"Nothing in the profiles could have predicted this."

"When can we schedule an interview with them?"

Alex: "They left the program. They say they're happy and don't need any more *life advice.*"

"Can they do that?"

"But we need more information."

"More data would help us figure this out."

"Icarus has so much more to offer them."

I have no idea how this will play out, but I know that by the time I get back to my desk there will be more meetings scheduled in my Google calendar.

17. Is This Island Completely Surrounded by Water?

To learn about our customers and potential customers. To increase teamwork. To reduce the cost of labor. Because corporations are giant fraternities and you have to earn your approval.

Instead of the back end of a paddle, everyone gets headphones surgically attached to their brains and potential customers with itchy dialing fingers and plenty of time on their hands to ask questions. Questions are cheap.

"Can you connect me with my husband?" The lady from Arkansas asks.

"You don't have his number?"

"He died last year."

"The current version of our system does not allow this."

Now I know why so much customer service has been off-shored. Workers in India and Romania obviously have a higher tolerance for inanity.

I type: insane customer wants to be with dead husband, should I suggest suicide? I press enter and a new window opens: Remember we are collecting data that will help us provide a better service and hone our marketing strategies.

I yawn and the woman hangs up, but I don't think these events are related.

Is this a generic message or is the system actually responding to my input? I don't have to wait long, the phone rings.

The next caller is a wrong number looking for pet supplies. I type: woman is looking for a companion animal for her beloved schnauzer.

The new window states: thank you for testing the system. Probing minds like yours are good for the company. Please keep in mind that customer service is an important component of YNTBE.

How many are involved? I'm testing the system, the system is testing me, but who are the people on the line testing? Are they in on it? I promise, to no one in particular, to keep my mind on task and be the best customer service representative that I can be.

My father had no tolerance for silly questions. So of course my brother and I asked as many stupid questions as we could think of. We tortured him with serious inquires about the inhabitants of Grant's Tomb and what crystal balls were made of—jokes that, to us at least, never seemed to get old. Is it hotter in the summer or the city? Did you take the bus or your lunch to work? What color was George Washington's...

We thought that our queries made sense—father loved books and kept a library as eclectic as it was disorganized. A man with so many books on history, science, philosophy, religion, should have all the answers.

"Dad, I need to know what is..."

But there were no quick answers in my father's office; there were only reference books, guarded by a man who would have been more in place as headmaster of a boarding school than 2nd in command of a modern family.

"Do you thirst for knowledge..." At this point he would place his mechanical pencil on the desk and slowly turn towards me. "or do you just want a quick answer that will be forgotten as soon as your pen leaves the paper."

I want to view my porn stash in the privacy of my own room. You could say that I thirst for forbidden knowledge.

"Great minds have always….." But I was zoned out, waiting for him to finish so I could look up what I needed to know to finish my busywork.

It took years to kick in, as these things often do, but my father did pass on his love of books, mostly fiction, and dare I say, thirst for knowledge or at least a strong curiosity.

My rotation in customer inquiry service and response (CISR) is scheduled to be over in about 20 minutes. We didn't call it customer service; that would be too normal. The system just asked if I would mind working a few extra hours. I agreed and was rewarded with a screen with helpful hints to keep me alert: stretching exercises, remaining hydrated, light & healthy snacks…

I take a swig of coffee and hit the button on my keyboard that lets Icarus know that I am available to receive telephonic communication. Within seconds I have a call from a potential customer that is worried that we may require too much information about "personal matters." As soon as I type this in, a screen pops up with suggested talking points, but I play it by ear; I've been down this road before.

"We collect all the data that we can to insure that the suggestions we make are the best possible..." I pause. "...for the rest of your life. There are reasons why more than 50% or marriages end in divorce... Individuals simply chose to ignore the information that is available to them, but our computers don't." I wait...

"But," the caller says, "I think that it's important to, you know, be somewhat attracted to."

"Yes attraction is important, very important."

"It is." He says to confirm it to himself.

"Our system understands your need to be attracted to potential life partners." He wants to be hooked up to a babe, but doesn't want to come right out and say it.

"Yes, attractive women—that are looking to improve their lives, use our services all the time, enter your data and you can meet some in a few days."

"Really?"

"Today could be the beginning of a new, and better you."

"Thanks," he seems reassured so I verify his email address so we can follow up. The system will now only harass him with items that directly relate to his concerns and encourage him to finish entering his data and give us permission to collect more.

No matter how hard we tried, we didn't kill father with our teenage inanity. Our stupid questions remained unanswered. The lung cancer did him in. He died at the exact moment of my life that I could finally appreciate him—and needed him the most.

Smoking kills. Who knew?

18. Where Have You Gone Joe DiMaggio?

Superstars have theme songs, music that is associated with them so much so that it must be played at their funerals, something to listen to when the B-Roll flashes across the screen. The rest of us are on our own.

What to play while I read from Joe's memoirs?

I'm a cliché' Brandy to sip. Sitting next to the fireplace (hasn't worked since the Eisenhower Administration). Like the rest of us, Joe doesn't have his own song. I choose *Hallelujah* by Jeff Buckley. If I drink enough, I'll change it to Dylan's *Knockin' on Heaven's Door* (the live version), but I'm not there yet and too many drinks and I'll end up falling asleep on this chair.

"What can a man write about death? It's not like we can die and return and tell you all about it. It is, as the kids say, what it is. And then it isn't.

I know what you want to read about. You want to know about my past. My story. You want to hear about poor little Joseph and his brothers. You want epic tales of the journey to America. I have no

332

*time for fairy tales. No desire to use my remaining
words to lie.*

*You can skip ahead and try to find what you
are looking for, or continue reading. The manuscript
is in your hands. It's now your problem.*

The manuscript is in my hands. As he was
dying Joe had what was written of his memoirs
printed out and bound like a real book. I and all his
relatives have signed copies. The difference is that
my copy has his notes and corrections in the margins.

I won't skip. I'll read every word in the
order they were handwritten and latter transcribed.
Just one more drink and I can read this:

*When the terrorists explode the atom bomb
in lower Manhattan let it be during the month of
October. Please God, if it must happen, let the
Yankees be playing at home for the World
Championship.*

*After the 500 degree heat has melted the
flesh from thousands. After the winds from hell have
run their course through the concrete canyons,
ripping steal beams from skyscrapers and limbs from*

bodies. After the radiation has been scattered for miles and jump-started a trillion cancer cells in the breasts and internal organs of millions. After the ashes of the dead have been gathered and buried in mass graves. After the living have been medicated with Potassium Iodide.

Let there be baseball. Let them play in valley of the shadow of death, but let them play.

Before curfew is made permanent, before the constitution suspended and martial law declared, let the games continue.

There will be calls for the games to be postponed or cancelled. All the king's horses and all the king's men will solemnly declare that there are more important matters than a ballgame. As usual, they are wrong. Let our leaders hold their committee meetings, their hearings, give them their fifteen minutes on CNN, Fox News and MSNBC. Let them promise security and take away our freedom an ounce at a time. Let them make their speeches, draw their flow charts...

334

If the games are forfeited, postponed, or canceled, the assassins win.

Our bodies have already been exposed to the fallout, the river has been crossed, the die cast. We will now fear life more than death.

Let them play. Let them play. Let them play. If all the regulars are dead, let minor leaguers substitute. If minor leaguers are unavailable insert the batboys, the groundskeepers, the ticket takers, the hot dog vendors, the beer men. Let them play. Let them play because when we play there is hope. When we play there is life. When we play we ward off death for an hour, an inning, a mere swing of the bat.

Let them play for the sake of playing. Let them finish the World Series so we don't have to face the coming nuclear winter without our season coming to its natural conclusion.

Let each player walk to the batter's box knowing that once they were young boys dreaming of playing in the big leagues.

Let each of them stand in the batter's box believing that they are about to hit the gaming winning, series ending, home run.

Let them play as fast and hard as they can. Let them run out ever hit, because in fact, it may be their last.

Let them make plays that seem impossible to make even after they have been made. Let them catch balls that were not made to be caught. Let the balls fly out of the park as if gravity never existed.

Let them play until their uniforms are covered in dirt, sweat, tears, and blood.

Let the rest of the world listen on their radios, wishing they were there to witness a small piece of history.

Skip the pregame festivities, the bullshit symbolism and pageantry. We've had enough; all the flag waving in the world was unable to stop the chain reaction from reaching critical mass. Let the politicians have their symbols, let the rest of us have our beloved pastime.

Don't invite the celebrities, for the only thing worse than a self-serving, sanctimonious speech about love and understanding, is a self serving sanctimonious speech about love and understanding delivered via satellite. While the revolution was televised, the wake for the revolution can only be experienced in person, face to face—no pain will be felt via long distance, no comfort will be received over the airwaves.

Forget the captains of industry who will speak about rebuilding, while they are secretly thinking about how they can line their pockets in the process.

And last but not least, don't turn the recently incinerated into heroes. I assure you, they were not heroes. They were just folks, no better or worse than most. They were not selected to be assassinated, they just happened to be at the wrong place, at the wrong time.

Let the players play, and we will remember the dead for what they were and not what they would

have been if only. They didn't see it coming and
neither did we. Bad luck does not a hero make.

Let the games begin. And when, and only
when, the game is over will we be able to say
goodbye to the dead and mourn the loss of what
might have been. Until then, let them play ball. Let
them play nuclear baseball.

Knock, knock, knockin' on heaven's door.

19. Case Study 516

Question: Why is this case study different
than all other case studies? Answer: Because this
one is attended, via video satellite, by The Doctor.
His image projected on the front wall.

Alex: "No matter how much we tweak the
data, we have a subset of users that refuse to believe
that we can help them. 85% of this population would
not only find a match...."

"Sometimes you just need a hook," The
Doctor interrupts, "something to make them believe
that we not only have partners that are perfect for
them, but the ability to improve every aspect of their

lives." I have no idea from which part of the planet the Doctor's image is being beamed from.

Alex: "Suggestions?"

"Have you considered entering the signs of the Zodiac into the matrix?" Tropical plants in the background provide some clue.

"Astrology?"

"About as predictive as head shape or tea leaves."

I can swear I heard a parrot squawking in the background. I've heard he has an estate in Costa Rica.

"It's been demonstrated that a monkey with a dart board is a better predictor than astrology." People are almost shouting at the Doctor. Not sure if the uproar is a result of his huge face projected on the wall or a corporate culture that encourages challenging the status quo, questioning authority, speaking up, stating different points of view—up to a point. In other words, it can get loud, but no one really knows when the line between insubordination and creative thinking is crossed. It's like running up to an edge of a cliff, once you've gone too far, it's too late.

"The magic of Astrology is that some people believe that it works, and that's all that matters," The Doctor continues. "Sometime we just need to jump start the process."

"It seems just a tad deceptive." I suggest.

"Isn't that what you wanted to do with your research grant, jump start the love process."

"Somewhat similar." How does he know this? And why? We never even submitted the proposal. I can't even remember how many years ago that was.

"Icarus is real. Icarus works. Some people just need a little convincing, a different approach." The Doctor takes a long pause, looks of off screen. "Think beyond the logical." His face disappears and we are blinded by the white light from the projector.

Think beyond the logical. Have I just witnessed the birth of a new acronym?

20. How to Pronounce YNTBE: A beginner's guide.

"EEE TV"

"WHY N TIB"

"N TUB E"

"END TABLE"

If asked to stare at a random inkblot and describe what one sees you are merely projecting your state of mind and/or thought process. Followers of Rorschach believe that their test is 100% accurate. These are not meaningless inkblots; these are the film and radiation necessary to capture the image of your psyche, the X-ray of your soul.

Same with YNTBE.

There is no right answer. There is no wrong answer. There is no answer. There is no official pronunciation. Never has been and never will be. It's an acronym that is used to rally the troops and tease new employees who don't have a clue. When someone insisted on "knowing" the answer we answered with "You're Not Thinking Big Enough."

We tease newbies and if we are perverse enough we attempt to figure out their thought process, an inkblot with letters. What part of their brain were their answers coming from? Were they thinking about TV? Did they fixate on the Y. or just ignore it? How much did they care about solving the mystery? If they were a coder did they attempt to hack into Icarus? Icarus is waiting and can't be bribed. More than one staffer was plied with many rounds in an attempt to find the true pronunciation. I'm not sure if I believe the rumors that someone even got laid to get the answer. By the time the new employees figured it our there were more new employees to torment with the non answer. Secrets are only safe when there is nothing to reveal.

21. Case Study 518

Sally: "How come we are not taking into account menstrual cycles?"

Crickets.

"Everyone knows that women are more receptive to new relationships during specific times in their period."

More crickets.

"I did not know that." I say just to break the silence.

"Maybe you should consider it; it might boost our success by another 7 or 8 percent."

"This information is not in any of the data sets."

"Really?" She folds her arms across her chest."

"I've been over the data many times. I'm sure it's not there."

"Really?" She just loves that word. "And you were probably in the honors class. Yes?"

"A few." Biology was never my strong suit.

"Have you considered that you have all the data you need?" Sally doesn't give me time to think, let alone answer. "You have shopping patterns and when they purchase specific products: feminine hygiene, pain medications, chocolate. Perhaps you could correlate this with a decrease in visits to the Gym, shopping for luxuries; it all should give you a range of when a client is most likely to be ovulating or menstruating. Need I say more?"

Wish you had said less.

"I think we got enough to work on."

"Well, what are you waiting for? Go."

I can't read minds, but I know what every male in the room is thinking.

22. Case Study 585

You are gay. Closeted, but still a homosexual. This is not a value judgment; it's what you are. You are simply not sexually compatible with women. In other words, you don't really want to have sex with them. For you, women make good friends—not life partners. This is the way either G*D or evolution or nature or nurture created you. You are gay. This is not an opinion. It's the result of millions of calculations, based on solid data. The chance of error is less than one tenth of one percent. Ignore us at your own risk. You have been faking your interest in the opposite sex for too long. Pretend that you are straight and be miserable, and make everyone in your life even more miserable. Here's a list of qualified therapists who specialize in helping people come out of the closet. When you are ready to accept who you are, please come back and we would be happy to help you find a partner and many additional suggestions on how to improve your life.

23. Insert Reference to Dante Here

This is my nightmare. Welcome. I'm sitting at the main conference table at YNTBE. The table is shaped like a giant horseshoe and I'm seated at the ass of the U, the armpit of the V, the focus of attention.

The meeting starts off slow, and like all good nightmares, pleasantly.

"We like your work."

"You have really surpassed all expectations."

"What do you think of your contribution to the project?"

"It's a start," I say. "All of it is a learning experience—we can redefine everything with each trial.

"Do you believe?"

"I believe it can work."

"And that's enough for you?"

"I think that would be enough for most people."

"You are--"

"—not most people!"

"You are someone that wants to do his best."

"You do want the best for yourself, don't you?"

"More testing," I mumble. "A little trial and error would help. Never being completely satisfied with the results never hurt—like The Doctor says *there is always room for improvement.*" I hope that quoting our CEO will get me out of this.

"What else?"

"I'm not sure that there is anything else."

"How about trying it on you?

"Not just the lab, but letting Icarus have all your data and making the most appropriate recommendations."

"I want to remain objective," I thought, wrongly, of course, that this was the answer to put the matter to rest. False hope, the other necessary ingredient of great nightmares.

"Objectivity is important, but it has often been said that to fully understand, to fully achieve one must jump in. You can't swim unless you get wet."

"Without trying, you'll always be an outsider."

"Ham and eggs."

"Ham and eggs?" I ask.

"The chicken is involved, but the pig is really committed."

At this time I was aware of the dryness in my mouth, I was willing to drink just about anything to quench my thirst.

"Does everyone have to be an insider?"

"Everyone is entitled to be what they want to be?"

"Your work and you deserve the best."

"Be open to it."

"You deserve the most out of life."

"Don't you want someone to grow old with, to share your thoughts, your dreams?"

"I have someone."

"Where is she? On the road?"

"How do you know that she is the one?"

"Only one way to find out."

They are all starting directly at me. I swear that I can see them all mouth the words "what are you afraid of," and "submit to Icarus," over and over. I wake up alone, sweaty, and thirsty— very thirsty.

24. Case Study 607

"Of course the relationship got off to a rocky start; they completely ignored the dating advice supplied by Icarus. A quick read of the data and it is obvious that this couple needed to do something exciting to get their serotonin levels to an elevated level to facilitate attraction. Dancing, an amusement park, anything with action. Their choice of an art museum is great for impressing someone—NOT for attraction."

25. Case Study 631

Alex: "He's a construction worker…with an above average IQ."

"And?"

"Icarus believes that he would be happier in a different job."

"He'll be happier if beer came out of water fountains."

"Or breasts for that matter."

"Free beer may keep him satisfied, but will not help him live up to his potential."

349

"Not everyone wants 'to be all they can be."

Alex: "The fact that he is resisting means that deep down, he would really like to do better. To have more."

"How do we convince him of this?"

"No idea."

"The Doctor wants us to find one."

26. Case Study 646

Alex: "In Kansas City, Icarus set up a brother and sister on a date."

"If it was only in Kentucky—"

"—In some states, people might pay extra for a computer to give them permission." The room floods with nervous laugher.

Alex: "And yes, they had different last names and lived at different addresses—there is no easy fix. This is a real problem that needs a solution. Today."

"Maybe we should introduce genetic testing to eliminate the possibility of siblings ever dating." I quip.

"Brilliant!" Scotty says from the back of the room.

"It was just thinking out loud." Really I was joking. A little humor never hurt. Until now.

"It fits in with everything we have been attempting."

"I don't know why we haven't thought of it before." Sally adds.

"It's just so simple and perfect—I'm going to send an e-mail to The Doctor." Scotty starts typing into his phone faster than you can say D N A.

One could argue that humans are predisposed to NOT pick relatives for mates. In studies, subjects rated distant cousins less attractive than subjects not related to them. Evolution has encouraged us to mix up our genes with non relatives. A little swap of DNA and ICARUS would insure that you would never be introduced to a cousin, even if you didn't know you had a cousin.

"We'll need your report on how to accomplish this be the end of the week." Scotty looks up from his tablet.

"It was just an idea." What are the ramifications of matching via DNA?

"It's ideas that make companies great; if you could have the report sooner it would be appreciated."

"OK."

"If you don't mind, try to include cost estimates, resources needed, etc."

I guess I am finally thinking, or joking, big enough. Lord help me. Lord help us.

27. Big Enough

"Many of our clients are not very sophisticated investors." Brad is the first presenter. I think he's new here, but I can't be certain. I'm on my laptop reading about DNA and checking e-mails from vendors that do genetic screening.

"That's why we created the finance module of YNTBE." Brad yawns. Unprofessional, but can you blame someone who has been up all night preparing a presentation that may or may not be the difference between becoming a full timer or not?

"As you can see from the slide, if we encourage clients to increase their savings by just 8% and help them invest at current market rates…" If I was looking at the slide, I could see it, but who has time? Everyone in the room is doing at least two things at once. Depending on your point of view we are giving half our attention to Brad, or half ignoring him.

"The next slide represents stock market growth during the past 80 years."

Every week, in addition to my own assignments, I attend presentations where some staffer suggests another feature that we should shoehorn into the equation: 401k plans, life insurance, interior decorating, music clubs, automatic shopping, fitness training, life coaching, family planning, dog walkers, booze of the month club…

Hello from the road. An instant message from Susie.

Hello from hell.
???

I've created a monster, and I see him every morning when I shave. I type to Susie. It's not the long hours or the work I take home that scares me. I've become what I've always hated. *I'm a multitasker.*

It's about time. Susie responds. We usually do the full video conference; since we are both in meetings we are in chat mode. I can see her, but the sound is off.

"Our inside intelligence will help us keep ahead of the market."

YNTBE is connecting men with women, people with jobs, places to live for happy couples. Ambitious yes, but that was just the start. For if YNTBE was anything, it was a company that not merely encouraged suggestions, it insisted on them. All employees were graded on the number of, and quality of their ideas. To not participate in the process is career suicide.

The background seems to suggest that Susie is backstage somewhere with the band, but I can't be sure.

I have 72 hours to learn all about DNA.
Thinking of having a baby?
We live in a society that frowns on sibs
dating.

Some rules are good.
I made a joke.

Can O Worms.

"My name is Warren and my presentation
provides a unique opportunity for us…"

How could it end? Once you start perfecting
lives, can you ever take a break? Would it be ethical
to not complete the mission? Alex wasn't kidding
when he wanted to sell caskets, along with funeral
plots and weekly flower delivery. At least lunch will
be served soon.

It's fairly easy to prevent distant relatives
from dating, but what do you do with the rest of the
data?

You will figure out something.
Got e-mail from The Doctor. Loves my idea.
That's great!

355

Now he wants to know how we can use the
information to develop additional services.
Healthcare options. Life insurance. Diet and
exercise programs that are customized to an
individuals lifestyle AND genetic background.

Interesting.

I'll never talk in a meeting again.

IDBY.

Thanks.

"As you can see from the slide," Warren
continues, "we have the opportunity to be number
one in this market just from our current client base."
If, and they always leave out the *if,* 100% of the
target audience do as you predict. This happens
never.

It's great that your work is getting noticed.

Until I remember that I'm helping a
computer learn how to destroy humanity.

Drama much?

Just a little.

"Not just travel, but total travel: trips, excursions, retreats, based on the unique needs of the individual."

In theory we could match up people for complete genetic compatibility, eliminating nasty diseases caused when both parents pass on recessive genes to their offspring

???

Not sure if it's ethical or not, but the world doesn't need Cystic Fibrosis or Sickle cell anemia.

Interesting.

Tay-Sachs used to be a "Jewish Disease" passed on to a baby only when BOTH parents are carriers. With screening none of the ten babies born in North America last year with the condition had Jewish parents. Genetic screening is here to stay.

Sounds like you're trying to convince yourself.

Perhaps.

Isn't this a discussion for the management of YNTBE?

They just want to know if it will work, the ethical considerations come later. Much later.

Luck with that.

"I call this the Total Travel Module or TTM." Another three-letter-acronym.

A staffer hands me a bento box from Mystery Sushi.

A few years ago I complained about having to attend presentation after presentation. I rejected idea after idea. Now I'm tasked with integrating them. I type, but I really want to eat. Chopsticks, online chatting, and pretending to listen don't mix.

Irony is your bitch. Susie replies.

In this life it seems that we are punished by our sins, not for them.

True.

I'm positive that at some future meeting someone will suggest that we attach protein shakes to those baseball helmets with the long straws so we don't have to stop working to receive sustenance. Someday soon, someone will make a joke about this in a meeting, but it won't be me.

28. Meetings

"You're late."

"And you are?" I ask the strange person sitting at my new desk.

"I'm your shadow." He stands and offers his hand.

New day. New location. A shadow? I drop my box on the desk and shake his hand.

"Hello shadow."

"My name is name is Ian. I was assuming you read the e-mail."

The almighty ICARUS has assigned me a new desk. An opportunity to interact with different coworkers. If this trend continues, I'll need an app on my phone to tell me where I'm supposed to sit on a daily basis. Does Icarus not know that I hate change? Perhaps she does and wants to alter my mindset. Maybe he does and just wants to fuck with me.

"I had to pack. And now I have to unpack."

My box is light. Not many personal items. A picture of Susie, the signed copy of Joe's memoirs, a stress ball that couldn't reduce the stress of a corpse.

"I'm new here, been assigned to follow you for the rest of the week."

"And?"

I take my time finding the perfect spot for the photograph of Susie. The company supplied the frame. We are encouraged to demonstrate that we have a life outside of work. *Photographs convince investors that we are well-adjusted, normal human beings.* For three months I kept the frame with the picture that it came with, but it didn't convince anyone.

"What's the first thing you do in the morning?" Ian asks as he straightens his tie.

"Get Coffee."

"After that?"

"Drink it."

Ian gives me a look that would make a puppy jealous. "I'm here to learn, not earn."

It's too early for a new slogan. It's always too early for a new slogan.

"You do realize that most of what I do all day is stare at my monitor and attend meetings." Often both at the same time.

We head towards the break room. Ian needs sun even more than I do.

"Where were you working before this?" Why do new employees insist on so much morning conversation?

"Federal prison." I say, hoping this will quickly end the conversation.

"Why?"

"Asking too many questions." Actually it was for asking too few, but that's not going to shut him up.

"I was in rehab." His gaze shifts towards the floor. "Alcohol mostly, but there were drugs of course. Marijuana. Pills, amphetamines mostly, some downers. I did Cocaine, a little crystal meth. Sex with strangers. Nothing unusual for an addict.

I've been clean and sober for almost four months."
He barely pauses between sentences.

I make my coffee selection and place the cartridge in the machine.

"We have cream, half & half, soy milk in the fridge. Help yourself to any of the snacks."

He eyes the piles of fruit, chips, and other assorted goodies, and starts piling them on his plate. I help myself to a banana. "Rookie mistake."

"What?"

"Taking more than you need to eat. It's not like they remove all the goodies after breakfast."

"You never know." I do and tomorrow he'll take less.

"I have a sponsor." Talking with an addict is easy, just pretend to listen and they do all the work. I motion for him to make his coffee selection. "I have a meeting at six, but can come back after that." He pours six packets of sugar in his coffee. "I was an addict since my early teens. Bottomed out halfway through college. I was living in my car before... You get the picture."

"Think so."

We head back towards my desk.

"I'm recovering. Always will be."

"It's OK." I say, because I got nothing else.

"Thanks. Most people are a little judgmental."

I judge in silence. You might say I'm a recovering judgeoholic—and always will be.

"Here it is." I point to my screen. *Ian is assigned to you...* I scan the rest of the e-mail. *New employees, learning curve, different life experiences, different abilities. Embrace them. Learn not earn.*

"Any advice, before we start." Ian asks.

Look both ways before crossing the street. Avoid women with too many tattoos. Never draw to an inside straight.

"Relax. And lose the tie."

"Thanks."

Today's schedule is promptly displayed on my monitor.

"Everything is electronic, especially the scheduling. Meetings. Meetings. Meetings."

"Must be important."

"You would think."

"You saying that meetings are a complete waste of time?"

"I'm saying that the distance between two points is never a straight line." I hope that by the time he figures out that what I said was meaningless he'll be somebody else's shadow.

"Interesting."

"It would be if I had more than 15 minutes to prepare for my 8:00."

"Our 8:00." Ian adds as he takes a sip of his coffee.

29. Case Study, Case Study

"How did we utilize what we learned from case study 716?"

It was only a matter of time; a meeting to discuss the effectiveness of case studies.

"We learned nothing," I volunteer.

Alex is once again the conductor, the assembled are the choir, PowerPoint the guiding light.

"Why is that?"

"Everything worked."

"I see your point about A to B Ian whispers to me."

"David." Alex says. "Do you or your assistant have anything to add to the current discussion?"

"One. He's not my, assistant, he's my shadow. Two. Am I the only one who reads his morning e-mails?" The silence is priceless. Thank you Ian.

"My name is Ian. I'm here to learn." He smiles.

"Hello Ian."

"Welcome."

"Speaking of learning, it's impossible to not learn something." Alex flips through his electronic file. I can imagine the gears turning in his head; a Swiss watch in a digital world.

"They met. Fell in Love. Got a new place to live. Got married. Found better jobs. If every variable stayed the same, they would be our model, but that's not how it works." I say. "Everyone's different—too many variables. STYK. Success teaches us nothing." Shit. I just created a new acronym. I've been absorbed by the collective. Is it impossible to turn back now?

"Are you claiming that we only learn from our failures?" Alex finally looks up from his computer.

"A blind pig can occasionally find truffles." Although his comment is cliché, Ian is the gift that keeps on giving.

"That makes no sense." Amanda says.

"Why not?" Ian resorts as he checks out Amanda.

"Pigs don't see truffles, they smell them. You should have stated: 'an olfactory challenged swine can often locate the fruiting body of an underground mushroom." Never heard her speak before. She's the one that never has anything to say during the meeting, but as soon as you get back to your desk, you can expect an 8,000 word e-mail— with footnotes.

"I stand corrected M'lady" Ian says as he gestures like an actor performing Shakespeare in rural Ohio. A touch of color has returned to his cheeks. They both hold the glance and smile.

Did I just witness a love connection in a meeting to discuss the effectiveness of case studies to help us better understand computer-generated love-connections?

Alex: "Moving on to case study 718."

I think I did.

Alex: "A few people were unhappy when they found out that their new employer was in fact the maker of the program that has promised them a better life. How should we handle this? And what did we learn from the case study."

We learned the number one thing in business: that when all is said and done more is said than done. We learned that projects that should take a few hours can take days, weeks even. We learned that our labor is cheap. We learned that free coffee, like free candy often comes at a price. Although the price is not as high as the nice man in the van would like you to believe, there is a price.

30. On the Waterfront

"You want a coffee before I go to my meeting?" Ian asks with the nervous energy of a sprinter at the starting gate.

"I'm good. Thanks."

"Working late?"

"Depends on what you consider late."

Ian hesitates and asks: "So, how do you pronounce the name of the company?"

"That's your question? You don't want the 411 on Amanda."

"Can't"

"You can't ask questions about a woman you recently flirted with?"

"Can't have intimate relations with anyone until I've been sober for at least six months."

"Did not know that."

"I have a large porn collection."

I wonder if they have support groups for individuals who consistently dispense TMI?

"You're not thinking big enough."

"That's your answer?"

"There is no answer."

"How can there be no answer?"

"It's a trick to get people thinking."

"Really?"

"Just pretend you care."

"Thanks. I'll be back after my group."

"It can wait till the morning."

"I want to help."

"Shadows don't work, they...." I'll never be good at repeating slogans.

"Can I ask you why you do it?"

"Do what?"

"Work so hard."

"Right now the computer is doing all the work, compiling data."

"You seem to spend a lot of time here."

"If you want to help on the project and don't mind bending the rules, pick up a laptop in morning and I'll find you something."

"Thanks. I can't be late" Ian says, turns and jogs away.

Why do I work so much? Why don't I do what Susie suggests and just quit.

Every time I think of quitting YNTBE, I remember Wally Pipp. Jack Parr comes to mind. Who could forget the very promising early career of percussionist Pete Best? I imagine that one day all three will meet in a pub in heaven and talk about the only thing they have in common. At first they will avoid the subject, making small talk about the nice weather in paradise and the many opportunities they each have to catch up on their reading or golf.

No matter how hard they try, they will not be able to avoid what has brought them together, the life circumstances that give them something in common, that few of us will truly understand, the fact about their lives will mostly be remembered for what might have been.

Jack Parr walked off the Tonight Show and was replaced by a newcomer named Johnny Carson. Wally Pipp had a headache and rookie Lou Gehrig replaced him for 2,400 straight games. Mr. Best was the drummer in a group called The Beatles before being replaced by Richard Starkey, better known as Ringo Starr. The rest, as they say is history; a long history for those left sitting on the bench, watching their replacements get all the fame, all the glory, all the riches.

When I think of walking, or running away from YNTBE, every story of the person that could have worked at Yahoo or Apple or Google when they were garage start-ups comes to mind. I think of the secretary at McDonalds who was paid in stock. There is no phrase in the English Language sadder than: *Might have been.*

I imagine it's like being an executive at Decca Records. Several years after refusing to sign The Beatles to a recording contract because "guitar bands would soon be out of style," Decca signed Pete Best. They even released an album titled, "Best of the Beatles," a play on Pete's relationship with his former band. Fans were disappointed. Sales of the album were dismal. Decca Records never recaptured any of its early glory.

You want to change the world; you want to be a millionaire. You do your best to serve two masters in order to not spend the rest of your life not having to tell everyone that will listen that: I could have been a contender. If only I had stayed a little longer, put in some more time, worked harder (and smarter), stayed the course, was really dedicated, put in just a few more hours. If only I had truly believed in the project.

Thankfully I don't have to shadow Ian to his AA meeting because as soon as I finish at the office, I'm having a beer. Or two.

31. Primates

"I'm working on a new project." Susie on video chat. She's in a hotel that seems a little too fancy for the band's budget.

"New project." I'm afraid to ask what mischief she's up to.

"I can't talk about it now, but I'll send you a link when I can." When she's on a computer that can't be traced back to her. I fear that our roles my someday be reversed and I'll have to visit her in the pen.

"Nice room." A part of me fears that some guy in a fancy hotel robe will appear in the background and say hello to me in a foreign accent. And then go on to tell how he loved my Susie all night long and made her scream so loud that the hotel called the cops because they thought someone was being murdered. And they're going to do it again tonight and the next morning.

"I got us upgraded." She takes a sip of her room-service coffee.

"Cool."

"You're *up* early this morning. You must miss me." There's my tease.

"My DNA report is due."

"What have you learned?"

"We share 99% of our DNA with chimpanzees."

"How does that help you with the project?"

"I'm thinking of suggesting that we use ICARUS to match monkeys with better partners, find them better jungles and zoos to live in, and most importantly, better jobs. No more lab experiments. I call it: You're Not Thinking Primate Enough."

"Not much sleep last night.'

"There's only one rule in our employee manual: *We'll sleep when we die.*"

"You need help."

"My shadow should be here any minute."

"Don't abuse him. Or her." Perhaps she misses me too.

"It's a he." Although you would think that shadows, like clouds, would be asexual.

"You're always too hard on yourself."

"Don't say it."

"You have alternatives."

"Wow she's even more beautiful on video."

Ian.

"Who's that?"

"My shadow. He's all primary process, holds nothing back."

"Don't feed him after midnight."

"Of course."

"See you latter." She blows a kiss. Why not, she has an audience?

"Seems nice."

"Ready to start?"

"How do you know I'm qualified to do this?" Ian asks.

"Your profile is on the network."

"Everything?"

"No personal details. No Address or social security numbers. If I wanted to stalk you, I would have to work to get those. Not that I would want to. Or have the time."

"Weird."

"Openness is the new normal."

"Can I look up?"

"I'll show you later. In the meantime you can start analyzing the last data set."

* * *

"Did you find her through Icarus?"

"Who?"

"Your girl."

"No."

"You created love all on your own."

"Only a fool would take credit for love."

"Really?"

"Just happens. Like the man who inherits a million dollar and thinks that he earned it."

"Are you saying you don't deserve it."

"I deserve it, but I didn't create it."

"Deep."

"We've been here for 14 hours. Someday you'll look back at this conversation and think that we're all idiots."

"Hopefully I'll be on an island in the Caribbean after cashing in my stock options."

"In the meantime, can you make a coffee run? They seem to be out in the break room."

"I thought ICARUS ordered supplies automatically."

"Perhaps the system has not taken into account company growth or the increase in employees working overtime."

"Must be."

* * *

"Where's your shadow?" Looks like Susie is back stage. Somewhere.

"Twice in one day."

"I'm worried. All work and no play."

"I have more fun when you're in town." And more sex, although I guess that's implied. If not, it should be. Sex should be implied. Always.

"Just a few more days. Is everyone looking forward to the concert?"

"It's going to be huge." Glad she mentioned it, because it has slipped my mind completely.

"The band thanks you and I hope we pass the audition."

"It's just a corporate gig."

"Pays the rent." This from a woman who makes great money producing bad advertising and more bucks with deals on the side. Has she gone native? She waves goodbye and the screen goes black.

If we share 99% of our DNA with chimps, it can also be said that they share 99% of their DNA with us. Not sure which one of us benefits from that extra 1%, but I'm beginning to think it's the monkeys.

32. OTG

"David. How are you doing?"

I turn and see Scotty and Sally.

"OK. Although it seems the break room on my floor is now out of milk and I haven't heard back from you about the report, I e-mailed the files to both of you." God, I miss paper.

"Would love to show your report to the Doctor, but he's not in." Scotty taps his pad acknowledging that he received my findings.

"We're looking into the temporary shortage of a limited number of office supplies that the team requires to perform its daily functions." Either Sally has been replaced by a robot or she too has been deprived of sleep. Perhaps both.

With paper, when you finished a project, you got to hand someone something.

"Where is The Doctor?"

"OTG?" Scotty says.

"Where's that?"

"Off-The-Grid." Sally says slowly. "It replaces AFK, only to be used when you don't want to, and absolutely can't be reached."

At least when you handed something in on paper, it had more mass than a collection of atoms. People could judge it by its weight. It's real. An accomplishment.

"When's he coming back?"

"OTG means OTG."

So the acronyms are now defining themselves. I'll be really impressed when they start reproducing themselves. Forget machines, the world is going to be destroyed by business lingo.

"So in the meantime, I'll just say nice job." Scotty glances at Sally.

"Nice job." Sally agrees.

"It was a lot of work."

"We know." They say in unison.

"Ian helped."

"He's not supposed to."

I'm not supposed to work 80 hours a week.

"Wasn't it The Doctor who said that you can't learn by watching, only by doing."

"True."

"Very True."

I could print out the entire report, place it on my desk, but besides feeling good about it, what's the point?

"It would be nice to get some feedback."

"You seem stressed."

"Maybe you should take a few hours off." Scotty suggests.

"Take a walk, see a movie, we have discount tickets at the concierge desk."

"Cool."

I hope the trees are happy.

33. Saturday in the Park

"The times are a changin" sings the aging boomer with the guitar.

The only change I detect is the lack of pot sellers. Recent police crackdowns on low level drug peddlers in Washington Square Park have made it nearly impossible to purchase enough grass for a measly joint. This did not stop the pushers from selling, they merely moved indoors and sold drugs out of their dorm rooms and student apartments. Unfortunately, they didn't arrest the singers. The groups that think the sixties ended yesterday and are three parts short of a four part harmony. They sound terrible and sing about things that are no longer relevant. They are protesting the last war and ignoring the next one. Listening to these holdouts would make anyone want to smoke something.

"The answers my friend, are blowing in the wind."

A man in a long robe hands me a pamphlet. "You seem lost; this will help you figure out why you are here."

Why am I here? O yes, I work for a company that thinks a few hours off is the same as a two week vacation.

Why am I here?

Because Washington Square Park is as good place as any to take a mini vaca.

A few hours is not enough to even try to get off the grid. I find an empty bench to go online and check my e-mail. Vacations are for the weak, days-off for the non-committed.

First order of business, check out the link from Susie.

More shaky video. Looks like a marijuana plant. Same location, but the plant is much larger and starting to flower. The camera zooms back and we see the plant is on the side of a non-descript building.

The camera pans to show the name of the building: West Topeka Police. This could be interesting.

The video fades out and more plants and more police stations, sheriff offices, highway patrol, state troopers. The only text is the tagline: *The seeds are in the ground.*

The video ends with links to more videos and a URL for a site that's hosting a contest for best video. Entries will be judged by: *maturity of plant, location, type of institution.*

Nice. It's not enough to simply undermine the corporate world; she needs to take on the war on drugs. It's not illegal; it's just tilting at windmills.

What do you call this type of activity? I guess it beats singing protest songs from 40 years ago. Or maybe it's exactly the same thing. Each generation protests in its very own way.

The good news is that she and the band will be back in town. The Doctor will give his spiel that was developed OTG, Tequila Mockingbird will play at the after party. And the next day will all get up and get back to work.

383

"If I had a hammer."

Perhaps the singers are on to something or perhaps they simply haven't learned any new songs.

34. Rawhide

The music stops and the lights dim.

"Are you a maverick?" The Doctor asks from offstage.

The video screens go from an MTV montage of modern history to a simple YNTBE logo.

"A true maverick?" The spotlight travels left and right searching for its target.

We all know exactly what he is talking about, for the schedule in yesterday's e-mail clearly foreshadowed today's theme. Buried in yesterday's missive--between a listing of all our amazing accomplishments and everything that we are going to achieve (with just a little extra effort) was the story of Maverick.

The Doctor enters the spotlight. He is dressed in an off-white linen suit. No tie.

384

Virginia born and Yale educated Samuel Augustus Maverick was (in no particular order) a lawyer, politician, slave owner, signer of the Texas Declaration of Independence, husband and father. He knew people that knew people that fought, and died at, the Alamo.

The spotlight fades and the house lights come back on. The room is silent.

"In this life, a maverick is the true leader."

During his long and prosperous life, Maverick accumulated more than 35,000 acres of ranch land in the San Antonio area. He steadfastly refused to brand his cattle. None of his Texas Longhorns were scarred with a *Lazy B* or *Rolling R*. You would never find *Suzie Q* or *Mad Cow* markings on any of his bovine investments. His Texas neighbors, being equally stubborn, continued to brand their animals. They considered Samuel Maverick a nonconformist, an eccentric, a rebel, a...

"To brand or not to brand?" The Doctor continues from the podium. "When all you have is a brand, what do you really own?" His silk shirt

385

almost shines. "Only mediocre companies depend on a brand." When he pauses, there is enough silence in the room to hear air flowing through the vents.

"Lets produce the best services and then improve them. And then improve them some more."

The audience nods in agreement—all 852 of them.

"Never be satisfied. This will be our mark on the world."

If you would have passed a plate, people would have donated their meager paychecks to the cause.

"We must improve today..."

Praise the lord and pass the ammunition.

"Tomorrow doesn't exist."

Smoke 'em if you got 'em.

"You must ask yourself, is that a branding iron in your hand or a crutch?"

I once was lost, but now am found

Applause. The Doctor exits. No encore. The video screens display a new montage of happy YNTBE clients: smiling couples, wedding pictures, satisfied workers, new houses, babies, lots of babies. And more wedding pictures. REM's *End of the World as We Know It* blares on the speakers.

I was willing to throw out my branding iron, but could I ever be truly free? Can anyone?

35. Just Call Me Yoko

"I'm with the band."

The fact that I can honestly say this *and* get to sleep with a member of the band means that I can die a happy man, or at least a man with a smile on his face. To you, she's a part time lyricist/assistant manager/marketing guru/assistant roadie, but to me she's a member of the Mockingbirds. Tomorrow we get back to work, but tonight we party like indie rock stars.

I'm sure that real rock stars have more glamorous back stages, with groupies, tons of food, alcohol, drugs, and a room larger than Giant's Stadium to store their egos. We have bottled water and imported beer.

"You seem a little nervous," Susie says and squeezes my hand.

"Looking forward to the show." Trying to get my mind off work. When I close my eyes I see equations that need to be changed, ideas that need to be tested, and data that hasn't been interpreted. I fear that we don't know what we don't know.

The band starts with something from the 2nd Album, *If I tell you I'm gay can I see you naked?* Nothing like a song about sex to get an overworked, sleep deprived crowd going. Susie and I smile at each other, as only couples can. I only fear the encore, the novelty song. The signature song that they must perform or they will die as a band or something.

"I've never been backstage before."

"Technically we're next to the stage on folding chairs."

"Today it's bars and ballrooms, tomorrow stadiums."

The crowd cheers as the band finishes the song and immediately starts the next. Something from the first album. So far, so good. My former coworker, Dave on lead guitar plays like he was born for the role.

"Dave is sharp tonight."

"He's been on fire since he quit his day job."

"I can see."

"When you leave here, whatever this company is called you'll have time to practice or do whatever you want."

What the hell does that mean? What could/ should I do? Write a novel? Open a restaurant? Join the Peace Corps? Any there any whales left to save?

Rebecca, on drums, twirls her sticks, waiting for Lee, the lead singer to finish his intro. Something about being inspired to write the song during an epic marathon of Zombie films and premium tequila. The crowd cheers, but I'm not sure if it's for the Zombies or the alcohol.

"I wanted to ask you about your latest video project." And yes, in my mind, *project* is in air quotes.

"Ask away." Susie keeps her eyes on the band.

"Why?"

"The war on drugs is a joke, a very expensive joke."

The band starts the next song. Something about Hitler's diet and the end of civilization as we know it.

"Why you?"

"It's a political protest, if you have to ask, you don't really get it." She withdraws her hand and stands up to cheer.

Did I just get rejected or did the song end at the wrong time? She sits down and keeps her eyes on the stage. Something in the back of my mind tells me that I need to say something, but it doesn't tell me what to say or how to say it. It never does.

The lights dim, it's going to be a ballad.

"I do get it, I just don't understand." I'm beginning to think that talking is overrated. I take another swig from my beer, and realize that it's

empty, but now is not the time to get a new one.
More beer and everything might start making sense.

"You do remember that I wrote the lyrics for the last song."

I really need another one.

"And I'm proud of you." I am. I am. I am. What am I supposed to do to acknowledge this? Send flowers? Hallmark doesn't do cards for girlfriends who write lyrics about the culinary choices of egomaniacal dictators.

"It meant something to me for you to finally hear it live."

She never told me, her heart was cold. Lee croons from a song I've never heard and have no idea who wrote the lyrics for.

It's high school all over again, the fact that it's legal to drink is only a slight improvement.

Lolita, Lolita, Lolita.

"Interesting choice of names." Susie says nothing. It's going to be a long cab ride home, might as well grab another cold one as the band plays on.

For their first encore, the band does their rendition of *Twist n Shout*. Next comes another cover song, The Rolling Stones, Rock n Roll. Another song that keeps the crowd dancing.

When the applause dies down, the band is ready for the finale. Here goes everything.

The song starts and it sounds like a riff on The Band's "The Night they Drove Ole Dixie Down."

I don't get the words from the first verse, but the chorus is unmistakable:

> *The Night they tore old Zabars Down*
>
> *And the Jews were screaming*
> *The Night they tore old Zabars Down*
>
> *And the Jews were screaming*

Zabars?

Why shy away from controversy, when you can invite it to spend the night? It won't just steal your wallet after it screws you, it will demand breakfast before it leaves. Trust me: the smile on your face disappears long before it starts hurting when you pee.

> *May the Yankees Beat the Braves*

At least they're keeping with the New York theme. Zabars the premier shop on the Upper West Side deserves its own song, but I'm not sure if this is the one. They are "Jewish" in that they sell lox, bagels, and babka. I guess there are worse things to sing about.

> *And the people were singing*
> *They went, "Oy, Oy, Oy."*

36. The Long, Long Cab Ride Home

The city shines like the stars, no the stars shine like the city. The city is here, the city is real. I'm not sure about the stars. If I didn't know better, I'd say they were fakes, manufactured by some over competitive billionaire who wanted to prove that he could really light up the sky.

The cab heads north.

90% of New York City cabdrivers were not born in this country. I find this statistic to be useless and amazing. And at this moment in my life, with my girlfriend giving me the silent treatment, I wish that I was in one of those foreign countries, a faraway place where if someone refused to talk to me It wouldn't matter because I couldn't understand his, or her, language.

"Speaking of the concert, we'll be passing Zabars soon."

"It's faster if you go up Amsterdam," Susie tells the driver.

Let go of my ears, I know my business. I know New Yorkers love to give directions, but to me it's like telling the counterman at Zabars how to slice your smoked salmon. They've been doing it for years and don't hang out at Carnegie Hall giving tuning advice to Itzhak Perlman.

This should be a great cab ride, we are slightly buzzed. At least, I am. The band mostly nailed it. I don't need this. Work does not stop just because you are having relationship problems.

"I said Amsterdam."

Please god of cities and stars no more red lights. The light turns yellow and the driver hits the gas.

How to play this? I want to say sorry, but if I say it too soon, it will sound insincere. Of course if I piss her off some more, she'll give me more silent treatment. I can buy a few days till the weekend. Get some work done if not in peace, than at least in quiet.

I keep my eyes on the meter and wonder if I had 50 years could I develop a computer program that would accurately tell me how to avoid situations like this. Maybe 75 years, but only if we assume that computing power doubles every 24 months and 80 hour work weeks. The car stops in front of our building.

"You pay, but no tip." She leaves the cab as if it was on fire.

Maybe 100 years.

I pay the driver and yes, I give him a tip, because he's come a long way to be here and didn't kill us for telling him how to do his job.

37. B2W

"Wanted to ask you about Ian."

"He's only been with me for a week."

"It's actually been three weeks."

Working at an Internet start-up is like living in a cave or working in a casino. There are no clocks on the walls. Time loses meaning when you are always inside. Sometimes you can't tell if you are working or dreaming about work.

"That's long enough to know if he's a C or a T?"

"C or T?" I ask, but I'm just stalling, because I have no idea what they are talking about.

"Using the OW method of evaluation."

"The OW method" I ask. I probably have more wrinkles on my forehead than a Shar Pei puppy.

"OW stands for Oscar Wilde." I can't understand how this is supposed to clear things up; did I forget the assigned reading again? Was I late for class? If my eyes roll any further back would they be able to see my brain?

"Charming or tedious. —'People should not be judged as good or bad, just charming or tedious.'"

"Charming or tedious? Tedious or charming?"   If my eyes could see my brain would my brain know it was being spied on?

* * *

"We need to TBV."

"Can we communicate without using TLAs."   Me again.

"THLS."   Or even FLAs.

"Yes."

"IRNC"

"There's none in my break room."

"Why"

"Don't know."

* * *

"We at YNTBE can solve all but FWP."

"Really?"

"But do we really want to?"

"FWP? Is that a new TLA?"

397

"It replaces. I forget what it replaces, but its

NAI.

"I never heard that."

"DGTM?"

"Guess not."

"Soon we will be able to solve all problems known to man, but until then we'll stick with the basics: jobs, housing, partners, life insurance, health and medical needs, entertainment, vacations, family planning, retirement and estate planning, special events, hobbies, sporting activities, cultural events, life coaching, politics, …"

Politics? What does this even mean?

And when I wake up, I realize it's another nightmare—not because it's unbelievable, but because it isn't.

38. Live Long and Prosper

Alex keeps tapping on his tablet; apparently he has lost touch with the mother ship. "The network is down people. It should be back up in a minute, in the meantime, what case study are we on?" Alex is always the most prepared staffer at every meeting, but apparently has no back-up plan for a network crash.

"It was number 845."

"I thought we had a network that could never go down."

"It's up more than 99% of the time." Alex says.

"The hours between 1 and 6 AM don't really count."

"They do if you live in another time zone."

"Good point."

"Back to the case study 845."

"No, that was last week. We're up to 914."

Alex surveys the room and looks back at his tablet. "The network is still down." Alex is completely lost. "914 it is."

"The server room is not answering my texts, IMs, or emails."

"Maybe we should Skype them."

"Or send someone down there to find out what's happening."

"Not me, the person they send always dies."

"This is not Star Trek."

"I'm sure the network will be back up in a few minutes." Alex puts his tablet down; he's a couch without a whistle, a hunter without a rifle, a bartender without a rag. "In the meantime case study 914 was about our optimization of worker productivity."

"That was Case Study 929."

"No 929 was the group who didn't want more suitable careers."

"I think you're right."

"Ungrateful bastards."

"All the data suggests that not only will they be happier, but their life-long earning potential would increase by at least 38%, not to mention extra retirement benefits and other perks."

"Some people just don't get it."

"Looks like the network is back up."

"And no one died"

"That we know of."

"Are you suggesting a company-wide headcount?"

"I'm suggesting that somewhere, something is wrong."

"Were running low on coffee."

"Again?"

39. The Rock

"You OK?" I ask Alex after the assembled have left the conference room.

"She wants the rock," he says.

"I assume you are referring to an engagement ring and not the prison in San Francisco Bay."

"Or the movie with Sean Connery and Nicholas Cage called, appropriately enough, *The Rock*." Ian just can't help himself. I think he'll be assigned to work with someone else soon.

"Did she say something?" I ask. Ian and I follow Alex as he leaves the conference room and enters the hall.

"She presented me with a printout from Icarus. It said and I quote:

Based on research, you are approaching the appropriate time to take your relationship to the next level." Alex stares at me.

"I only help program the machine based on the best evidence on long-term relationships that's available. I don't make value judgments." Who am I kidding? I judge therefore, I am.

"It makes sense; men have been comparing marriage and prison for centuries." Alex and I both stare at Ian, but he doesn't stop talking. I realize that I have more expertise behind bars than with holy matrimony, but that hardly seems relevant now. "They say that no one ever escaped from "The Rock" Ian informs us.

Alex takes a gulp from his coffee, but his expression tells me that he's disappointed that it's not tequila.

"After I get more coffee, I'm going to go back to my desk, and you know what I'm going to find?"

"No idea." So true. I not only have no idea, I really don't want to find out.

"Oh you do, you developed it. I'm going to find a note from Icarus with links to Jewelry stores that specialize in engagement rings, and that's only the beginning."

"On the plus side, I think that you are entitled to a discount from selected jewelers." I don't think that's the answer he was looking for. He takes one last swig of his coffee and throws the cup into the trashcan of the break room with more force than is necessary. Some of the coffee splashes on the wall.

"She says her clock is ticking." Mental note: Do not plan a double date with this couple. Ever.

"Even Al Capone couldn't escape from The Rock. Ian is a cornucopia of trivia, a flash drive of distraction. I might even miss him a little when he is assigned to work with another group.

I watch two drops of coffee race towards the floor.

"You telling me that no one every escaped from Alcatraz?" Alex asks.

"At least ten made it over the wall into the water, but they only found five of the bodies."

Alex opens the refrigerator and quickly. "Last week no coffee, today no milk."

"Sorry" I say, but it's not my fault that the break room is out of dairy products, or the network keeps crashing, or that most women on the planet seek to mate for life with a suitable partner.

"How am I supposed to drink my coffee without milk? Or cream. Or even that Soy crap. What happened to the other escapees?" He asks Ian.

"They say it's impossible to swim across the channel, the water is too cold, the current too strong. They claim the Bay never gives up her dead, so that's why they never found the bodies."

Alex searches the empty cupboards for some creamer. "Damn."

"Who says they swam?" I ask Ian, just to try to get Alex to think about something other than marriage or the lack of dairy and its substitutes.

"How else could they get across the channel, the current is strong and the water cold."

"Perhaps a friend with a fishing boat?"

"Brilliant." Ian makes some hot chocolate.

"So you are saying that it's possible that someone escaped from the rock?" Alex gives up his search for anything to lighten his java.

"It's more than possible."

"I have some research to do on diamonds." He looks directly at Ian and exits the break room.

"It's good to know that at least someone escaped." He grabs his cup and exits.

"You are brilliant. I would have never thought of an escape by boat. Explains why they never found the bodies."

"Just a theory."

"It's still brilliant," Ian says.

Am I brilliant? I can figure out how someone may have escaped from a federal prison more than 50 years ago, but have no idea why my girlfriend is pissed or even begin to resolve the problem.

Perhaps she wants/expects the rock.

Is Susie looking for more commitment than I want to give? I wonder if I can live without her? Maybe they're right, escape is only an illusion. We are all trapped, all prisoners, all doomed. Maybe I'm the one that needs more than coffee. Or a real vacation.

"He's not going to try going over the wall, is he?"

Ian has found yet another addiction: bad metaphors.

40. E-mail from another World

Keep working, everything will be better soon. That was the only line in the e-mail from The Doctor.

"What's it mean?" Ian asks.

"Don't know. I lost my cryptic to English dictionary."

"What do we do?"

"Keep working until they come to take away our furniture."

"And then what?"

"If I knew what to do next, I'd already be doing it." Or would I? Susie doesn't seem to think so. By her definition, I may be insane; doing the same thing over and over and expecting different results.

"There's another problem."

"My direct deposit didn't show up."

"Maybe there's a problem with your bank."

"Did yours?"

"Didn't check. I have people to do that."

"What should I do?"

"Keep working, everything will be better soon."

"Perhaps we should go OTG. Off-The-Grid."

"I know what it means Ian." Am I getting so old that everyone thinks I can't even keep up with the lingo? Maybe it is time to hang it up. The brain can only handle so many acronyms. One can imagine that in the not too distant future entire business conversations will be nothing but letters. People like me, that can't, or are not willing to adapt, will be forced to quit. Of course, they'll come up with an acronym for this too. Perhaps the only escape is a friend with a fishing boat or death.

41. Case Study I, Me, Mine

If it works for corporations, why not for individuals? A case study of one.

A quick analysis may shed a little light on my life. Input raw data, the results should speak for themselves. Start with the basics: Job, Relationship, and place to live.

1) Job. Still here, but for how long and why? Is the risk worth the reward? Besides new acronyms am I learning anything? Where does this job lead me? I know that I don't want to do this for the rest of my life, but what do I want to do? And when? It would be nice if the universe could send me a sign.

Everyone in this industry wants to change the world AND make tons of money. Enough cash to be able to go and spend time on an island and do nothing until they get so bored that they need to come back and do it all again.

They are called serial entrepreneurs. And they, like The Doctor, do it over and over again. The question is why?

Perhaps their sign from the universe was in the form of seed capital and stock certificates. The IPO is their Big Bang. And like the universe they do it over and over again. Infinity is their only direction.

They don't need the money or the fame. They couldn't spend their fortunes in their lifetimes if that's all they did; the interest is accruing faster than the money can be spent (not to mention the fact that for some reason we keep lowering their taxes). They own enough so that their great-great grandchildren don't have to work. As for fame, they have been on enough magazines covers so that their mug is more recognizable than anyone listed on the FBI's most wanted list. In the business world, they are the rock stars that never age or fade away.

Perhaps it's validation that they seek. They need to prove to the world, and more importantly, to themselves, that the first 3 or 4 times was not a fluke. It wasn't luck that brought them here, it was something else, and they still have it. They can do it again and again, with one hand tied behind their back.

When you were hired, you were lead to believe, and eagerly accept the idea, that you were helping them create the next big widget and change the world and get rich. But no, those are the symptoms, not the cause. Your main purpose is to help them feel deserving of their exalted position in life. The serial entrepreneur enjoys the rush, but they truly strive for the emotional hug at the end of the stock options.

You're the drug dealer/therapist. Enjoy your co-dependency. You, and your entrepreneur master, are never going to quit. The Universe is a silent film in the land of the blind.

I don't see myself ever coming back to work after striking it rich. For me it's a job, not a way of life. It's rent money, not a calling. Stock options are the mirage that will never quench my thirst.

2) Relationship. No idea. Relationships don't come with a guarantee or an owner's manual.

I know that I Love Susie and don't want to live without her, but I know that this is not enough.

3) Place to live. Somewhat of a package deal with the relationship. We have our rent-stabilized apartment together. If I lose one, I lose the other. That's the price of freedom. And don't think that I'm the only one in New York City that has considered rent in the relationship equation.

I could load all my data into Icarus and see what it says about my lifestyle choices or I could spend the time making dinner for Susie. What would be a better use of my time? Which would pay dividends in my old age?

What have we learned from this case study? No idea, but pasta and salad seems like a good idea for dinner. And wine. Lots of alcohol, cause getting a woman tipsy is not just for high school students.

42. The Apocalypse or My Dinner with Susie

"I love my pasta al dente." Susie says as she takes another taste of my famous bowties with tuna.

"That's one of the two phrases that I know in Italian."

"What's the other?"

"Al Fresco. I guess we can eat undercooked pasta outside--with vino, of course."

"We should plan a trip to Italy, the tour ends in a few and I can always take time off from my other gigs. I've always wanted to go."

"I don't know what my vacation policy is." I take a large sip, I'm not sure I like where this conversation is headed, but I fear it may be a one-way trip.

"You must get time off."

"I think when we die, or lose a limb, the policy is not clear." Actually the vacation policy is nonexistent. Vacation is for the weak, the barely committed. A true believer will postpone his days of leisure for another time in the very distant future.

"Everyone needs vacation."

"The company is going through a lot."

"Of what?"

"More wine?" Perhaps I should open another bottle.

"What's happening at Y?" Susie gave up on the holy acronym a long time ago. She simply refers to the company as "Y" as in why do you keep on working there? Or, why don't you consider leaving. Y? Y? Y?

"I have no idea." I pour myself another glass. "Sometimes I miss the big picture." Susie covers her mouth to hide her smile. I'm surprised she doesn't bust out laughing. "It started with the coffee." We both take sips of our Pinot Grigio.

"Coffee?"

"They started running out of it. Not the decaf, just the real stuff. Millions of dollars of computers and countless hours developing software and they can't keep enough coffee for employees who believe that working from seven in the morning to eight at night is a half-day." I have Susie's undivided attention. I'm not sure if she is completely interested or if she's plotting on how to get me to commit to vacation or worse. "Next, a few of the ladies started complaining that the bathrooms were running out of paper. The network crashed and it took hours to get back up. Another mistake, perhaps, but a couple weeks later and paychecks started not getting deposited on time. A few days, almost a week late. It's not like payroll is distributed by pony express." I take a swig.

"What is management saying?"

"What they always say: keep working, this will pass."

"In other words, prepare for the apocalypse."

"Apocalypse is not technically correct. In this situation."

"How so?" Susie asks. She's a sucker for trivia and perhaps this will distract her from vacation/ life planning.

"In addition to Italian, I also know a few words in Greek."

"I could marry a well-educated man." Perhaps not.

"OK." Hopefully that was the wine talking. "The meaning of the word apocalypse, for example is not what most people think. Literally it means 'lifting of the veil.' It is used to refer to specific individuals that were able to see or understand something that was hidden from the masses.

"So what do you see that is hidden?" Susie helps herself to another glass of vino.

"Nothing. I've figured out a lot of crap in my career, using several pieces of unrelated data to come up with a conclusion that will predict the likeliness of a future event. How many hard drives people will need or whether someone should change careers now or wait, but when it comes to my own job, I have no fucking idea. No fucking idea. If I could see the future, would I really want to go there? And would I buy a one way ticket?" Now I know I've had too much to drink. I should stop drinking, or at least slow down, but only on TV commercials do people drink responsibly. In life, too much is usually the preferred dosage.

"It's not the end of the world." Susie holds up her empty glass. I move to the kitchen and pick up a bottle without even checking the label. It's wet and has alcohol.

"Trust me, I'll be sitting at my desk when the world ends and I won't have a clue. I'll be clueless." I pull the cork and pour Susie another glass. "Perhaps an angel will descend and ask why I didn't read my memos announcing that the end is near."

"You don't have to be like that."

"It's a family tradition."

A moment passes. I glance down at the bottle I selected and notice its Italian. A warning sign perhaps?

"What are people doing about this?" She asks as she takes the bottle from me.

"What they always do when things look bad, they put in more hours."

"Sounds more like a cult than a business."

"Cults pay better."

We both smile and for a moment I forget about work and marriage and wonder why life can't always be this simple and this good. But I know the answer. Because it can't. And if it could we would both soon become bored, and want more, and more costs money, more requires commitment and responsibility. More invites risk to your doorstep and insists uncertainty stay in your guest bedroom and use the good sheets and towels. This is life, and whether or not you use a program like Icarus or you do it all yourself you can't escape the complexity any more than rain in the city can escape the sewer. I can't say this to her, I've been not saying it for too long. Perhaps, she knows, or at least understands.

"Why the silence?" She asks.

"I heard that a group of investors were demanding to see results—sooner, rather than later. The company is not a factory where you can produce a few cars to demonstrate that you can and perhaps bring in a little cash. It's all or nothing. Until everything works its all practice and theory. The fact is we are getting close, but no one knows if we are getting there fast enough. We believe that this can work."

"I'm going to stick with cult." If I tell her she's wrong, that an outsider will never understand what we are trying to achieve, will I sound like a member of a cult? Am I one step away from handing out flyers for YNTBE on the subway? *Here's a Web site that will change your life, solve all your problems, make you a better person. We have the all answers, trust us.*

While it is true that any new technology starts as an act of faith, and most nonusers think the users are crazy (who needs a computer, people will never bank online, my typewriter never crashes) they eventually catch on and accept the latest advance. Eventually people wonder how they ever lived without what they had just recently scoffed at.

"But if it works, we all benefit. I'm talking about stock options, of course." I say as if stock options is the answer to any question, including the meaning of life.

"If is the key word."

"OK when."

"I'd like to check it out, are you free for lunch on Thursday?"

"Looking forward to it." I look into her eyes and see the warmth of suns, but fear that if I'm not careful I will get burned. Perhaps the wine has made me well-educated, or at least let me think that I'm an educated man. If I was responsible I would stop drinking, at least for tonight, but I am not and I won't.

43. Kiss

KISS is how the world *should* be run.

Keep It Simple, Stupid.

Kiss is not how the world has been, is, and perhaps never will be run.

As my old boss Joe used to point out, you can't win a ball game in the first inning. Unfortunately the world hasn't been run by people smart enough to keep it simple since Eve had a conversation with a snake. Perhaps the snake was a business consultant and used a PowerPoint presentation to convince Eve to take a bite out of that juicy apple.

The company does not require that you always be here.

In what sane world does management put this in a company-wide e-mail?

YNTBE does not ask you to give up your personal life.

They just don't forbid it. Why should they? Slavery may be over, so they can't show you the stick, but they can offer the carrot, in the form of stock options. Stock options that seem to be closer and closer to being worth more than the paper they are printed on, but never within reach. You can dream about what you would do with all the money, but the bank still considers them worthless.

And why are we putting in so many hours? Perhaps it's because we lack, what's the word for it? Focus—it's how you keep it simple.

"You coming to the meeting?" Is it really a question when the only answer can be yes? Me, and my hangover want to scream NO.

"Yes, Alex." I want to just say 'Y' because I know that's what Susie would say.

"It's important." Alex stands waiting for me to move.

Y? Y? Y? All meetings are important, even the extra-long meetings to discuss how the company must be more efficient. I slowly gather my stuff. Perhaps Alex wants to impart his newfound knowledge of engagement rings or wedding planning on the way to the meeting. "Ready." I say.

"Have you read the latest SWOT analysis?" He asks. "I've been busy and hoped you can catch me up."

SWOT. Strengths, Weaknesses. Opportunities. Threats. An overview of what the company is doing, should be doing in relationship to what our competitors are doing and what we think that they may do next. Its war planning for people who have never been to battle, people that love planning for the sake of planning. I glanced at the report, but compared to Alex, I'm the expert.

"Opportunities mostly." More opportunities = less focus.

"What else?"

"The DNA work was also featured." Less Focus = more time at the office.

"Props, my man. I think that what you are working on will blow away everything that we have done to date."

"Of course it was also featured in the threats category."

"What's the concern?"

"Survey data suggest that people are reluctant to have their genetic makeup used to guide their lives."

"But it already does."

"No one wants to believe that."

We head into the break room; going to a business meeting without coffee is like scuba diving without oxygen, mountain climbing without rope, presenting without a pocketful of cliché's.

Alex checks the refrigerator for milk before he makes his coffee.

"Of course if we get the process accepted, we can't have a patent on DNA so anyone could do what we are doing. The people in counter marketing think it can be used against us." I say as I make my cup.

"Counter marketing?"

"You have been preoccupied. CM is a new unit, excuse me function, that attempts to figure out how our brand can be used against us and be prepared."

"Like counter terrorism."

"More like counter intelligence."

"You know what this means?" Alex straightens up slightly as if the answer to his question is not only obvious, but life changing a well.

"Not really." But I think it means more work and less carrot.

"I'm going to Tahiti."

"One way or roundtrip?"

"Seriously. I will soon be able to cash in stock options to pay for an extended honeymoon."

"I'm not sure if that's what it means."

"You can count on it."

If I had a dollar for every time someone in my life said I could count on something and it didn't happen, I could buy Tahiti.

We leave the break room.

"You ever think that we're trying to do too much?" I ask.

"You can't achieve greatness by doing the minimum."

Alex opens the door to the conference room and it looks like either the meeting has already started or the previous meeting is running late. Although the two are not mutually exclusive— meetings are like mutant DNA that often combine to form new, and unrecognizable, life forms.

"The tech guys are always making excuses." Scotty says from the front of the room.

"They work 18 hour days, some of them are even sleeping here," says the Head Nerd.

Sometimes the end of one meeting is a preview to the theme of the next one.

"I think that's because their paychecks are late." It's my old friend Ian.

Sometimes meetings are previews for movies that will never be released.

"They still have a job to do" Scotty insists.

"Everyone needs sleep to function."

Scotty and Head Nerd continue to stare at each other. Neither one wants to take a step back. A few hundred years ago, they would have challenged each other to a duel to the death. Today's equivalent would be a combination of solving calculus equations and answering Star Trek Trivia in Klingon, but neither seems to be in the mood.

"We are working on the problem." Scotty says as he takes half a step back. "In the meantime the next meeting is scheduled to start."

Head Nerd relaxes slightly, waits a second longer than necessary to turn around. Scotty looks at Alex and me. "We need to discuss some new features."

New features is the arch nemesis of KISS. New features means that you can kiss your stock options goodbye, because you choose to make things more complicated than they need to be. New features means it's going to take longer to get your service to market.

"You're late" Scotty says. Alex and I glance at each other, neither one of us wants to point out that we are late for a meeting that was destined to not start on time.

"I need you here on time, every time."

"Ok."

"We are accelerating the schedule" Scotty says.

"How?" Alex asks, although I think that why would be the more appropriate question.

"We are also adding a few new features." Now would be a good time for Y.

Now it's Alex's turn to stand his ground against Scotty. He does his best not to tense up, but it's impossible to not notice that he is bothered. "We can add more features or go faster, but I'm not sure if we can do both."

"You have more staff than ever before." Scotty glances in my direction and then at Ian. Scotty is correct, but the part of equation that is missing is that each new feature adds complexity that can't be factored into the workload until you do the work. If you don't know where you are going, it's impossible to know how long it's going to take to get there.

"And we appreciate the additional staff."

Sometimes going faster just means you got lost sooner.

"So what's the problem?" Scotty has not relaxed from his confrontation with the Head Nerd; Alex has no room to maneuver. Now is not the time to agree, but if he acquiesces, he's stuck with more work than the staff can handle.

"I'm not clear about the need to move up deadlines."

"Decisions had to be made; there was no time to consider additional input."

More is better I say to myself, but it's a mantra that I will never believe. Faster is better is equally inane.

Alex has questions to ask, statements to make, but he remains silent, because he knows that whatever he says Tahiti will have to wait.

"It's all here in the PowerPoint." Scotty motions for us to sit and be enlightened.

* * *

The presentation is over and all I want to say to Alex is: More is better. More is better. More is better. Followed by: We must move faster. We must move faster. We must move faster. I remain silent in anticipation of Alex taking the lead on this. He can't possibly believe that we can make the new deadlines AND add new features. No reasonable person could.

As we exit the conference room he takes a deep breath and exhales. "How about a stroll?"

"I'm always up for a road trip."

We exit the building. "Uptown or down?" Alex asks.

I think of a story that Susie told me. She was visiting her aunt in the city and they pretended that when they were walking uptown, they were walking uphill and when going downtown they were heading downhill.

"Up," sounds good, I say. We're always walking uphill at work, might as well extend the metaphor to its illogical conclusion, the land of unicorns.

"Do I work hard?" He asks.

"You are here all the time."

"Not what I asked."

"You work very hard." I notice that the sun is shining, but I know that I don't have much time to enjoy it.

"The past few days I've spent a lot of time on marriage stuff."

"A few hours over the past week."

"I could be more dedicated." Maybe I should suggest we head downtown.

"You're one person, you only have so many hours in the day, the week."

"Maybe if I tried to inspire my coworkers more."

Is he talking about me? There are only so many hours in the day, the week.

"I think we can do this, thanks for hearing me out."

He turns and faces downtown.

"Sure."

Kiss, as in kiss your free time goodbye.

Kiss as in the rock band that is known for mediocre music and too much make-up. The band's detractors went so far as to claim that Kiss stood for Knights in Satan's Service. Seems to be the correct equation, keep it simple or serve the lord of darkness, because you can't do both.

We increase our pace; perhaps there is something to this downtown/downhill thing.

44. The Beat Goes On

"You actually wrote a paper on fucking drummers?"

"Yes." Susie takes a bite from a carrot stick.

"An academic paper?"

"Is there another kind?" She brought lunch, because I'm too busy to leave the office. We're not the only ones. The room is a collection of wives' visiting overworked husbands, boyfriends visiting significant others who have been asked to put in a little more time. The only difference between this and a visitation center at a federal prison is our walls are topped with stock options, not barbed wire and we don't need guards to keep people from escaping. The only security we have is to prevent someone from trying to break in, to attempt to become a member of our little community.

"Why?" I have the urge to repeat the question. Y? Y? Y?

"You asked me if I was sleeping with a musician."

"I only asked because you stated, and I quote: 'drummers were not always the best lovers.'"

"Did I just see someone walk through the cafeteria in a bath robe?" Susie turns her head and follows the Head Nerd as he makes his way across the lunch room with a plate of dessert.

"That's our chief technology officer. He's not going to leave the building until he's finished his projects."

"Really?"

"He's also saving money on rent, but don't change the subject."

"Are things really that bad that people are forced to live here?"

"It also saves on commuting time, we have showers and everything. Again, you are changing the subject." Susie returns her gaze to me, but my guess is that her thoughts are someone else. "How do you now about the sex life of drummers?" This conversation needs alcohol, but I'm at work/in prison/a member of a cult that discourages alcohol during work hours.

"It depends on if they are bangers or beaters."

"Bangers or Beaters? What's the difference?" I may regret asking this.

"They play and make love very differently. I can send you the paper we submitted to."

"You wrote a paper on fucking drummers?" I really need a drink. Of all the things that have changed in the business world since the fifties and

433

sixties, why did they have to take away the three-martini lunch?

"A venation blind is not the same as a blind venation."

"What?" Although WTF comes to mind.

"Not fucking drummers, drummers fucking __"

"You wrote a paper on having sexual relationships with percussionists?"

"Yes, and we submitted the paper to modern feminist quarterly."

"You said, you never."

"I didn't actually have sex with any of them, I just interviewed a selection of some of their conquests."

"Glad to hear it."

"Although some of the stories were so graphic, that I felt like I had – I do have my preferences. For example bangers and beaters, it's all about rhythm..."

"I think I've had enough."

434

"I'll e-mail you the paper, it's a quick read. You are the data guy."

"Not really my cup of tea."

"Don't judge. You're the one who works at the place that allows bathrobes in the lunchroom."

"No judgments, it's just that you never mentioned the project."

"You never asked." Behind Susie another programmer struts through the lunchroom wearing what looks like a bathing suit and flip-flops. He hasn't shaved in weeks, his skin is pale, the color of a government office last painted in the 1970s. Like his boss, his plate is full of items with a main ingredient of refined sugar.

"How does a question like that come up? By the way have you recently authored any dissertations on the sexual proclivities' of percussionists and how was your day?"

Susie notices the bathing suit. "I'm still going with cult."

"What do you have against cults? Have you ever tried one?"

"I could name a lot of things that you never tried"

"Like?" Once again I know that I've said something foolish, but I can't take it back.

"Escargot or marriage, for example."

"Do I get to pick just one?" Susie smiles. OK. Dodged another bullet from the guns of matrimony. Unfortunately, the marriage gun is always locked and loaded and ammo is never in short supply.

"Do you smell smoke?"

"I haven't noticed, but I don't hear the alarm either."

I look into Susie's eyes, something is different, brighter perhaps, but she always knows something before I do. Call it intuition, call it being able to read the signs on the road that state the obvious and yet everyone ignores, but Susie is wise and sharp. She will know if the apocalypse is coming long before I do. The Alarm screams.

"That is an alarm." She says,

"We should get out of here."

I'm about to nod, but I remember there's something I left on my desk. "I'll meet you outside. It's probably just a drill." I stand and turn before she has a chance to respond.

"Be careful" is all I hear as I head toward the stairs.

45. Flying too close to the sun or my near death experience.

I've read that it's not the smoke that kills you. Or the flames. Or the heat.

Fire marshals report that stupidity is the number one cause of death in fires. It's not the individual that returns to grab a child or a pet, it's the fool who goes back into the burning structure to retrieve his prized baseball or stamp collection or bowling trophy or some object that although irreplaceable, in the scheme of things is completely meaningless—as far as I know, there are no trophy cases in heaven or hell.

The alarm continues to ring. I move up the stairs while team members head down. Each one gives me the *you're going the wrong way look*, but can't articulate it quickly enough as I take two stairs at a time.

Once again I'm moving against the crowd. I'm no longer a salmon swimming upstream to catch a train. This time, there can be no doubt that going against the crowd is the wrong thing to do. I'm on a mission to collect something that can't be replaced: my signed copy of Joe's memoirs. It's not the words I fear losing, it's the handwritten notes in the margins, the comments that I have only just begun to decipher. The ramblings of a dying man that only serve to remind me that he existed. Like reading graffiti in a foreign language, all they say is that someone, at some point in time, was alive.

The landing on the 2nd floor is empty. Ghostlike. My brain has tuned out the sound of the fire alarm.

The stairs up to the third floor are empty. Still no smoke. No smell of burning anything. At the top of the stairs I touch the knob. It is cold. The only rule I remember, don't open the door if the knob is warm. A warm door knob can mean one of two things: The room is still burning or worse, all the oxygen has been depleted from the room and opening a door will result in an explosion when fresh air is added to the mix. It's called a back draft and firefighters fear it more than just about any other hazard.

The handle is cold to the touch but I open it slowly, expecting something surreal and I'm not disappointed. The floor is covered with a white mist that swirls around, and covers everything up to my knees. It's as if the room is being used for filming a poor man's Sherlock Holmes.

No smoke, no flames, but I do detect a whiff of something metallic. If aluminum had body odor this might be it. The mist seems to be rising, but I know the way. I can find my desk while sipping hot coffee, checking my e-mail and having a conversation about conversion rates for our newest clients.

Joe's manuscript is right where I left it. As I pick it up I realize that something in the room is different. When did the alarm stop ringing? And why? Is this a fire or not? Doesn't the fire department have to come and turn it off?

No signs of life on the floor and the mist is now up to my hips.

Holding the manuscript against my body I quickly turn and head towards the exit. I can no longer see the desks and everything they contain, including the photographs that only serve to remind us that we have a life outside of the office—if only we had the time. My ankle feels something that doesn't belong on the floor. Perhaps this was not such a good idea. I grasp for something to hold onto, but all there is mist and I'm losing balance... With every mistake.

* * *

I'm on my back, immersed in this cloud of unknown origin. Perhaps the vapor is the soul of Icarus escaping. If I get out of this I may have supernatural powers or at least be able to whistle loud enough to hail a cab during rush hour.

I probably should sit up, but my body doesn't feel ready for the exercise. My brain, on the other hand, is racing. How long have I've been on the floor? What was I thinking about before I fell? Something about life and mistakes.

Yes.

When my ankle got tangled up, I thought this might be a huge mistake, which reminded me of the demo of *While My Guitar Gently Weeps* with the extra verse. My ankle may be busted, but for better or worse, my brain still functions at normal capacity.

Recently I listened to the "missing" versus of "While My Guitar Gently Weeps." Songs usually change from demo to final album cut, but the demo version is completely different than the published song on The White Album. The published song is much more upbeat and polished and an altogether better song, but I wonder what it would sound like with just one more verse.

I wait in the wings of the play you are
staging
While me guitar gently weeps

441

Sitting here doing nothing but aging
While me guitar gently weeps

Why were these verses written? Why were they left out? Was George trying to tell us something? Is this his version of an Easter Egg? A secret message written in a tomb only to be discovered many years latter?

My ankle aches, but I can completely move my foot, so I must be OK.

I'll think I stay with the original version of the song, but I wonder why George thought, even for a second or two, that he was doing nothing but aging. I would hope that he understood that it didn't fit and that's why he edited it out of the final mix.

George Harrison may be dead, but somewhere he is still learning, as we all should be, although I can't be certain that this is always the case. With every mistake or if not with every mistake, perhaps, if we are lucky with every other one. It's the perfect song and always will be.

Susie. I need to discuss this with her. Wonder if she had a similar reaction when she first heard the unused verse?

I lift my head to discover that the mist is only a few inches thick, barely enough to reach my ankle if I was standing. I sit up, not ready to test my leg.

I could have left Joe's manuscript to burn in the flames, but I don't think that the flames were up to the task. The fire seems to be a nonevent. Another drill perhaps. Or maybe a test from Icarus, an opportunity for programmers to see daylight, get some exercise and then get back to work and be even more productive.

I use the side of a cubicle to pull myself up, favoring my good leg. I look around and I see that the mist was not the soul of Icarus, but rather the gas that is used to extinguish fires in server rooms. For some reason the system didn't stop emptying its contents. Not sure what the stuff is called, I used to know or if it is toxic or not, but I'll worry about my Agent Orange another day.

I slowly put more weight on my injured leg and realize that I may walk again, although marathons may be out of the question. I hold Joe's manuscript and limp towards the stairs.

The door to the stairs opens easily; the air has a memory of smoke, like your clothing the day after a campfire. Something burned somewhere.

I hold the rail and ease my way down the stairs, promising myself that I will never do something this stupid again.

Between the 3rd and 2nd floors and I figure I'm safe: no smoke, no alarms, no fire. No reason to worry, I'm only a floor and a half from the street and the woman I love and want to spend the rest of my life with.

The fire alarm starts squealing louder than before as if the gods were reading my thoughts and wanted to make a point about attempting fate or counting chickens or whatever gods need to make a point about. I want to cover my ears, but I need them to hold on to the rail and to the manuscript.

I wince and continue. Pain is not my bag. I would die if I had to give birth. I think most men would. The truth is that women are stronger than men and always have been.

A drop of water, but it hasn't rained for days. The sprinklers. As if on cue a drop becomes an inside thunderstorm as the alarm screams and the sprinklers release every drop of liquid they been holding. The stairs become slippery as water rushes down. At least this time, I'm going with the current.

Second floor and the sprinklers are still creating a flood. Nothing is dry. I turn, only a half floor to go.

My elbow catches something and I realize it's someone heading up. "Sorry," I say and turn to realize it's the Doctor. His white suit and silk shirt are soaked.

"For what?" he asks.

Does he think that I'm apologizing for the fire or the flood?

"Just sorry" I say.

The muscles on his face move the slightest such muscles can move, but I can't really tell if it's a smile or a grimace. I look down to check my footing. When I look back up, The Doctor is gone. I wonder what piece of crap that he needs to retrieve from his rarely-used office.

I look down and realize that the manuscript that I've been clutching is becoming soaked, ink runs like a watercolor in the rain. Water continues to rush down the stairs and I hold on the rail like it was my lifeline. I only let go when I reach the bottom. I open the door and haven't been as glad to see sunlight as when I was released from the pen.

I scan the crowd but see no sign of Susie.

Fire trucks. Ambulances. Police. Lights flashing.

The YNTBE faithful each has the look of cattle waiting patently in line to enter the slaughterhouse, not sure what's going to happen on the inside, but upset that they have to wait so long to get in.

Susie blindsides me with a hug and I almost lose my balance. I drop what remains of the manuscript.

Hushed whispers from the crowd, but no one is saying anything I can decipher.

"It's over," Susie says.

"I don't think it was a real fire."

"No, it's over. Finished. Done."

"We have copies of everything." I look into Susie's eyes. "We can rebuild." What's left of Joe's manuscript is swept in the gutter like a newspaper soaked overnight in a bathtub of tears. I wanted to keep it, but I realize it's not that important. It's not what we hold in our hands that counts, it's what we hold in our hearts. Susie continues to hug me as if she understands. Perhaps she does or perhaps it really doesn't matter.

I catch a word or two of the ambient noise. Can't believe. Never.

The alarm stops.

I am alive.

46. Hallelujah

"Hallelujah," I hear from the street, but the years and the shouting have softened his voice. Or perhaps it's the guilt. His victims will never forgive him for the pain and suffering that he afflicted upon them, but perhaps the people of New York would be willing to. If only he had spent his time helping rather than preaching he could start to make amends. Instead of walking up and down the streets of New York and screaming about the wonders of god, perhaps a simple demonstration: Work in a soup kitchen, volunteer at a hospital, build housing for the homeless, pick up trash in the park. Even if he never achieved forgiveness, he could make the world a slightly better place, but instead day after day he marches to the demons in his head and proclaims that god is here to save us, if only we obey.

"Hallelujah." If his voice was any softer it would be a whisper. Or perhaps god needs better messengers.

* * *

"Am I the only person in the room that thinks it's extremely ironic that when Icarus crashed it was running on a Sun Workstation?"

Susie looks up from her electronic crossword puzzle. "Yes. Of the two people in the apartment, you're the only one."

"Icarus was destroyed by The Sun. The situation screams irony."

"Last week it screamed, today it's just whimpering. Irony doesn't age well." Susie looks up from her screen and smiles.

"The system would have been saved if the backup system was online. It was destroyed by a small fire. No one knows how that started."

"It wasn't the fire; it was your burn rate. You were spending more money than you were bringing in, investors were pissed. The fire only sped the process up by a week or so."

"But here was a real fire."

"In a trashcan. Before you start looking for men on the grassy knoll, you might want to ask yourself what happened to the doctor."

"OTG and I still have stock options."

"Worthless. It's over. Finished. Kaput."

"Is it really over?" As if that could be a real question. The only thing I suppose that could have been more appropriate is if the entire server room caught on fire and was extinguished by fire extinguishers filled with Kool-Aid. Instead, the world was saved not by Icarus, but from Icarus. Is there anything that can be added to the story—not unless you believe that something can be more than perfect. Not if you believe that stories rarely end perfectly, they just end.

I don't pretend to claim that I saw it coming. I just mean that when it happened, it made perfect sense, like the myth. Perhaps this is how we know when we have arrived, and must now move on--it's when our myths and our lives collide and we are forced to move in some new direction.

I would like to think that the server exploded because I added one too many algorithms to its matching matrix, that I was the data straw that broke the camel's back. It would be nice to believe that a mere human could feed a computer too much info, but we know this is not the case and never will be.

Soon, someone else will try to do a project that is even bigger than Icarus. They will put even more human and financial resources into the effort. They will work as if there very lives depended on the outcome. They will claim to be changing the world, while secretly or not so secretly, hoping to cash in and never have to work again.

In the business world, every man only has one eye and believes that everyone else is blind.

"Finish your breakfast, we need to pack."

"I was going to start with the books."

"I'm giving them all away," Susie says.

"All of them?"

"We've read them already." I'm about to say something about their importance, how they were carefully selected and how they were all related thematically by suicide, but Susie interjects. "I've moved on." I guess she has. What was once a fine collection of suicide authors will be a random assortment of fine reading for someone to pick through at a *friends of the library* sale. Perhaps someone will buy them and make their own library that has a meaning that only they understand.

"I still don't get how we can afford this. I worked my ass off, had stock options and everything, you get asked to leave your job and still have tons of money."

"We have lots of money."

"How?"

"They wanted me to leave and they didn't want any embarrassment."

"They're paying you to leave?"

"They're paying me to stop fucking with them." God I love this woman. For the next 24 months she'll be making more to not work than I ever did working.

"Hallelujah," I say, but no one is listening.

47. To Look for America

If several years ago, you would have asked me if I would ever get married I would have laughed in your face. If you have also mentioned that my girlfriend at the time would stop taking the pill and I would be OK with that, I would have suggested that you need to be committed. If you also suggested that I would be both happy and unemployed, I would have called for an intervention, because you are obviously addicted to something or your brain chemistry was so far out of balance that you needed professional help, or some time in a institution.

I can't be the first male in human history to rail against matrimony and then end up tying the knot. I consider myself lucky. You know what Susie wanted for an engagement ring? Hint: It didn't cost two months salary. Diamonds are for suckers, she said. I swear the woman would have been happy if I shop lifted something from Wall-Mart. Instead we bought the plainest of bands at an estate sale. Someone died, we got a bargain. All that glitters is not gold. Or maybe it is.

453

If you would have told me that I'd be on the open road with the woman I love. That we had no maps, no GPS just a few belongings, new books to read and the rules developed to live by, I would have protested, but here we are. No plans, just ideas.

We intend on finding the highway attractions, the largest balls of twin and giant frying pans that everyone has heard about, but no on makes time to visit. We will seek out the places in the desert like the guy who owns the only known copy of the Rock n Roll Bible. I'm sure it has much to say about the demo version of "While My Guitar Gently Weeps."

Road trip rule number three: pancakes for dinner.

My guitar may not be weeping, but I will continue, correction, we will continue in the play that *WE* are staging.

I hit the gas and wave goodbye to no one or nothing in particular and head west. Here comes the sun.

***The Final True Story about a Thirsty Man
(in which we promise to explain it all and change
your life forever.***

*Every year, in the middle of the Moroccan
Desert, they stage a six-day, 151 mile marathon.
Don't bother to ask why, just accept the fact that
some men are either very brave or very stupid, or
both, — stupidity and bravery have never been
mutually exclusive.*

*The event, held in March or April, attracts
more than 700 entrants, who believe that they have
the stamina and fortitude to brave the 120 heat and
sand dunes and scorpions and win the "passion
prize."*

*One year an Italian runner was lost in a sand storm.
He survived for days by eating snakes and drinking
bat blood and even his own urine. After days of
agony and not wishing to die a long, drawn out
death, he attempted to take his life by slitting his
wrists, but his blood did not flow onto the sands of
the Sahara. He was too dehydrated, his blood was*

too thick to flow properly and his self-inflicted wounds quickly clotted.

He collapsed and was rescued by nomads who took him to the hospital, where he was slowly brought back to life. The thirsty man lives…

Author Unknown

Glossary

24/7/365   There are 24 Hours in a day, 7 days in a week, and 365 and a quarter days in a calendar year. If you are working less than this are you really committed to the organization?

Albert Einstein. No doubt that the Special and General theories of relativity were game changers, but one can argue that Albert was really a business consultant disguised as a theoretical physicist with bad hair. Consider this quote: "Anyone who has never made a mistake has never tried anything new." Sounds more like a guy who gets paid in advance to disseminate mediocre business advice than a scientist. If you need any more evidence, you're probably also skeptical about gravity. Consider this: "A clever person solves a problem. A wise person avoids it." Indeed.

Alphabet City   A neighborhood in Manhattan that is known for its hipsters, drug dealers, and streets named for the first four letters of the English Alphabet. (Parents beware: this is not the home of Sesame Street). It is rumored that anyone walking in Alphabet City after midnight that does not have a tattoo or numerous body piercings will be ridiculed by poorly dressed kids from New Jersey.

AMO   Acknowledge, Move On. Accept that a mistake has been made and get on with your life. Accidents happen. Milk gets spilt. AMO is always easier to say than to do. We at the glossary have developed our own coping philosophy: TAFI (Tequila and Forget it). Writer and resident barman Simon West-Bulford has suggested that Gin can be substituted for Tequila. We're going to have to get back to you after additional research. In the meantime, L'chaim.

B-Roll Can you really tell the difference between hurricane Lucy and hurricane Ricky? We can't either and the accountants that run network TV are counting on it. They recycle used video like some men recycle women. Not us. We like women. We also like old sitcoms, that's why we name all our hurricanes for television characters. Lucy you have some splaining to do.

Book In the world of publishing a book is just a magazine/trade publication. Why do they call it a book? Makes them sound important.

Burn Rate The difference between how much money your company is spending vs how much cash it is generating. In the earlier stages of most start-ups, the cash that is generated is in the form of capital from investors. Too fast of a burn rate and you will not survive, too slow and no one will know that you even exist.

Coincidence. Coincidence is God's way of remaining anonymous. Another gem from Albert Einstein.

Comdex. Once the largest computer trade show in the world. That was when the only a fraction of Americans owned PCs and the smartphone was a gleam in Steve Jobs eye. Today nearly everyone owns multiple computing devices and Comdex no longer exists. Irony? Poetic justice? Was Comdex a victim of its own success or part of a larger conspiracy?

Cube farm (Cubical Farm). How modern offices are divided up. Individual employees sit in separate cubes and pretend they have a real office when in fact they have three partitions and a desk manufactured out of fake wood. According to industry expert Amanda Gowin, when an individual stands up in a cube farm they bear a striking resemblance to a participant in a life-size version of the whack-a-mole game. Unfortunately the leaders of corporate America do not think this is a metaphor.

Deck. A PowerPoint presentation.

Digerati. The term is a portmanteau word, derived from "digital" and "literati." The Digerati are the kids that sit at the cool table. If you needed to look this up, you're probably not one of them. Don't worry, we'll sit with you. We're not he coolest, but we're old enough to buy beer and young enough to enjoy it. Cheers.

Donner Party It was cold, they were lost, they were stuck in the snow, they ate their dead. Please don't judge them too harshly, some of them survived to tell the tale.

DGTM   Didn't get the memo. Remember if you don't get the memo, the memo will get you.

Easter Egg. A gift to the masses hidden in a software program. Can also be a metaphor for tidbits of clever knowledge hidden in a novel. We're just sayin'.

Fax Machines All you need to know about this evil piece of technology is that it was invented when Calvin Coolidge was President of the United States. 1924. It can't die soon enough, but may outlive us all.

FWP   First World Problems. Your garage door opener isn't working and you have to get out of the car and do it manually. Perhaps you lost the television remote or your pool boy didn't get all the leaves out of the hot tub. These are the problems that most of the world would love to have. Think

about it next time you order your soy latte
and the barista forgets the extra whip.
Remember, someone in China can only
afford basic cable.

Gatsby, Jay   You really had to look this
up? You need to get out less.

IDBY   I Don't Believe You. If you get too
many of these you have a believability
problem and should not seek employment as
a lawyer, politician, or member of a
religious cult that attempts to convert
commuters on the subway. Trust us, people
do not use underground transportation to
find god.

IRNC   I really need caffeine.

L'chaim   To life. What else are you going
to say when drinking?

MacGyver   An American television
program that ran from 1985 to 1992. In

short, there wasn't a life-or-death situation that Mac couldn't get out of with a Swiss Army Knife and a roll of duct tape.

McBucks. The merger of Starbucks and McDonalds has produced the world's leading producer of tasteless burgers and burnt, but very expensive, coffee.

Miracles. "There are only two ways to live your life. One is as though nothing is a miracle. The other is as though everything is a miracle." Albert Einstein.

NDA Non disclosure agreement. Sign this and promise not to divulge any secret information you learned while doing business with us (except to your best friends who promise not to say anything, but for a drink or two will spill the beans to impress their friends).

Numbered Case Studies   In business, the case study is often used to provide an in-depth overview and analysis of what works and what doesn't. As far as we know no case study has ever been written to discuss why top CEOs are overpaid and often refuse to work hard unless their taxes are slashed…

The question you should be asking yourself is what is the significance of the numbers of the case studies in this novel and am I smart enough to figure it out?   We know you are.   A simple Easter Eggs contained within this project.

OTG   Off the Grid.

Programmers, The secret to getting what you want from.

We only have two tricks.

The first can't be overused, but it never fails.   100% success rate guaranteed. You just need two things. Caffeine and this: Tell them it can't be done. Challenge is their only motivation. Guaranteed to work the first time you try it. Sometimes it works the second time, but after that that tend to catch on. They are super logical people with great memories for unrelated facts. No one has found anything else that is guaranteed to be as effective. After all, deadlines are arbitrary, seldom logical, and never their problem.

Trick number two. When it comes to comic books, science fiction, or any other form of nerd entertainment, they are never wrong. Never. If they claim their grandmother can beat up Batman, you must agree with them. Always. If there are two programmers and one likes Batman and one favors Superman (or Star Trek vs. Star Wars) choose carefully, because for the rest of your career with this organization you will be stuck with your choice. It's like marriage without divorce, life without parole, a weekend with your in-laws without alcohol. Superman may be able to reverse time, but you can't.

Portmanteau Word A word composed of two or more words. First used by Lewis Carroll. Spot the portmanteau words in the following sentence: I *chortled* while she browsed *Wikipedia* during *brunch* with her parents.

PowerPoint. A wonderful program from Microsoft. It helps managers make simple things sound complex. Full Disclosure: We once "partied" with Bill Gates. By partied we mean we watched while nerds asked him technical questions and soaked in his wisdom. Not our definition of a party, but we are only honoree nerds.

Meme. An idea that travels around the planet like a cold virus runs through a school of runny-nosed toddlers—fast and out-of-control. The speed of travel is in no way correlated with the accuracy of the information or the astuteness of the scheme. It just travels fast.

Quotes from Einstein

Any intelligent fool can make things bigger, more complex, and more violent. It takes a touch of genius - and a lot of courage - to move in the opposite direction.

Any fool can know. The point is to understand.

If we knew what we were doing, it would not be called research, would it?

RDZ Reality Distortion Zone. An organization that refuses to see, or deal with reality. "Our products are the best, because we said so." "What are you going to believe your eyes or our advertising." "We are losing money on every sale, but will make up for it in volume." "If we build it, profits will flow." "We are the leading…"

RTW   Reinventing the Wheel. If you need this defined, you are obviously unfit to live in the 21st century and should move.

Sisyphus   Man. Rock. Hill. Repeat forever.

Skinner Box   A box in a laboratory that is used to train rats how to perform tasks like pushing a lever or pulling a chain. The rats are rewarded with treats. At the time this was considered serious science and NOT a metaphor for capitalism.

SOHO   A neighborhood in NYC that used to be cool, but now is merely trendy. You can enjoy art galleries and expensive lattes or head to Bushwick in Brooklyn and see the real thing before it too becomes trendy.

STUN   Success Teaches Us Nothing. We only really learn from our mistakes. Plus when we are successful, we assume we are geniuses, but perhaps, we just got lucky. Of course, if we are extremely successful and think we know it all we cockily move forward with our next big scheme and make a big mistake, which of course is a potential learning experience and the cycle is complete. Thanks for playing.

Symbionese Liberation Army (SLA) A left-wing militant organization active between 1973 and 1975 that considered itself a vanguard army. The group committed bank robberies, murders, and was most famous for kidnapping Patty Hearst (the granddaughter of William Randolph Hearst). WR Hearst was used as the model for publisher Charles Foster Kane in Orson Welles's masterpiece Citizen Kane.

TBTL   Think beyond the logical. We have no idea what this means and we don't care. We accept the fact that business gurus need to say things that no one understands. Gurus need to be worshipped; most of them already have enough money. We could turn this into an acronym, but that seems to violate even our sense of ridiculousness. Of course, if we were paid by the word, we would write more, much more.

TBV/Trust But Verify/Ronald Reagan. The 40th president of the United States. Reagan was a big believer in small government. He believed in it so much that the federal deficit tripled during his eight years in office. He said, and we quote: "The most terrifying words in the English language are: I'm from the government and I'm here to help."

Side note: After an earthquake and tsunami devastated Japan, The USS Ronald Reagan was dispatched to provide aid and comfort to her citizens. The $4.5 billion aircraft carrier is built of the finest steel, but apparently she is powered by irony.

THLS Train has left station. This acronym has no meaning if you are at the airport.

TLA Three-letter-acronym. If you can't reduce a business idea or process to three words, you have no right to call yourself an executive. If this is the case, when you show up for work tomorrow, please beg HR to lower your salary and start doing some real work. In a few weeks, the firm that employs you will be sending us a thank you note.

Tontons Macoutes A Tonton Macoute was a member of the Haitian paramilitary force created in 1959 by dictator François 'Papa Doc' Duvalier. Haitians named this force after the Creole mythological Tonton Macoute (Uncle Gunnysack) a bogeyman who kidnaps and punishes unruly children by snaring them in a gunnysack (macoute) and carrying them off to be consumed at breakfast. A Tonton Macoute stopped at nothing to enforce order and help their masters turn a tidy profit. War pays.

YTD   Yours to Discover. From our point of view the greatest TLA ever. It means exactly what you want it to mean, and in this crazy world, it works for us.

Violence. Bob "I once beat a man for spelling my first name backwards," Pastorella believes that violence is sometimes the answer, but never the question. Interesting. If we are ever in a bar fight, we want boB on our side.

WMT   Wasting my time.

Year of the Cat. The hit song from the album of the same name by Al Stewart.

During the first draft the novel quoted both Year of the Cat and While my Guitar. "The missing quote is from the song's opening: *On a morning from a Bogart Movie, In a country were they turn back time, you go strolling through the crowd like Peter Lorre, contemplating a crime.*" Apparently the author was hoping that the songs attempt at mystery would jump into the pages of his tome. Perhaps the author was trying to capture the I-grew-up-on-70s-pop demo.

For reasons unknown the song was scrapped and While My Guitar was asked to stand alone. We believe that WMGGW deserves this honor and look forward to defending the choice in the bar of your choice (after you buy us a drink).

Year of the Cat is filled with fantastic images, including: *like watercolors left in the rain,* which the author stole in one of the scenes of his novel. He thinks he borrowed it, paid homage to the song; we'll go with outright theft, like in a Bogart movie.

Xanadu. The summer house of Kublai Khan. Also the name of the estate in the movie Citizen Kane. Charles Foster Kane was modeled after the real life publisher, and yellow journalist, William Randolph Hearst. Hundreds of movie stars were invited to spend long weekends at Hearst Castle in San Simeon, CA. The most famous houseguest at Kahn's Xanadu was Marco Polo. No one knows if Marco ever used the pool.

Zabars The place to get gourmet food on the Upper West Side of Manhattan. Warning: do not tell the man at the counter how to cut lox. He knows what he's doing.

Zyklon B. The gas the Nazis used to exterminate 8 million men, women, and children. At the end of the war the Nazis still had enough of poison to kill an extra 6 million humans. At the time there were not that many Jews, Gypsies, homosexuals, and political prisoners left in Europe. To whom was the extra Zyklon B intended? The Nazis were too methodical to produce more than they needed. It is a great question, but the wrong one. The Nazis knew exactly what they were doing. Many German Generals owned stock in the company that produced Zyklon B. Extra poison meant extra sales. Why wage war if you can't make a profit?

Acknowledgments

To Ben and Sasha. You deserve a book dedication all your own. Until the next one, I gift you the four rules for the prefect Gibbel family road trip. 1) Always listen to classic Rock-n-Roll. 2) Make frequent stops for diet cokes and other food of dubious nutritional value. 3) Pancakes for dinner! 4) There is no rule number four. I firmly believe that if these rules were adhered to, the world be a much better place. Ignore them at your peril; enjoy them at your leisure.

To Mario Cianci (Author, *In a given moment*) who dragged my ass across the finish line, for reasons that I may never understand or need to. Keep writing and rocking, rocking and writing.

To the distinguished musicians, artists, dreamers of The House (Matthew Volz, Juan Wauters, Tall Juan Zaballa, Jose Aybar, Ben (Katzman and Trimble)) thanks for all your encouragement and for teaching me this: if it's not amplified, recorded, sung, printed, or published—it's not art, it's just a sequence of electromagnetic impulses running through your brain. Turn it up to 11 and set it free.

The book would not have been possible without the support of the cool kids in Write Club.

To the crew that wrote the glossary: if words are not enough, get a bigger dictionary.

To Nikki Guberman for giving me Tequila Mockingbird—I know that if you were here, you would read the novel and say you loved it (no matter what you actually thought).

To all of you that fired/downsized/ kicked my ass to the curb I give you Dorothy Parker's best quip: "living well is the best revenge." As soon as I'm living well, I'll send an e-mail, until then—thanks for the raw material. If any of you think that you have been misquoted, keep in mind this is a work of fiction.

479

Stuart Gibbel was born in Hollywood, California. His work has appeared in *Menacing Hedge* and *In Search of a City: LA in 1,000 Words*. This is his first novel. He has worked in the corporate world and for several Internet concerns, but can't remember why. Currently he is working on a piece about the place he calls home, the coolest house in Far Rockaway, NY where he lives with some talented musicians/artists who are doing their best to reinvent reality. When he is not drinking Mate' or watching the sunset fall over the Manhattan skyline from the couch in his backyard he can be reached at sgibbel@yahoo.com.